VALEDICTION RECORDS

R PETER DAVIES

CRANTHORPE
—MILLNER—
PUBLISHERS

First published by Cranthorpe Millner Publishers (2024)

ISBN 978-1-80378-150-1 (Paperback)

www.cranthorpemillner.com

Cranthorpe Millner Publishers

In memory of my father, who was also a writer

PART ONE

THE LOST GIRL

2017

ROY

I have had a realisation. No one understands what I'm saying anymore. This shocks me less than you might imagine, because something has felt wrong for a while now. I can't explain that feeling, other than to say it's in the details.

People are appearing where I didn't expect them to, and I'm sure there are others who have gone away. The clocks stop, and start again, but the hands have moved. There is a cat here; I can see it now, sunning itself by the door to the garden. I never liked cats, but this one I do.

I think I must have played the guitar at one time, I'm not sure, but the one I've been given by Kelly (she has a badge with her name on it, for some reason) isn't what I want. I want that other guitar, the one I used to have, and I find myself crying for it in the night.

So I am thinking all of this, and I am saying it to myself, but no one is understanding me. That alignment has shifted.

The memories, though, are more vivid than ever, and they are coming to life.

I can smell pink roses as my first love comes to me.

My daughter clings to my leg as I turn to the door.

My brothers.

The glorious sound of vinyl in 1977.

My God, I can feel the pulse of everything.

I am dreaming of going home, with all the notes and chords and lyrics finally coming together in a perfect pattern, that I never quite saw when I was young.

I am remembering the mystical.
But no one understands.

KELLY

Kelly was waking up alone, for the first time in months. The silence filling the house was overwhelming, and she curled up under the sheets, as she emerged from another dream of her mother.

She had always felt this an unsettling place to be, even dangerous, that shadowy road to the morning. Her eyes were shut, but she was still looking back over her shoulder at the distant figure waving to her, reaching for the arms that no longer held her, and she knew that she needed to wake up. She never felt so close to death as at these moments.

Perhaps she might talk to Roy about her dream later, although she was on an evening shift today, and he was unlikely to be responsive by then. In the meantime, there was an essay to finish, ironing to do, and a baby to collect.

Certainty, order.

The life between the dreams.

Okay, she thought, but why the need to mark the end of every year like this? Why draw a line, as if to say that all was done, over, and that now we can move on? Had the past twelve months been wrapped up neatly and consigned to history when they had bawled 'Auld Lang Syne' in Grace's crowded living room last night? No one knew the words to that ridiculous song anyway, and, just fifteen hours into the fresh, new world, the day was taking a familiar shape, as were the days ahead. She sipped coffee from a chipped Wonder Woman mug, with a John Donne anthology open on the kitchen table.

Grace's mother had almost wrested Evangeline from her when she took her sleeping daughter there yesterday evening, such was her enthusiasm to have the little girl stay over. Grace, who had left the large family home to share a flat, had always told her that her parents would have happily adopted Kelly, and it seemed that their focus had now switched to Evangeline. They were warm-hearted people, and their lights were always on, and the kitchen smelled of baked bread, but Kelly had been as reluctant as always when Grace had made the suggestion.

"Work, college, baby... you can't keep on like that without a break, Kel."

It was the jolly tone she always found so irritating (that and the shortening of her name), and it was her remorse about feeling like that that pushed her into a New Year's Eve she had not planned, which had involved her shaving her legs with a blunt razor.

Evangeline seemed none the worse for her first night away from her mother, although she looked different, in some way hard to define.

Just two hours, and the unfinished essay on the poet's 'Devotions Upon Emergent Occasions' would have to be put away again, and the two of them would be making their way down the road to the bus stop.

Perhaps Grace was right. Last night had been no break, particularly as most of the people at the party were the ones she saw daily, but she did wonder about those days ahead, and whether she could keep running to stand still for the rest of her life.

ROY

Sometimes I wonder if this is how the afterlife feels, if I have even died without knowing, or whether I am seeing the world in this way for a reason. Perhaps I am meant to do something before I leave, before I sleep in God's acre. Perhaps I need to tell someone what I know before I am lost to sight. For truths have been revealed to me, as I have been sitting here in the morning room.

All along, it turns out, there has been a God, and he does sit in judgement. There are angels, and they are not worried-looking human figures with their wings folded under shabby coats, they are as in Renaissance paintings, serious of countenance. I have seen them over the sunlit garden, and the sword of Michael was unsheathed, for the reckoning will soon come.

I am a child again, looking up from the pew as my father preaches from the Old Testament, but the Word no longer terrifies me. I understand now that all we're ever meant to do is to love, to be loved, to try to do the right thing, to honour the lives we've been given. Honour our lives. That's it. Nothing else matters much. I wish I had known this all along, but I suppose that's the thing, you never do, not until you're near the end.

And in the end, I imagine the final years of my life falling away, like discarded clothes. I have less need of them, and of my worn and lined skin, with each day that passes now.

I see a small boy running, turning to wave, then running

on toward the sound of a familiar voice, toward the sun, running home, under the bluest sky.

KELLY

"I will lift up mine eyes to the hills, from whence cometh my help."

As always, Roy silently mouthed the words to Psalm 121, as Kelly read from the battered King James Bible.

"He that keepeth thee will not slumber."

It had to be the King James Version. Roy had once misplaced it and, inconsolable, had refused the alternative modern version Kelly had brought from the lounge, by jabbing his fingers into his ears and howling, until she had found it, incongruously, in the middle of a stack of birdwatching books under his bed. Between readings, the Bible lay open at the page on the table in his room, next to the only other item he permitted to be on the table, an old black and white photograph of three young men, in an antique gilt frame. On her first night shift, Kelly had been directed to the table, as she got him ready for bed.

"Mister Roy's a sweetheart, he'll be a nice easy start for you," Mrs Flaherty, the deputy manager had said. The patronising tone of several of the staff had immediately grated, and, from the outset, Kelly had refused to address him as anything other than just Roy. She had initially thought that she was meant to look at the photograph, and went to pick it up, but his agitation made it clear what he actually wanted her to do.

"No, no! The psalm! That psalm, there!"

At the end of the first week, she realised that he knew the

psalm, and was following her, word for word, as she read, his eyes closed. When she stumbled over the unfamiliar text, he would simply pause, and wait for her to catch up, but she no longer did that. She wondered if she now knew Roy's psalm as well as he did, but she knew that he would not countenance her simply reciting it, and that her sitting there next to him, with the Bible in hand, was as important to him as hearing the words.

When she mentioned what had happened after that first night, Mrs Flaherty had expressed surprise but no interest.

"Our Mister Roy, a Bible basher? Who knew? I daresay he's just reverting to childhood. Most of them do, you know."

Kelly could not argue with the woman's brisk, almost abrasive manner, nor with the logic of what she had said. The Grange seemed at times to be filled with the awful sounds of old souls calling for their lost homes and lives. She knew, though, that Roy was not just reliving a church-going past, although she couldn't say why she knew this when she talked to Grace about him.

The seventeenth century language had moved her intensely when she first read it aloud – her English tutor had often spoken of the importance of the Bible, how it underpinned Western literature, why they should read it – but it was only now that she began to appreciate the austere beauty, and to truly understand it to be poetry. She found herself making progress with her Donne essay.

She was also unable to say why, though she did not mention this to anyone else at the home, she had felt drawn to the old man, since the first time she had looked into his face, etched by age and trouble, but also reassuring, even wise. She had seen there something that she could not yet

10

name, and it unsettled her.

For now, she realised that these moments of her night shift, with her child sleeping fitfully in the cot in the live-in room, with hours of lonely and stressful work ahead of her, had come to mean as much to her as to him.

"The Lord shall preserve thy going out and thy coming in from this time forth, and even for evermore."

ROY

There is always more than one way of looking at a picture, always more than one way of remembering what was happening then.

Three young men looking back at me like they know me. Two of them are holding cans of beer.

I remember summer evenings in a garden, drinking beer. Perhaps they were with me?

I remember the warmth on my back, and the gentleness of my father. Where did he go?

I remember benign Northern voices, from a time lost to me, from before darkness appeared at the edges of the photograph.

There is something about this photograph, there is another way to look at the picture, and it's about what you can't see.

That's what is really important, it's what you can't see, what is really there, and that is what I cannot remember.

I will lift up mine eyes unto the hills.

KELLY

Psalm 121 aside, Roy's vocabulary appeared to be diminishing. Kelly had only been at The Grange for six weeks, but he had now stopped thanking her for the Bible readings, and no longer returned her 'Goodnight'. Nobody at the home seemed concerned when she made her observation known, not even Grace, a kind-hearted young woman.

"It's sad, Kel, but it's what happens. They have an illness, and that's a symptom."

Kelly had worked in retirement homes since enrolling in the Open University, and she had thought she was used to the infirmities of old age, and the desolation that sometimes came with it. She had not imagined that The Grange's dementia care specialist status would mean any significant change to her working life, despite the warnings of Grace. After all, she had alerted her to the vacancy, the increased money, the overnight accommodation for babies, and had no doubt spoken for her friend to Mrs Flaherty.

If anything, Kelly had felt a surge of hope for a future in which she and her daughter could settle into a comfortable rut, depending on no one else to get through each week. By the end of her second day, she was wondering how long she could bear this: the uncompromising brutality of the disease, stalking its prey relentlessly along corridors reeking of piss and disinfectant, the endless howling, the hopelessness of lives collapsing all around her.

It was only when she met Roy that she began to believe

that there was worth to what she was doing there, and she still believed this, although she could not explain it, not now that the old man had lapsed into ever longer periods of silence, broken by the occasional disjointed word. She found this almost unbearable, especially because of her conviction that someone was still there behind the fading eyes. She did not say this to anyone at The Grange, not even Grace, but in the silence of the evenings, as she sat with him, Bible in hand, she would talk to him as if she expected responses, not in the infantilising manner used by the other staff with their wretched charges (nor by her when she was with any other resident). She told him about her adoptive parents, how unhappy she'd been at school, how she moved out and lived with Grace's family for a time. She explained why she had not wanted Evangeline's father to be involved in the child's life, and how relieved she felt when she heard about his drugs conviction before she'd come to a decision as to whether to tell him she was pregnant.

Occasionally, when she knew that Mrs Flaherty was not going to be in, she would take in the guitar she'd been given as a twenty-first birthday present from Grace's parents. It was a cheap model, and she had never mastered the tuning, but she'd learned three chords, enough to bash out a couple of bedsitter classics. She'd heard that dementia sufferers could still respond to music, but Roy would not, almost as if he'd decided not to. She nevertheless continued to sing to him, and began to leave the guitar in his room, where she somehow felt it belonged.

Mostly, as they sat and drank tea, before she helped him into his bed, she talked to him about her degree course and what she wanted to do afterwards. Grace would have told her she was mad, she thought, but she knew that Roy was listening to her as he watched, of this she was certain. She was just as certain that he was still communicating with her, trying to tell her something, and one January night she realised what it was.

ROY

The picture, I know something about the picture.

My little brothers, that's who they are, my little brothers.

So is that me with them?

So long ago, I don't know what I looked like.

But I remember my little brothers, that's who they are.

This is all to do with Kelly.

I remember her from way, way back.

There is something about Kelly and my little brothers that is important.

Oh God, I'd forgotten how beautiful Kelly was.

I loved her more than anyone I ever thought I'd loved, and I thought she'd gone away.

Now she's come back, and she showed me the baby.

I can't remember the baby's name. My daughter, I can't remember her name.

But the picture, there is another way to look at it, there's something you can't see.

It's what is really there.

Someone else is there, that's it, only you can't see her.

Her.

Kelly.

No, not Kelly, Kelly is here, now.

Emma! It's Emma!

Emma is there, somewhere.

KELLY

"Emma! It's Emma!"

Kelly had been turned away from the old man, switching a lamp on for the reading of the psalm, but the shock would have been no less had she been facing him. In the immediacy of that moment, the light and the voice, she imagined that she had touched an exposed live wire, and then that she had somehow inadvertently switched on Roy's television.

When he next spoke, she was looking at him.

"Emma is there, somewhere!"

Roy was not looking back at her, however, but at the framed photograph on the table. It came to her that he had been doing that a lot in the last few days. Now that she realised what had happened, she sat down in the chair opposite him, gripping the Bible as if for reassurance, and tried to slow her racing heartbeat.

"Roy?" was all she could say, as she contemplated what had happened. She could not take her eyes off him, just as his gaze was fixed on the picture. As her thoughts took shape, and less rational explanations were firmly suppressed, she began to feel a sense of vindication. Grace had suggested that Roy would not talk again, but she had never been able to accept what was a reasonable assumption. Far into his deep-set, weary eyes, she imagined that she had seen her own reflection, and now she was sure of what she had sensed for some time, that he had been thinking about her in his silent world, that she was a part of that world, and that he had always been going to speak again, to her.

Vindicated, but unsure, and a little shaken.

"Roy?"

It occurred to her that this was perhaps the longest sentence Roy had spoken to her, maybe even the only true sentence, and yet it made no sense. She had also, as if it mattered, picked up on a surprisingly strong Mancunian accent. She supposed that this had registered with her because she had been born in Manchester, as far as she was aware.

"Roy, who is Emma? Where is she?"

Finally, he turned to her.

Outside, the gloaming of a late winter afternoon in the North of England closed in on the Victorian house, and Kelly shivered. In the sepulchral silence, nothing moved except for the ticking clock. Finally, she released her breath.

"Roy, where is Emma? Who is in the photograph?"

She was meant to be doing something, to be helping Roy, she was certain. A part of her felt ridiculous for imagining it, but it was as if this moment had been coming, she was in this place at this time, at his behest, and the stars had aligned. Slowly, she stood up from the chair and reached for the frame, noticing for the first time the dragonflies and flowers tangled in the design. She sat back down, with the photograph on her lap, and looked up at Roy, who was now smiling expectantly. Of course. He was one of the three young men, the one who was smiling. He was wearing aviator sunglasses, but it was unmistakeably him.

"Were these your friends with you, Roy? I can't see Emma."

She wondered how long ago the photo had been taken,

and thought of decades rather than years, although she struggled to pin down a younger Roy in any precise period of the past. When had people stopped taking black and white photographs? Perhaps Emma had taken it, perhaps that was what he meant.

It appeared to be summer, and the young men were in a garden. Two of them, not Roy, were holding cans, of beer she assumed. One of them was dark and slight, handsome but indefinably sad looking. The other, standing in the middle, was seriously posing for the photographer, she decided. Roy, on the right, had his hair tied back in a ponytail, and was as gaunt as he was now. One way or another, he had not aged. She looked back at him once more, and he was now pointing at her, jabbing his finger. No, not her, he was pointing at the frame.

"It's beautiful, Roy. Art nouveau. Older than the photo."

He began to howl, but she had experienced his frustrations before now, and knew how to respond, sotto voce.

"Roy, it's alright, hush now. Just try and tell me what the matter is. Who is Emma? Did she take the photo? Is that why you think she's there?"

To her relief, as Mrs Flaherty was on duty this evening, the howling stopped abruptly, just as the back of the frame came away in her hand. It had not been properly fastened, and there was a piece of paper between it and the photograph. On the back of the frame was an adhesive label inscribed 'To Rev C Rogers, with grateful thanks. May 1986'.

She looked back at him, as if awaiting confirmation, or permission. He was smiling again, like he had been when the photo was taken. She turned the paper over and read the words aloud: "Look behind the guitar."

19

She had turned to look where her guitar had taken up residence in Roy's room, propped up in the far corner, before she reminded herself that the note must have been wedged behind the photo before she had ever met Roy. Then she realised that the back of the frame was insecure not only because of the note, but because the end of the photograph had been folded over, and was pushing the back out, as if it would not be denied. With trembling hands, she slowly prised the card from where it had been affixed and unfolded it. The lamp flickered briefly, before illuminating the garden from long ago.

There were now four people there, and the fourth person, hidden for so long, standing next to Roy, was a blonde-haired woman in a leather jacket, who was not looking at the photographer but away from the group.

Tears were running silently down Roy's bowed head.

"Emma," said Kelly, as she took in the face, her heart missing a beat, then another.

*

Roy never spoke again, as far as anyone knew, but his last words, and the revelation they had set in motion, were reverberating inside Kelly several days later.

He had not cried for long that night and was again smiling broadly when she left him. He's happy, she realised, he's happy, that's why he was crying. He had made it very clear that the restored photograph was not to be folded back into the frame, and so she had the next day brought in a bigger one, in which her adoptive parents had once resided.

So four pale young people from a lost world now stared

20

out from Roy's table, and one of them was Roy, and one was Emma, who had ceased to be an unnamed ghost.

Roy now actually looked like an old man, it seemed to Kelly. His almost constant agitation had ebbed away with that evening, and the air of worry that had always hung over him had dissipated. In some ways this was a relief, at least to other staff at The Grange, but Kelly felt waves of sadness over her fear that Roy was now beginning to disappear. She did not want him to go gently into that good night.

She also needed to talk to him, about what had happened that evening, about the hidden image of a young woman, about the note, about Emma. It was all still too much to take in, and there was no one else she could tell, not even Grace. Other staff had made comments about 'Mister Roy's special girl', and she knew that Grace wondered about the time she spent with him. She now realised, though, that she had not been drawing closer to him in these recent days, but he to her.

She was on a day shift, and helping him to wash and dress, but he had dozed off in his armchair. She picked up the photograph and examined it properly for the first time. In the cold morning light, the same thing struck her again. It was Emma's eyes. Her own hair was long, neat and light brown. Emma's had been short, just out of bed, and wonderfully platinum, and she was tall, at least as tall as Martin. But the eyes.

She had never known how to assess how she looked, how attractive she was, or wasn't. She had had boyfriends, and there was Evangeline's father, but the feral young men she had grown up with could not have cared less, so long as you made an effort (a phrase, oddly, that Grace's mother sometimes used when trying to persuade her to wear a dress and mascara). The thought, then, of a slight resemblance to the prepossessing young woman Emma had been was incredible to her. The lost girl from Roy's past reminded her of the sixth formers she'd admired from afar as a twelve-year-old: casually beautiful, effortlessly glamorous, forever beyond an adopted child with a lisp. Yet the eyes, the turn of her neck as she looked away, the pursed lips: they were familiar from so many adolescent holiday snaps.

"For God's sake, child, can you not just smile for once?"

She tried to put this to the back of her mind. So much about the evening now felt like a dream, and she needed to think about the mysterious note and the instruction to look behind a guitar.

There was something else about Emma, though, something that hung over the affected world-weariness. She was unhappy, thought Kelly, and no one knew.

*

She had kept hold of the note. If Roy had noticed, he hadn't cared. Emma, whoever she was, was there beside him, and now he was sleeping through the afternoons. Even the reading of the psalm had ceased to be a nightly ritual, as if the help sought in the verses had now come.

The note perhaps pointed the way forward to discovering more about the photograph, about that long-gone summer, about Emma. It could also have meant nothing or referred to a guitar that no longer existed. It could have been something of no significance. It could have been a mislaid joke. Kelly ruled out all these alternatives, partly because they made no sense to her. Why would the note have been placed so deliberately and carefully within the folded photograph? There was also the handwriting, which was in an old-fashioned cursive script. She felt certain that Roy was the writer, and that the formality meant that it referred to something important. The other reason for not screwing up the piece of paper was that she did not want, in so doing, to let go of Roy, not yet anyway. She believed that this was mutual, or that it had been mutual. So where to go first?

"Kel, no! No! Don't be stupid! You'd lose your job if Flaherty found out!"

Grace's response had been predictable, if in some way reassuring. The risks could not be denied, but it was all Kelly could think of. Roy had been at The Grange for longer than most of the current turnover of students and underpaid migrant workers, and anyone she had asked had known nothing much about him. No one visited him, although that was far from unusual. Mister Roy was just one more old man from a lost history, and nobody else much cared, least of all Irma, Mrs Flaherty's secretary. Kelly, however, finally saw a chink of light during a rehearsed conversation with her. Irma zealously followed the management line on resident confidentiality, to the point where she had had run-ins with visiting doctors, but she could rarely resist letting staff know how much more she knew about the people in their care. As expected, she had stonewalled the initial questions about Roy's background, but she had eventually conceded.

"Of course, you know that's not his real name?"

"What?"

"Mister Rogers. Roy isn't his real name, didn't you know? You're too young to get the joke."

Kelly had known but had forgotten his surname.

Surnames were packed away with suitcases upon arrival at The Grange, and she felt a pang of complicity, but she did not get the joke. Irma's condescension rose another notch, as she explained.

"He arrived here with a couple of old bags, a few dog-eared birdwatching books and a guitar. He never played the damn thing, I'm not sure he could, but that's how he got the name. Roy Rogers!"

The hoot of laughter was one of derision, and Kelly had to swallow hard, and wait until the day she would leave the place before calling Irma a hateful bitch. In that very instant, she realised that, by avoiding looking at her, she was staring over her head at a rack of keys, and then the idea came to her.

"Martin, Grace, Martin. His name is Martin, and all the time he's been here, we've treated him like a clown, for a cheap joke! And a joke that isn't funny."

"Kel, you're right, okay? But please don't do this, and don't ask me to lie for you if Flaherty finds out."

Grace knew that Kelly would not be talked out of this, hence the second request. She had seen this often enough since they were teenagers. Calm, clever, quiet, but unafraid in the cause of what was right. She remembered her slapping a boy in class for snapping Grace's bra strap. Most of all, she remembered her on their doorstep one night, rucksack in hand, determined not to cry even when Grace's mother had started to, and had put her arms around her.

"I would never ask you to do that. I just wanted you to know why I'm doing this."

"Kel?"

"Yes?"

"Remember the name we used to have? Our little two girl

24

gang?"

"You mean Grace Kelly? Of course I do. Now that was funny!"

They both began to laugh, and Grace put her hand on her friend's arm, as she remembered how much she loved her, and often worried about her.

*

When it came down to it, she couldn't believe how easy it was, a thought that came back to her often in later years, when she reflected on that long winter night.

Irma's office was never locked, although the inner sanctum of Norah Flaherty, where the residents' records were filed, certainly was. All she needed was two minutes with her torch – the lights on would be noticeable from the staff room on the other side of the courtyard – and no one else from the night shift wandering the corridors. She had checked on Evangeline just after midnight, then taken the longer way around the old house, in order to avoid the staff room, where she would have been expected to join the others for a cup of tea. In the office, all the keys were still there on the rack behind Irma's desk, all neatly labelled. 'Storage Room', with a bright red fob, was on the end, and the torch was unnecessary. She realised that she'd been holding her breath as she closed the door behind her, and sighed heavily, just as Kalina, one of the students, came around the corner.

Before she even had time to panic, and perhaps resort to an unprepared explanation for where she was, she realised that the young woman was crying. They both stopped, frozen, Kelly apprehensive and Kalina clearly flustered.

25

"Kalina, whatever's the matter?"

Kalina appeared to be too choked with tears to respond, and instead she crumpled onto Kelly's shoulder and sobbed. Taken aback, and now wondering if she could feel the key in her pocket as she pressed into her, Kelly could do nothing other than hold her gently, and hope that nobody else came around that corner.

Kalina had only been at The Grange for the last month. Kelly had spoken to her once or twice in the staffroom. Thin and anxious-looking, she was probably no more than twenty but looked older, hollow-cheeked and constantly drawn. Kelly had asked tentatively about her background but, even allowing for her shyness and accented English, had made an early judgement that there were areas of conversation not to be explored. Kalina was from Warsaw, and she had left Poland with her mother two years previously. As far as Kelly could understand, there had been some trouble to do with the mother being a journalist and being involved in an abortion rights campaign, but she did not press her any further on this. She was now enrolled on an NVQ course, as were several of the staff, and that was as much as Kelly knew about her that night.

"Kalina, tell me, what is it?"

"I did not take tights. I did not."

Relief at the girl's preoccupation mingled with confusion.

"Tights? Whose tights?"

"Sarah's tights, drying in staffroom. She said I have taken them. She says she will tell Mrs Flaherty. I will lose job and be sent back to Poland. I did not take tights."

Everything now became clearer. Sarah was another of the students, a woman with an ear-piercing laugh and forceful opinions, particularly when it came to her 'foreign' colleagues.

"Kalina, listen. I know you didn't take them, and Mrs Flaherty won't sack you just because Sarah says you did."

Kelly was not certain of that. Sarah was a favourite of the deputy manager, who perhaps recognised a like-minded soul. Kalina was becoming calmer, however. Together they walked back round to the staffroom, Kelly holding on to the key in her pocket, Kalina blowing her nose. Nobody was there, and so no explanation of how and where she had found Kalina was necessary, nor was a defence of her required, to her relief. Sarah could be intimidating.

"Thank you, Kelly. You are good friend."

I don't know about that, thought Kelly. Sarah's tights had gone missing at just the right time, as she crept around the house that night. She made her way back towards the storage room.

Roy had come to The Grange with a guitar. No, Martin had. She liked the real name much better, especially now that she knew that Irma had thought the moniker so amusing. It was as if a slave name had been shed and an identity reclaimed. She wondered how he might react to being called by a name he might have forgotten.

Martin. Martin Rogers. "Look behind the guitar."

There should be a guitar in the storage room, tagged with that name, although what she would find behind it mystified her. How could Martin have known what would be behind it when he wrote the note? Perhaps something was stuck to the back of it, that would make more sense, although it was now past two in the morning, and she wasn't thinking very clearly. Once Kalina had been persuaded not to phone her mother, and to lie down for a couple of hours, Kelly had decided that the whole thing had to be done tonight.

No residents had gone for a midnight walk, there had been no unexpected medical emergencies, and Sarah was not actually on the overnight shift, but had apparently called in en route to a Manchester club to pick up her favourite tights. Kelly didn't care to imagine why they were here, but Sarah had left without them, talking pointedly about shortages in Communist countries. Along with the tights, thirty years of European history had now gone missing, but they would all have to wait to be retrieved, as Kelly reached again for the key. She had only been in the room twice, on both occasions to recover cases for bereaved relatives, and her torch confirmed her recollection of a disorganised left luggage store, crammed with luggage never to be reclaimed by the owners. She could not, however, see a guitar.

She had almost completed a second sweep of each shelf, and concluded that it had been stolen, when she realised that half a dozen suitcases were protruding from a top shelf. Pulling over the stepladder she remembered using, she took down the cases. She hadn't thought about the guitar being in a case itself, but there it was, of course. Black, or once black, under dust and cobwebs, and with a guitar inside it, judging by the weight as she slowly eased it down, and placed it flat on the floor. There was the tag, tied to the handle: 'Mr M Rogers'. She shone the beam across the matt body, and picked out the faded, silver stencilled letters 'EDC'. Hoping that it had not been locked by a missing key, she released the three catches along the side and swung open the cover.

Three floors above her, Martin turned over and opened his eyes.

To her disappointment, but also with a sense of relief, she could see immediately that there really was only a guitar in the case.

Roy had gone, he had never in truth been there, and she had brought Martin back, and found Emma for him, but she had felt disquieted since that night she had picked up the framed photograph and opened up its secret, the secret girl. Yet here she was, in the darkness, looking for something else a younger Martin had hidden, but had wanted someone to find.

"The someone is you, Miss Ackroyd."

The torchlight flickered, and she started at the sound of her own voice, using the surname she tried to avoid.

"Oh, for God's sake!"

That felt more like herself, and she tutted, hit the torch with the flat of her hand a couple of times, and examined the guitar. It was an electric one, she could see that, and much bigger than hers. It looked to have been originally as plain black as the case but was mostly covered with peeling stickers – 'Rock Against Racism', 'Sandinista', 'Vote Bobby Sands' – and another stencil of 'EDC'. It also only had four strings, very thick ones.

So this was Martin's guitar, the one that had earned him the disdain and humiliation, and which had been stowed away out of sight, along with his life and self. She wiped her eyes, and carefully picked it up. There was nothing on the back, no message, no clue. "Whence cometh my help?" she whispered, as she knelt in the shadows, shivering.

She was lowering the guitar back into the case by its neck, when she noticed the small compartment upon which the neck partly rested. The torch picked out the strip of ribbon protruding from the felt-covered lid. This time, she lifted the whole of the guitar and took it out of the case, gently leaning it against the shelf to the side of her. Adjusting the torch again, and taking hold of the ribbon, she stopped still, and listened.

The night shrouded the Victorian house and filled the passageways with silence. The town beyond was still. Under the starless sky, in the near foothills of the Pennines, a red kite slept in the susurrating branches of an oak, waiting for dawn. In Martin's room, three young men stared out from a bygone summer.

Kelly pulled on the ribbon, and a faint sigh drifted down the halls, as a clock chimed the hour.

*

Norah Flaherty had always prided herself on her ability to read people. This, she supposed, was why she remained unmarried at the age of fifty: men were easy to read. As a young woman on a Salford estate, she had resisted all earthly temptation, and her confession had rarely involved any more than uncharitable thoughts. Membership of the Catholic Women's League had been the outlet for her energies, before she had followed her sister into nursing. Her parents, both from the West of Ireland, died when she was in her twenties, and both her sisters were now in Australia. She believed she had an aunt in Liverpool, but she was otherwise quite alone in the world, and that suited her.

The sign on her door read 'Deputy Manager' but, in reality, she was in charge of The Grange, one of a chain of homes owned by a London company. She was of course answerable to the employers for her running of the place but, so long as the accounts were legal and healthy, and nothing worthy of media interest was allowed to happen, they appeared to be happy to leave the day-to-day practices to her. She had duly made The Grange in her own image: all was orderly and efficient. "Shipshape," she sometimes said to herself, with immense satisfaction. She had allowed the 'Mrs', by which she had been mistakenly addressed when she had first arrived, to go unchecked, believing that it magnified her authority over the silly girls who worked there. Kelly Ackroyd, for example.

There was something about that girl, thought Norah that morning. She had just endured a formal complaint from Sarah about her missing tights, during which she had had to repeat several times that she would not be calling in the police, and that accusations could not simply be made on the basis of disliking a colleague. Sarah was a feather-brained 'eejit', as Norah's father would have said, and she'd once again told her to put on less make-up for work, but still. Kalina was too quiet for her liking, always creeping around like a church mouse. Norah had felt sorry for her when she turned up for interview, looking like she hadn't eaten properly in days, but had later heard of her mother's involvement in some pro-abortion movement, and had now decided that she couldn't be trusted. Maybe it would be worth checking her locker.

Kelly Ackroyd was another matter. There was a sly one, she thought. Sarah was right about that, she was too smart for her own good, and a bit of a bleeding heart, too ready to side with the foreign girls whenever they complained. Probably voted Remain. Always bloody reading, too, and far too popular with the residents, especially that weird old man on the top floor. That was always a bad sign, staff getting too close. Sarah had heard that Kelly had been seen with her arm around Kalina last night, and the suggestion of an unnatural friendship had completed the picture for Norah. She would have to be watched.

For now, there were two locker checks to do. She stepped through into Irma's office and, as she reached for the master key, she noticed that another key was missing from the rack.

By the end of the day, the locker searches had revealed nothing of any interest: no stolen tights, no residents' jewellery, a book of poetry (who had time for that nonsense?), nothing. Norah's focus was now elsewhere, however.

The missing key had been found within minutes, still in the lock of the storage room door. Irma had come in late, after Norah's realisation that it was missing, and her secretary had reminded her that when she went home yesterday evening, Norah had been there. In any event, Irma had seen no one in the office yesterday, and she had not used the key herself, and why would she? Why would anyone? Why take the key and go into a dusty room full of empty cases? It made no sense, and Norah had to have sense.

She briefly imagined one of those little trollops sneaking a boy in there, or maybe even the Ackroyd girl and her little Polish friend, but there were easier places in the house for that sort of carry-on, God preserve us, and none requiring access to keys. Having decided that a sweep of the various nooks and crannies one evening might be worthwhile, she reverted to her consternation at what appeared to be a break-in with no purpose, resulting in no damage or theft. Not a thing was out of place in the room. It was as if nobody had been in there for a long time, but somebody had, and the somebody knew something that Norah did not know. That would not do.

*

Only one week in three was a night shift, but Kelly was still struggling to organise her life around those weeks. She had never been able to sleep during the day, and often abandoned the idea, to sit in her dressing gown at the kitchen table, with an overdue essay on her laptop. The Grange, which had at first seemed like the answer to several questions, was wearing her out. Even the day shifts had become part of a vicious circle, closing in around her. She needed the job, it was just about covering part-time nursery fees, and there would soon be a residential summer school to pay for, but she was increasingly aware that she was not doing it very well. Mrs Flaherty had noticed as much as soon as Kelly had realised it.

"It's fine to be nice to the old dears, but we mustn't forget that they all need to be taken care of. Cups of tea, the toilet, the washing up."

The woman managed to make 'taken care of' sound harsh, but Kelly knew she had a point, especially about the old dear everyone else still called Roy. She also fretted about how Evangeline might be affected by an overwrought mother, but the 18-month-old appeared to be thriving on the attention of a widening support system. She was at a heart-stopping and irresistible age, teetering into the outstretched arms of Grace, Grace's parents, the nursery staff, several of the young

33

women at The Grange, even Sarah, who had promised to take her out on her eighteenth birthday. Only Martin had shown no interest in the little girl on the two occasions he'd seen her, and had on the first occasion become upset, asking where the baby had been.

Martin was saying nothing anymore, but he continued to overshadow the disarray of Kelly's life, along with the recurring dreams of her mother.

She had two more night shifts after her discovery of his guitar, and then the blessed relief of a weekend off. It would of course be no such thing, Evangeline and John Donne would see to that, but there would be breathing space, time to sit still, to collect her scattered thoughts, and time to look again at what she had found behind the guitar.

*

Grace had not asked her anything about the storeroom. Kelly had regretted confiding in her, not because she thought that Grace might betray the confidence, but because she had made her feel uncomfortable and torn, and not for the first time. She thought back to an incident at school, when no one had joined her in skipping classes to join the local Iraq war demonstration.

"We can't all keep to your principles, Kel!"

It was around that time that her mother had caught her trying to unlock the bureau where she knew any adoption papers would be kept, and here she was again, breaking in somewhere in search of secrets.

When Kelly had asked her friend if she could take Evangeline for a couple of hours on Saturday afternoon, she knew that Grace suspected the story of an essay to complete, but she also knew that for Grace the subject of the break-in was closed, and the disagreement filed away, just like the one they'd had ten years ago.

She sat at the kitchen table, on which she had placed a folded sheet of paper, marked 'In Blood', a sealed envelope, addressed just to 'G27', a scrap of paper with a name and address scribbled on it, and a guitar pick. She had barely thought about what she had taken from the compartment in the guitar case that night, but the oddments of Martin's life looked no less mysterious in daylight. Even the blue pick was inscribed with something, mostly faded but still partly legible. The second word was 'Records'. The name on the paper was Phil, and the address was in North London by the post code. She unfolded 'In Blood' and immediately dropped the sheet, as she realised that the rust-coloured patches at the bottom were actually dried blood. She had seen enough blood at The Grange, and had cleaned up enough cuts after falls, but this blood had been shed a long time ago, apparently by intent, which disconcerted her. The writing above was in red, although it was in pen, she noted with relief, possibly for dramatic effect, and had not faded at all. What made it painstaking to decipher, however, was the script. Was it called copperplate? It was similar to the note behind the photograph, and so she decided that Martin was the author.

Alexandra Palace
4th May 1977

We, the undersigned, do now bind ourselves in blood to each other, in perpetuity.

As we have not worried to be born, we do not worry to die.

Our art will live on forever.

We are Generation 27.

So long as we live, wherever we are in the world, should one need the others, that one will send a Valediction Records plectrum and a date on to the next, in the order as set out below, and that next one will in turn send it on, and so forth, until the plectrum has returned to the original sender. The undersigned will then duly meet on the given date in London, at this place where we sign our names on this day.

The names underneath were M. Rogers, P. de la Croix, S. Elijah and E. Dehasse-Carter, and each one was signed and bloodstained.

Forty years ago. Her guess at the age of Martin's photograph seemed to have been about right, if you could assume that the boys and the secret girl in the garden were the four bound in blood. So that meant E. Dehasse-Carter had to be Emma, Martin's Emma? Emma Dehasse-Carter, to whom she had imagined a faint resemblance. Of course, she thought, how stupid of me! That's why Martin was so happy to see me, that's why he wanted me to pick up the photo frame, to find Emma, to find his instruction. It was so obvious now. The old man had possibly even conjoined two young women, the one before him and the one he had known. The two other names (the three of them sounded exotic, she decided) were therefore the two young men in the garden with Emma and Martin. And again, of course! EDC! The stencil on the guitar case and the guitar. Had that been Martin's tribute to her? She had no doubt that he had loved

36

her, although she could not have said why.

She looked again at the plectrum. Yes, now she could see it, 'Valediction Records'. That's why it was there with the oath.

"In blood," she repeated. To Kelly, this was more than agreement, much more. Four people, at the age she was now, had committed their hearts and souls to each other. She could hear Grace making a joke out of it, and Mrs Flaherty calling her a 'silly girl', but she wished she could have been a part of something so pure, so life-enhancing, so truly romantic. In blood.

Who or what Generation 27 was, she did not know, but that led her, finally, to the letter.

*

"Are we keeping you up, Kelly?"

"I'm sorry, Mrs Flaherty, I had a bad night. Didn't sleep much."

"What did you say? Speak clearly, girl."

"Mrs Flaherty, her lisp gets worse when she's tired or upset."

"Thank you, Grace, but she's perfectly capable of telling me that herself. Aren't you?"

Oh, Grace, I don't deserve you. That witch. Come on, don't cry. Do not cry. She'd love that. Calm. Take your time. Breathe. Okay.

"I'm sorry, Evangeline kept me up. I am listening."

Kelly did not believe that anyone present at the weekly staff meetings ever listened to much of what Norah Flaherty said. She had once bumped into one of her former teachers in the pub, who had delighted in letting her in on various staffroom secrets, none of which surprised Kelly, including the description of the head teacher's addresses to them all as 'hortatory gibberish'. She had to check the first word in the dictionary and had then loved the phrase ever since. Anybody could safely glaze over and think about other things – applying for Housing Benefit, a late period, buying milk on the way home – during Norah's rallying of the troops. Since when were the ill old people in their care to be regarded as impediments to the smooth running of The Grange? Why were vaguely possible future pay rises presented as an incentive to work harder? Anyway, she thought, looking around the room, most of the girls here don't care. They want to get on with stripping beds, changing pyjamas, returning mislaid jewellery to their correct owners, stopping Arthur, who wore his medal ribbons on his Fair Isle tank top, from pulling down his trousers, and then they want to go home, maybe by way of a supermarket or a bar. So shut up, you witch. It's not just me who isn't listening to you.

And she had had a bad night, several bad nights. Evangeline had taken to waking in the early hours and shouting for her. She had no idea why, and had sometimes woken up confused as to whether she or the little girl had been calling for their mother. All this was happening as she suddenly found herself close to the deadline for handing in her Donne essay. John Donne, poet, cleric, misogynist, to whom women were just objects in his poems. That was her steadfast line, despite the note of caution sounded by David Millhouse when they had last exchanged emails. She had met her tutor at the last summer school and had found him charming but intimidating. Evangeline, a babe in arms then, was in the creche, and he had been solicitous and generous with his time when he became aware of her fretting about this. He had, however, made it clear that no dispensations were available.

"Miss Ackroyd, I admire the commitment you have made, but you do need to understand that you will be assessed as rigorously as any other student."

She had appreciated that frankness at the time, it was why she was there, but she knew that her research was consistently lacking. She had done little of the extra reading around the course that had been recommended.

Typical, typical, she thought, I've decided my conclusion and that's that. I never learn.

In her braver moments, she told herself that Millhouse was just another chauvinist in a suit, and what the hell? I'm sticking with it as it is. Mostly, though, she was worried and weary. She hadn't even thought any more about Martin's mysterious guitar case. Listening to Norah Flaherty's 'hortatory gibberish' that morning was beyond her.

*

Norah left for home early that evening. She wanted to watch the episode of a new drama she'd recorded the previous night, so she could watch the next episode live, and she needed to stock up on cat food on the way. She hated the staff meetings, and she knew that the staff did – none of them listened to her – but it had been made clear to her that the requirement was part of the corporate identity of Golden Years Homes plc, and so she steeled herself each Wednesday morning, after which she regarded the heights of the week as conquered. It was then a downward slope to the weekend, assisted by a glass of sherry in the evening. From lunchtime onwards, Wednesday was a red letter day.

On the drive home today, however, there was no sense of escape. She could not get that damned Ackroyd girl out of her mind. Yawning like that, just as Norah was reminding them all about keeping an eye out for strangers on the premises. The stolen tights, the hug with the Polish girl, the storage room key – she knew they were connected, and that little Miss Smarty Pants Ackroyd was involved. She just knew. And then she was home, turning into her road, and she'd forgotten the cat food.

She sat down in her coat, as an expectant tabby jumped onto her lap. Maybe two glasses of sherry tonight, she thought, and then her shoulders slumped and her head dropped.

"Dad," she said in the silence, "Dad."

*

On the last day of January, Kelly pressed the Send button on her laptop, and her critique of 'Devotions Upon Emergent Occasions' was consigned to the lap of the gods. That felt like an appropriate description, and one that she thought might have appealed to John Donne: her words cast out into the ether, to be judged by an invisible, all-knowing presence. Millhouse always insisted upon his students posting hard copies of their work but was prepared to consider a deadline as met if an electronic version was in his inbox by the date in question. He was as immutable as Donne's God in this, and she had only briefly considered requesting an extension, before deciding that the request would be pointless, and that it might even add to his apparent concerns about the quality of the essay.

As she trundled Evangeline's pushchair to the post office – Millhouse also insisted on registered delivery – she felt the lifting of a heavy weight and the anticipation of a short respite before the next deadline appeared on the horizon. She had just promised herself fish and chips as a celebration tea when she remembered that, of course, she was back on an overnight shift at The Grange and that she needed to give herself time beforehand to deliver her daughter to Grace's parents. She had left Evangeline with them a couple of times recently. She suspected that Grace had passed on her consternation about how tired Kelly looked, prompting the offer of childminding, but felt that she was simply unable to turn it down. She was tired, to her bones, and it was so much easier than taking the child with her, especially with her ongoing habit of crying for her at precisely three o'clock each morning. She was also increasingly uneasy about leaving her in that room. Norah Flaherty had recently been making it clear that Kelly had been granted a huge favour, and that it was a temporary one, but it was more than that. Since the night she had opened Martin's guitar case, she had discerned a difference in the way Norah spoke to her, as had Grace.

"You're on her shit list, Kel. Be careful. She can be a vicious cow."

She had wondered if Norah knew about the night in the storage room but then realised that she would already have been dismissed if that were so. Still, she had begun to think about moving on, getting another job, doing something completely different with her life, and she knew that this sense of restlessness somehow had its origins in that day she had read 'In Blood'. John Donne had written about a recovery from sickness being like a visit from God, and a rebirth. She did not believe in his God, but she knew exactly what the poet had meant. On her way back from the post office, she decided what she had to do.

*

"Martin? Martin? That's your real name, isn't it? Martin Rogers. I'm so sorry I ever called you by that awful nickname, I didn't know. I'm so sorry."

She was meant to be getting the old man ready for bed, but she knelt before him, as he dozed in his armchair.

"Martin, I don't know what you can hear, or understand, but I have to talk to you. About Emma."

The lamp on the stand behind her flickered, and she looked back over her shoulder. When she turned back to face Martin, his eyes were open.

"Martin, I want to know about her. Who is she? Where is she now?"

He blinked, switched his gaze to the guitar in the corner, then back to her. She felt as if someone else was behind his eyes, watching her. Maybe he'd finally left, just gone. So who was she talking to, and why? She continued.

"The note behind the photograph," she pointed to the table but to no avail, "you left that there, didn't you? For someone to find. You wanted me to find Emma and find that note, but I don't think you remember that anymore. It's just that I don't understand what I'm meant to do now."

From the inside pocket of her Golden Years Homes

anorak, she took out the Valediction Records plectrum, the London address, the sealed envelope marked 'G27', which she had decided she should not open, and the document 'In Blood', which she unfolded. She placed them all on the floor in front of her, but Martin did not look down.

"So, Martin Rogers, this is what I think. No one remembers you coming here, except maybe Irma, but even she's a bit vague. I reckon that you were still," and here she paused to think of a sensitive way of putting it, but decided that there wasn't one, "you were still here with us back then, at least for some of the time. I think you were still having better days, when you had some idea of what was happening to you."

Her voice began to quaver, and she paused again, but Martin remained still, his hands clasped in his lap.

"That was when you put the note behind the photograph. You knew what was going to happen to you eventually, and that the day would come when you'd forget all about the guitar case and the things you'd left in it. So the note was a reminder, perhaps even a message for someone else, who turned out to be me."

She picked up 'In Blood' and held it open for Martin to see.

"You signed your name to this, a long time ago. So did Emma, but her name's been crossed out. And I think the other two names are the others in the photograph. Martin, did you want me to find this because you thought I was Emma? Because I looked a bit like her? Why did you ever hide her? I don't know why I'm asking you these questions that you're never going to answer. Here, you should have this back. It belongs to you and the others."

She took his right hand and placed in it the sheet of bloodstained, yellowed paper. He looked down, but with no sign of recognition.

"I can only think of one thing to do. The note behind the photograph was a message, and the message led to an oath, signed by the four of you. The oath is to contact the others if one of you needs them. Martin, I believe that you would think that this is the time to honour the oath, and I suppose, I suppose I'm here for your permission."

Her voice finally cracked and, as she welled up, she bowed her head. With his free hand, Martin reached out and stroked her hair.

*

"Oh my God, you call this live music? Half the people in here look barely alive, let alone the band."

Grace sipped her gin and tonic and made a face.

"This is warm! Why don't they have those huge glasses, filled with ice and all sorts of fruit, and cucumber?"

"Grace, for heaven's sake! This is The Albion, not that hipster bar you go to with Ryan."

"Sloe And Easy. I don't know what you've got against it. They do karaoke nights there. Much more fun than this."

They were talking over an uninspired rendition of something Kelly vaguely recognised. The Clash, maybe? Something from way back, anyway. Perhaps Grace was right, and they should have gone somewhere else, where other people in their twenties went. It was, after all, the first night out they'd had together in months, what with different rosters at The Grange, the demands of childcare, and Grace's burgeoning romance with a hotel management trainee. Her friend's face had fallen when she'd arrived earlier to drop off Evangeline.

"Aren't you getting changed? You're going out in jeans?"

So here they were, in what Grace called 'an old man's pub', drinking warm gin and yelling at each other above the noise. I am turning into an old man, considered Kelly, I don't want to be in a trendy gin bar. I want to be in a place like this, listening to live music I'm not old enough to remember.

"Oh, I'm so stupid!"

She slapped her forehead and turned to Grace.

"Don't beat yourself up, Kel. We can finish these and move on."

"No, no, no! I don't mean that, although we can if you want. I mean Martin. And the others. They were in a band together. Of course! How did I not see that?"

"Rewind, Kel, rewind. You've lost me."

Kelly recounted her night in the storage room and her discoveries in the guitar case, feeling guilty while she did so for not updating Grace earlier. She had been her confidante, after all, even an accomplice. With good timing, the band had taken a break, and the conversation dropped to a suitably hushed tone.

"So let me get this straight. Generation 27 were a band, and Roy, sorry, I mean Martin, was in the band, and so was this Emma, and two other guys. I've never heard of them."

"It was forty years ago. Why would we have heard of them unless they were really famous?"

"And they all swore an oath, in their own blood. That's just weird, Kel."

"I don't think it's weird at all. I think there's something

beautiful about it. You know? They all believed they were part of something bigger than themselves."

"And where's that got Roy? Living out his last days in that place, you wiping his arse, no memory of any band."

"That's why I need to help him, Grace."

"I knew you were going to say that."

"I know you knew. And I need your help."

"I knew you were going to say that too."

"Come on, let's go. Will they let me into Sloe and Easy?"

As they walked to the door, the band were about to begin the second half of their regular midweek residency. The singer leaned into the microphone.

"Thank you. We're going to start with a minor classic you might remember, if you're a discerning music lover, or just old. This is 'Trying To Explain'."

Behind the two young women, the wind caught the door of The Albion and slammed it shut.

It was not a karaoke night at Sloe and Easy, and Kelly was thankful for small mercies. Grace had what appeared to be an entire garden border crammed into a large, cold glass, and was much happier and more amenable. They sat in a dark corner, disturbed only by piped ersatz jazz.

"Why do you need my help? If you want to post this guitar pick – what do you call it?"

"A plectrum."

"Post it to an address in London, well, good luck. Just do it."

"No, listen. It needs to come back to me, Grace. I have to send it, in Martin's name, to this man, Phil. He has to be P. de la Croix, the next on the list on the oath. That's why Martin would have left a note of his address. But then Phil de la

Croix has to send it on to the next on the list, S. Elijah. That must be the other guy in Martin's photo. Then it goes to Emma, who is E. Dehasse-Carter, except there's a line through her name. Anyway, finally it gets sent back to me. That way, I know that everyone got the message."

"But why do you need my help? And what is the message?"

"The others on the list, they won't know where Martin is now, and I can't give out the address of The Grange for the plectrum's return. There's occasionally mail for a few residents but it always goes through Irma, and she weeds out anything for the ones as bad as Martin and passes it to Flaherty. I don't even want to think about that happening."

"Spit it out, Kel."

"Your dad, does he still have that PO Box?"

She had remembered Grace earning extra pocket money by often taking a detour home from school to collect the mail for her father's antiques business.

"Yes, I think so. He was saying just recently how appropriate it was that his customers wouldn't correspond by modern means. But Kel, if you're asking to use that address, I'm sure it would be fine, but why not use your own?"

"Because I'm sure I've lost post there. We don't have individual boxes, remember, it all just gets left in the hall. The plectrum will come back to Martin Rogers, not me, and if John saw a letter and didn't know the name, he might just throw it away or return it as 'not at this address'."

Grace nodded. Kelly's flat was in a former seminary, something Grace had always found amusing, but John, the landlord, who lived on the ground floor, could not be described as a saintly soul, and was not to be trusted. They

47

had both said as much in the past.

"And you wouldn't want to use our house for the same reason?"

"Oh no, Grace, that's different. Of course I trust your mum and dad, but it would need an explanation I just don't want to give, or can't give, not right now. What I'm doing, well, I'm still not entirely sure what I'm doing, or why, I just know I have to, and I'd rather no one else knew about it, only you. Does that make sense?"

"Of course it does. I think you're nuts, but you don't have to explain anything. Use the PO Box number and I'll make sure I do all the collections for the next few weeks. Dad will be happy, he hates doing it. But Kel, you still haven't answered me. What message?"

*

So it was that later that week Kelly sealed an envelope addressed to Phil de la Croix of Crouch End, North London. Inside was a blue plectrum with faded lettering and a folded page torn from her Open University planner. On one side of the page she had written a PO Box number, and on the other a date and "London".

She hadn't told Grace what the message to the other former members of Generation 27 was, because the sending of the plectrum was the message.

"Should one need the others… will duly meet on the given date in London, at this place…"

She had not read that part of 'In Blood' to Grace. She had heard of Alexandra Palace, it was something to do with the BBC, but she would have to find out where it was because she knew she would have to go there. The oath was clear on this. She could of course have included Martin's letter, because that was clearly intended to be read by the other three. Wouldn't that have amounted to a discharge of the duty she felt? No, she had no doubts about this. She could not risk sending Martin's letter to someone whose name she had guessed, to an address where he might not live anymore. She would wait for the plectrum to return and she would take the letter to Alexandra Palace, and hand it to whoever was there to meet her. 'In Blood' would be honoured. As to the date, she had decided to give everyone long enough to have the message forwarded to a new address, or to return from holiday, or just to be bothered to pass it on, but no longer than that. They would come or they wouldn't. Just over seven weeks from today was long enough and would allow her time to prepare. If the plectrum were not back with her by then, she would burn the letter, but that would not happen, she was certain of this.

On the third of April, she would be in London, and somehow Martin would be with her. Like John Donne, they would be reborn. She walked back from the post box with a lightening in her heart that was almost overwhelming. Far above her, in the clear northern sky, hovered a young kite, twisting its long, forked tail as it changed direction and flew to the distant hills.

*

Evangeline was the piggy in the middle, which was her favourite game, as it involved her two favourite people, a bright red soft ball, and a lot of running around and screaming. Three weeks had gone by, and Grace had been conscientiously collecting the PO Box mail, but nothing addressed to Martin had arrived, and Kelly was no longer certain that it would. A silly, romantic idea, a silly girl. Life isn't like that, young lady, her adoptive father would say. He would say it right now if he were here.

"It's March, so it's spring," said Grace one Sunday afternoon, "we don't have to wait for the twenty-first, let's sit in the garden."

She had recently moved back in with her parents, unable to meet a rent increase. So they sat throwing the ball to each other over the child's head, while she squealed with joy.

"Just imagine being that easily pleased. A ball, a garden, sunshine, no horrible boys."

"Oh dear, what's happened?"

"He keeps buying me things."

"Oh no! You poor thing!"

"Kel, no, I'm serious. It's getting too much. Every week it's another present, and he gets really upset if I don't like it. You know how sometimes I bring in a change of clothes and go out with him straight from work?"

"Lucky you. I'm sorry, yes, go on."

"I did that last week, and I brought those stockings he bought me. Well, hold ups. I drew the line there. Blokes might love all that stuff, but I could not be bothered with all that messing about with suspender belts."

"You told me all this," said Kelly, bouncing the ball off Evangeline's head.

"Okay. So they were really glamorous, with a rose pattern all the way up."

"To the giggle zone, yes, you said."

"When I came to get changed, I couldn't find them. I know I'm always doing this, forgetting where I left things, but the fuss he made. He sulked all night."

Half an hour previously, Kelly had told Grace about the A-grade for her Donne essay, and the positive feedback notes from David Millhouse. "Oh wow!" she'd replied and moved on. My God, Grace, you have no idea. You'll hand Evangeline back to me in a moment, and you'll carry on wittering about yet another vacuous young man, or your latest row at work, or your bloody hold ups. Oh dear, that's not fair, Kelly. I am so tired.

"But wait, hang on," she said.

"What?"

"Oh, nothing, you just reminded me of something, but I can't remember what. Something that happened recently. Never mind, it'll come to me. Sorry, Gracie."

"What for? You haven't called me Gracie in years."

"A lot on my mind. Go on, tell me about Ryan. You know he's not good enough for you."

"You're funny. All the years I've known you and I still think I don't at all sometimes. Anyway, this one's more important than whinin' Ryan."

She pulled Evangeline to her, and Kelly smiled at them both, the most important people in her world.

"I've never asked you since, about what happened with your parents, I mean your adoptive parents, and I don't want to know. I never liked them; you know that. But did you ever go back to trying to trace your real parents once you'd left home? I just wondered if they'd want to know they had a granddaughter."

"I never did. I don't think it ever really mattered to me,

not like it does with some people. I was just looking for a way out. I used to think that maybe they would come and rescue me if I found them. Once I'd got away, it just didn't seem so important."

She held out her arms to her daughter, who was running back to her.

"But I've been dreaming about her a lot recently. My mother, I mean. I hadn't done for years; I don't know why she's reappeared. Well, I don't see her face, obviously, because I've never seen a picture of her, of either of them, but I know it's her. I just know."

Her friend crawled across the grass between them and wrapped her arms around her.

"It's alright, Kel."

Kelly sniffed and reached for her handkerchief.

"I don't want to blow my nose on your shoulder. I do remember one thing. My name."

"Sorry, I keep forgetting. Kelly."

"No. The time I got into the Ackroyds' bureau, just before she came in and caught me, I did see something. A letter from the adoption agency, about me. My name wasn't Kelly. It was Eloise."

"That's a pretty name."

"Well, it's my name, or it was before they wiped out another part of my past."

"I could start calling you that, if you want?"

"Grace, you are sweet. I'm fine with Kelly. Anyway, your mum's calling."

Grace's mother was banging on the French windows and waving. While Grace went in to see why, Kelly hoisted Evangeline onto her shoulders and walked around the perimeter of the garden, pausing to watch two greenfinches on the feeder hanging from the apple tree. Caught in the sunlight, they fluttered their wings at each other as they squabbled over the sunflower seeds. Kelly thought that she had never seen anything so wonderfully, well, green.

"Mama!" said Evangeline, pointing at the birds.

"Birdies," said Kelly, then corrected herself, because she had decided that she would infantilise nothing for her child.

"Birds. Green birds. Viridescent, actually."

"Birdies," said Evangeline.

"Kel!"

Grace was running across the lawn, waving something.

"It's here! The message! It's come back!"

PHILIP

'Trying to explain why I think the way I do, trying to explain why I said those things to you.'

The first two lines of the first song they had ever recorded in a studio. That was 1976, when they were barely old enough to drink in the pub on the other side of the street.

Back home, it had been all he'd wanted since he'd first listened to The Velvet Underground, on his youngest uncle's cassette player.

"He was actually only a couple of years older than me. He saw it as his duty to oversee my musical education."

The younger man smiled and pushed back his paper boy cap.

"Someone would always have a guitar at the parties he took me to. I learned a few chords, and that was it. I was away. When I met the others, we all came from the same backgrounds, well, most of us, we knew each other from college, and you can just tell, you know? The places people go, how they dress, even how they walk. That was how it was then. It never entered our heads that we couldn't do this. We were kids, it was just an adventure."

It was a well-rehearsed story, if not recounted as enthusiastically as it had been, especially since his mother's younger brother had been lost to cancer some years ago.

The journalist paused his recorder and placed the phone down next to the accumulation of empty glasses, as he reached into his satchel and pulled out a photograph, black and white, of four thin, young people.

It was an image burned into Philip's heart, though he could never remember the time and place it had been taken.

"So what do you think, looking at this now?"

I think, thought Philip, that Steve probably no longer wears a narrow tie, with his shirt tucked in, but that he might still be that disbelieving lad from the Liverpool suburbs, that he was looking back at the lens that day, posing like a gangster, forgetting what I'd told him about acting like he didn't care. I think that Martin is already Marty, fully formed, full beard, hair less severe than Steve or me, eyes creased in a wide grin, utterly aware of the fun he's going to have in the next few heady months. There is an elemental joy in the realisation that he will never finish training to be a draughtsman. He can see ahead, much further than the rest of us could. Then again, he was older than us. I think, more than ever now, that I appear to be watching everyone, taking in everything. I want to control all this. Maybe that's why I'm not letting go of the guitar, as if that would drop my guard against the photographer. I think that I was sensing that something was about to happen, and that I needed to be right there when it did.

I think that there is someone or something else in that room that day, that it has caught her stare, that she really didn't care about any of this, that I never understood that at the time.

"This life is evanescent, Philippe, don't you see?"

He was no longer looking at the photograph and found himself wondering sadly how old the nervous boy opposite him was.

Philip could hear the damn phone – at least his hearing was holding up – but no amount of piled-up papers thrown from desk to floor had unearthed it.

Lottie, his younger daughter, in a pointless attempt to transform the spare room into the study he imagined it to be, had recently begun the process of filing away years of detritus into labelled boxes. She had reckoned without her father's lifelong predilection for disorder, more conspicuous since his last partner had left him, and in just one morning he had managed to cover the sofa, and most of the floor, with the contents of those boxes.

By the time the phone had been found, under a stack of bank statements, the Star Wars ringtone (Lottie again) had given out, a small mercy. The number of the caller, Felix de Vries, was a stored one, and he did not want to return that call right now, because that would mean a break in his concentration on the search for something he'd been trying to find for the last hour. Somewhere in the room were his old journals, and in one of those journals there would be a record of that photograph, the one that the young journalist had shown him.

"I lost count of the number of times important people told me I played from the soul, in the tradition, but it turned out that the tradition was to get all the critical acclaim and no money."

This was another old interview staple, and the journalist had laughed obligingly, but it was a bitter one for Philip.

"This guy in Amsterdam has a small label. He was a fan back in the day, he thinks he can get in on some sort of retro vibe that's out there now, do a rerelease of old material."

Even as he had been talking to the young man, he had listened to himself, and not believed a word. When had he started sounding like a caricature? He wanted to tell Felix that he was not going to sing 'Trying To Explain' again. He sat down heavily, sighed deeply, and stared at the phone for several minutes, before touching the call back button

The late winter sun was already low, and in his eyes, as he gazed absently across the rooftops of Crouch End, while Felix talked about schedules, distribution, and marketing budgets. Surveying the debris scattered over his desk, he realised that Lottie had left today's post when she'd brought him a pot of tea. He often left days' worth of bills and reminders but, uninspired as he was by the one-way conversation, he reached over and began a half-hearted sift.

"Phil? Phil? Hallo? Phil?"

In his favourite café, on Utrechtsestraat, Felix began to panic. Phil had not been in the best of health last year, he knew. The resident cat, irked by his twitching leg, now sidled off his lap and stalked off in search of a better place to sleep.

Back in London, the phone lay on the floor where it had been dropped, just the faint voice from across the North Sea breaking the silence of the darkling room, where Philip had torn open a handwritten envelope, and now held a note and a blue plectrum.

*

Felix was wheezing as he set down his bag again and drew breath. A tall man, he had carried his weight lightly until the last couple of years, when he began to feel that his earlier life

57

was catching up with him.

"The injustice of time!" he would grumble to his friends, who had mostly now settled into regular employment and family lives, and who regarded that point in the evening as the time to make their excuses and leave him alone in the café.

He had given up on his increasingly desperate attempts to bring Philip back to the phone, which had involved him shouting too loudly for the liking of the young woman behind the bar (and where was Hannah? she would understand), and certainly of the cat. He had eventually heard him anyway, seemingly muttering to himself, and decided that Philip had not had a medical emergency but had moved on to something he'd thought more interesting than their conversation (which had been arranged since last week!). He had also decided that his patience with this man was at an end. From the café, he had returned to his apartment, where he booked a flight and packed the bag he now regretted overloading.

He was on the Damrak, the central thoroughfare running through the city centre, and he could see Centraal Station in the distance, but it felt a lot further away. He cursed his doctor again, for the advice that he walk rather than take trams, and picked up the bag. On the train to Schiphol, he reflected on the day's unwelcome turn, and considered Philip de la Croix, or whatever his real name was.

How do I tell the man what he should already know, that the world has changed? That he depends on me, not the other way around?

Mostly, as the train approached the airport, he was wondering what in the name of God he thought he was doing.

The object of Felix's exasperation was at that moment regarding the photograph he'd been shown, and later given, by the student who'd interviewed him last week.

What was it someone once said about music journalists? Something like 'people who can't write, writing for people who can't read'? Actually, thought Philip, the kid had been nothing if not attentive and well-informed, and he'd paid for all the beers. Maybe he should stop referring to him as the kid. Maybe he should drink less, although he was sober now, yet weeping.

He stared incredulously at the single tear drop that had landed, too coincidentally for his comfort, on his younger face, and was now trailing across the black and white figures. So struck was he by this image that he forgot for a moment why he'd pulled the photograph from a desk drawer, and then remembered.

The unimaginable scale of the bigger coincidence, that of the photograph being followed by the note and plectrum, the need to work out what was happening, this was what was now consuming him, as the February afternoon died away, leaving him in an unlit room, alone with sorrowful memories.

*

As always, the kitchen had been left looking like no one ever used it, aside from a filled cafetiere and an empty mug beside it. Philip wondered yet again at the sheer randomness of the DNA inheritance that had produced a child so unlike her father. Lottie had eaten her vegan breakfast, put the washing in the tumble drier (he briefly wondered what the beeps announcing the completion of the cycle were), tidied away after herself, and left him all he needed for the start of his day, and all before leaving for college. Even the mug was his faded 'World's Best Dad' one. Chloe had bought him that, for a Fathers' Day back when they both still called him Daddy, and when he was married to their mother. Chloe now lived in Leeds (Leeds?!) with Alex, who designed computer games and called Philip 'mate'. She had decamped there at eighteen and not come back. He supposed that Lottie would continue to tidy up after him, and explain how to use his phone, so long as she was still here, but he imagined that she would follow her sister into the wide world once her History of Art degree was finished, although he tried to avoid thinking about it.

Even now, leaving Chloe at Kings Cross after an infrequent visit was something he dreaded, the familiar lurch in his chest as he stood and watched his child walk away, until she was lost in the crowd, another aching reminder that she had been lost to him for a long time.

Lottie, he admitted, had ceased to be his child when Maria had returned to Germany, and was now insisting upon being called Charlotte.

He took his coffee back upstairs. He needed to sit in his study and think about what had happened yesterday, and what he should do, but, passing Chloe's old room, he noticed that the door was slightly ajar, and impulsively walked in and sat on the bed. It still felt like she had left suddenly, just days ago. Dogs, bears, Philip's old bear, butterflies, not the threadbare panda, who always travelled with her: they appeared abandoned in the residue of a childhood past.

This room is filled with over twenty years' accumulated stuff, he thought, and I can't remember where she got half of it. Maybe I wasn't here when she did.

The dust was everywhere. There were builders outside, and perhaps the dust was theirs, but he knew that was not so. He heaved himself up, shut the door behind him, and carried on upstairs.

*

'A seasonal magazine which offers a pleasant read. The articles are tidily packaged into a full colour A5 magazine, which research has shown to be welcomed by our target readers for its benefits of portability and quality. Content is contributed by former and current students. It includes political debate, student issues, travel, entertainment, coupons and discounts. Please note that submitted articles not considered for publication cannot be returned.'

Theo pushed back his paper boy cap.

"Ha! As if!"

He regretted ever having begun this article, and certainly had no wish to see it again if London Grad, the magazine offering a pleasant read, weren't interested. He had initially seized on the opportunity presented to him by Charlotte, as they talked in the pub one night.

"What? Seriously? Your dad was in a famous band?"

"Well, a bit famous I think, for a while anyway."

"What were they called?"

"Generation 27."

"Never heard of them."

"There you go, not that famous."

Theo had been more impressed at this revelation than he admitted, however. Monday evenings routinely found most of Year Three Journalism in The Gaslighters, after the weekly guest lecture, and the gatherings were rarely happy ones, following as they did an hour of having cold water poured over their ambitions by an embittered subeditor with no pension plan. Theo always felt especially crushed on these nights. He had abandoned his ideals after his first term, deciding that no one from Ipswich could hope to write for *The Guardian*, but what he had seen as an alternative and maybe more exciting aspiration, writing about music, was proving to be no more attainable. His personal tutor had made clear her distaste for 'the showbusiness end' of the profession, enquiries about summer internships were ignored, and the unsolicited articles he had submitted to magazines had disappeared forever, as indeed most of those magazines had warned would be the likely fate of hopeful writers' efforts. He was a child of the millennium, who conducted large parts of his life online, but nevertheless felt that the grand old survivors of the paper age – *Mojo*, *Uncut*, *Kerrang!* – still carried a weight and a glamour that the glut of digital competitors would never have. Once they had made it plain that their continuing survival would not depend upon Theo, he had scaled down his plans, and, by the time he met Charlotte, he was concentrating his energies on submissions to free papers and the student press. He had even had a review published somewhere (though had not been paid for it). It was a start, but in an industry full of false starts. Charlotte, he rapidly concluded that night, could change all this.

She only happened to be sitting with the group because she was meeting her boyfriend, Tim, before going on elsewhere. Theo had a dislike of Tim for no reason he could have articulated, other than his public school drawl (he had actually gone to a state school) and the fact that he was a self-proclaimed vegan, but Charlotte was dark and pretty, and she laughed at Theo's journalist jokes. This was when she had told him about her father. It only took another fifteen minutes, and a half of cider, for Theo to have exchanged email addresses and left The Gaslighters with a promise that she would speak to her father and get back to him by the end of the week.

He had walked back to the student block with a head full of the possibilities that now lay ahead. An interview with a bona fide musician, a famous one (a bit), a suddenly open road, leading him away from miserable Monday nights to who knows where. By the time he got in, he'd forgotten the name of the band, had realised that he never asked the name of the man, and had decided that he was in love with Charlotte.

Two months on, that night belonged to a distant past. Charlotte had indeed come back to him within days of their conversation, to say that her father would be happy to meet. She had also suggested that Theo might want to embroider his journalistic credentials – 'Dad would never give his time to a college kid with no connections' – and that he take enough cash with him.

"Enough cash for what?" he wondered aloud, and he began to worry that he would be expected to pay for the interview. In a way, he was.

When a twice postponed meeting finally took place, Charlotte's father had shown little enthusiasm for a formally structured interview, during which he would be expected to answer Theo's carefully prepared questions, but a strong preference for craft beer and the sound of his own voice. During the course of a long afternoon, in a bar expensive even by North London standards, Theo's wallet was emptied, and a glass of red wine was knocked over his notes, which were by then redundant, as the man launched into another story of some or other tour. During a half hour of research into the band, Theo had even come across an old publicity shot of Generation 27, and had passed it over, in a vain attempt to exert some control over a situation in which he was now feeling out of his depth. All this had done was reduce Charlotte's father (Theo kept forgetting his name) to a morose silence, as he stared at the photo, then back at Theo in turn.

When he finally shuffled away, without a backward glance or a word of thanks for the drinks, Theo felt a sense of relief mingling with the deflation, together with a concern about whether he could afford to go out that weekend.

Now, as he stared at the familiar raft of polite rejections in his in tray, and contemplated the target readers of London Grad, he reflected bitterly on his first encounter with a 'proper' musician. He examined the photograph, a copy of which he had left with Philip de la Croix. What sort of a name was that? No wonder he could never remember it. Wasn't Charlotte called Cross? And what did Generation 27 even mean? Those people in the photo looked awful even back when they were young (except for the mysterious-looking girl standing to the side), and Charlotte's dad now looked no different to his own father, except for the earring. As to the music, the excerpts he'd located, on a website that hadn't been upgraded in years, were simply strange to his ear. You couldn't dance to that.

No wonder they were never very famous, and no wonder he still wasn't.

He pushed his cap further back, reached for his phone, and looked for Charlotte's number.

*

"Yes! Jesus, yes! Very interested! Go on…"

Lottie had stayed over at her boyfriend's, from where she was now calling.

"Well, that's about it, Dad. I don't know how these things work. All he said was that he could get you a show at the Union if you were interested."

"Is there a guarantee? And what about publicity? It's not that far until the end of term."

"Dad! I don't know! He just asked me to sound you out. You'll have to speak to him. And by the way, Tim and I won't come."

Philip had never quite accepted the idea that his children had no interest in their father's work, that they didn't even consider it work, not like the sort of work their friends' fathers and mothers did. He sometimes wondered whether they were embarrassed by him but dismissed the thought. What kid wouldn't want a rock musician for a dad, after all? Anyway, Lottie would probably turn up with that wet fish of a boy, but he thought better of mentioning a guest list just now. He scrawled the number in whiteboard marker on his hand.

"Just one thing, Lottie. Don't tell him I'm very interested. Leave it all to me."

"Dad, I have no intention of calling him back. He keeps on hitting on me, the little creep. Anyway, you are interested. And stop calling me Lottie."

Philip hadn't had an agent for a couple of years now. The last one had got him regular bookings, but almost all of them on the nostalgia circuit, as he liked to call it. A couple of promoters had refused to have him back, after he ignored all requests for Generation 27 songs at 80s revival weekenders.

"He just didn't get me," he told friends, "I am an artist, not some performing monkey. I've moved on, and people need to move with me."

Maria, a patient and resourceful woman, had tried to step into the breach for a time, but he was no more inclined to listen to her telling him that people were not moving with him. By then, she was hankering after returning to Berlin anyway, and a life not taken up by looking after the needs of a tattooed middle-aged man.

Philip had mourned her departure as he had those of both his wives and two other partners, dramatically and briefly, trailing clouds of cocaine and self-pity. His belief that it was only a matter of time before the world caught up with him, however, remained unshaken, and he felt an enormous wave of vindication now wash over him in the hours following his conversation with Lottie, or Charlotte.

The wave broke and subsided later that afternoon when he answered the doorbell, to find a bedraggled Felix De Vries regarding him balefully.

"You silly old fart! You might have let me know!"

"What? You mean call you? On the phone you never answer? Are you serious?"

The rancorous exchange had continued for ten minutes,

since Felix had put down his bag and unbuttoned his coat, which he was still wearing, but it was broken now by Philip being unable to suppress a snigger at the sibilant pronunciation of 'serious'.

"My God, Phil, you're such a childish asshole."

More sniggering, but Felix couldn't help but smile. Why could he never stay angry with this man?

"Well, you're here now. Come on, you old fucker, you can stop in the same room as last time."

"You mean the attic?" but Philip was already turning for the stairs, oblivious to the sweat on the other man's brow as he stooped to pick up his bag.

"You look terrible, Felix. You've put on weight. What time did you leave home? I've only just had breakfast."

Ten minutes later, in the kitchen, Felix had sufficiently recovered his breath to reply, but to ignore the personal observations of a man who looked considerably worse than he did.

"Phil, it's almost four o'clock, and anyway, I got in late last night. I stayed with my niece."

Philip raised an eyebrow and tapped the side of his nose.

"Son of a bitch, Phil, she is my sister's girl. I have told you about her. She works for ABN Amro."

"Ah yes, the family success story."

"Indeed. And she would not waste her time visiting clients who did not take her phone calls! Or talk to them while they were rolling a joint!"

"Come on, Felix! We've both been in this game long enough. Who wants to be like your niece?"

Felix thought back to the Lexus in which he'd been picked up from the airport, as the cloying smell drifted across the table and he stared into the mug of coffee. This was going to be a long day. He braced himself.

"Phil, I need to know whether you are committed to this project. I thought you were, now I am not so sure. You don't return my calls, you miss deadlines, I have to come to your house to speak to you, and all you can do is get high and laugh about the way I talk."

"Man, your English is good though. Have I told you that?"

"Often, but that's just what I mean. Always avoiding what we need to discuss."

"Lighten up, brother! This is just me! You've known me for years."

"Indeed, I have known you a long time, and now I am older, and so are you. I am sixty-one, I am overweight, I live in a one-bedroom apartment, and I pay interest on a bank loan. I need to look after myself better, and I need to work. You also need to do those things, Phil."

"Yeah, yeah."

"I mean, look at you! You were in hospital last year, but you're still smoking, staying up late, drinking too much."

He pointed to the empty wine bottles lining one side of the fridge.

"Phil, you'll have another heart attack."

"It wasn't a heart attack; it was just angina. Nothing like as serious."

"*Godverdomme!*"

"Bless you! Look, let's go for a curry. How about that? My treat. We can talk about the project for as long as you like."

Felix paused, decided that it was not worth the effort of responding to the insinuation that Philip was doing him a favour, and gathered up his papers from the table.

After two hours in a Muswell Hill restaurant, where all the waiters appeared to be on first name terms with Philip, most of the business in hand was done, to Felix's surprise and relief. The re-release of the Generation 27 back catalogue, licensed to his Centrum Records label, was scheduled for autumn, the artwork was agreed, and the costs had been divided. Felix had contacts in radio across the Continent – he even had his own internet show now – and he felt certain that there were enough silver-haired fans of the band out there in the suburbs of Copenhagen and Dusseldorf, keen to revisit their youthful infatuations, for he and Philip to more than recover their outlay. It was a kitchen table enterprise – or a restaurant table one – but wasn't everything now? There remained one last thing to discuss.

"No. No, no, no."

"Phil, I'm not asking you to re-form the band, I know that can't be done, but you have to promote the re-releases."

"I don't have to do anything. I own the songs, remember?"

Felix remembered, because Philip had reminded him repeatedly since they had first talked about the idea. He hadn't ever been a prolific songwriter, but somehow, and Felix didn't care to ask about it, he had emerged from the aftermath of a painful dissolution with all the publishing rights to the band's music.

"Phil, just a short European tour. A few clubs, some radio stations. It could be fun."

"It would not be fun, it would be Groundhog Day. Or Groundhog Jour, or Groundhog Tag. Felix, if punters want to buy the records again, great. I'll take their money. And so will you, I would point out. But I am not playing those fucking songs for them anymore! I have a professional reputation, I have artistic integrity, I have… dignity!"

Felix wondered at the spectacle of the figure opposite, grey roots showing and a curry stain on his silk scarf, lecturing him about dignity, but he suddenly felt exhausted, and decided to leave this battle until the morning. He supposed he had expected nothing else, after all. Philip, however, had not finished.

"Let me tell you something else. I've been offered a college gig, just this morning. I did an interview for the student magazine, or something, with a guy from Lottie's place, and now they want me to play. Kids, Felix. Receptive young minds. They won't want to hear stuff their parents liked. This is my future, not the Euro-nostalgia circuit!"

Felix rubbed his eyes, and thought of the heated seats in the Lexus, and Hannah.

"Felix, there's something else I wanted to tell you."

They were back at the house now. Philip's rant had finally run out of steam, and he was deep into the bottle of Talisker that Felix now wished that he had not picked up in the duty-free shop last night. Over the years, he hadn't found the morose version of the man any easier to deal with than the bombastic one. Neither could be stopped in mid-flow.

"That kid I mentioned earlier, the one who interviewed me, he gave me an old publicity shot of the band that he'd dug up from somewhere. I think I even remember it being taken, but I forget exactly where and when."

"Yes. And so?"

"So I was looking for my old journals when you phoned yesterday. I wanted to pin it down. You know I've been thinking of an autobiography, don't you?

"Yes, you have told me many times."

"I know, I know I still haven't got round to it, but there we are, that's why I still keep them. Listen, Felix! Try and stay awake!"

Philip leaned across the table, and Felix shrank back, overwhelmed by the whisky breath and the self-pity.

"Where are you going with this, Phil? It's late. You must see old photos of the band all the time."

"No, listen! I was bored, listening to you on the phone. Sorry, you know me. Anyway, I was opening post while you were talking. That's why I cut you off. Look."

He had reached into his jacket pocket, and now placed on the table a folded slip of paper and a guitar pick.

STEPHEN

The thought of the endless enormity of the passing of time, reduced to the ticking of a cheap clock, filled Stephen with dread, as he lay on his back in the dark.

The trick had always been to tether his thoughts as soon as he woke up, to occupy his mind with lists of capital cities and houses he had known, but this did not seem to be working now. He could not, or would not, return to sleep, and jumped about from referendum to election, from weight to health, to worrying about his children, and settling on a To Do list.

Drinking before bed wasn't helping, but all that year, his sixtieth, he had been feeling a gnawing sense of urgency.

Come on, Stephen! What? What is it?

Sometimes he thought he might get up early, and walk through the silent house before dawn, but he never did, and now he lay under the duvet, reeling at the approaching light and the decision he had deferred.

Kate was awake and checking her phone when he brought the tea tray up, an hour later.

"Sleep well?"

Of course she had; he knew that.

"So, all set for today?" she asked.

He wondered how set you were expected to be for a pre-retirement course. At any rate, he was on an early train, and reached for his wallet to check the tickets. He knew what he would also find in there.

A folded note was wedged in behind the credit cards, and

inside it was a plectrum. The plectrum was a deep blue colour and was inscribed in faded gold lettering: 'Valediction Records'. The note had a PO Box number on one side, and on the other it read 'London', and added a date, the third of April. Today's date.

*

It was still dark as the taxi passed along the familiar route, past the half-asleep houses.

Stopped at lights, the alternating purple and blue of the sign for a nail bar added to the glare in Stephen's eyes, and he remembered the barber's shop it had once been.

'It's not how long you wear your hair, it's how you wear your hair long!'

He had sat with his father, waiting for his turn in the red leather chair, and read and re-read the caption underneath the photograph. He thought it was clever, and a little exciting, because he knew that his father wouldn't approve of the sentiment. The photograph was of a young man with a dark, drooping moustache, wearing a cravat. He probably lived in London and knew the Beatles. His father had said that the Beatles would never get anywhere, as he listened to Nat King Cole and drank whisky with Dave Jones, who had lived opposite them. Dave's wife had left him, and he died a young man.

Where had nail bars come from, and what had happened to barbers' shops?

By the time the taxi had pulled into Lime Street Station's forecourt, Stephen was thinking of the two boys who had run alongside the train as it pulled away on that morning he left

73

home for university, forty years ago. He could see their faces clearly, they'd been at school with him, but their names were beyond memory, and it came to him in that moment that there were so many people to whom he had been close, but whom he would never see again. That train had left the station, and those boys were lost forever.

He slumped in the corner of four seats surrounding a table, and was thankful for the solitude, at least until Crewe.

He thought about his wife. He knew that Kate had always worried about him, and that she had further cause to worry with the upheaval of his retirement now in sight. He had been an unambitious civil servant in his mid-thirties when they met, but she had seen the fearful boy behind the reserved manner, and she had constantly surprised him. Day after day, night after night, she would take his hand and kiss his cheek, and he would return to her from that vast inner landscape where he had always wandered. He sometimes smiled to himself at the irony of someone with his mother's name coming along to rescue him, and he felt that he had been lucky. Deep down, though, he believed that someone from your past would always know you better than your present love. They were under your skin before the layers of the years were added, and it was this realisation that was occupying his mind this morning, together with the guilt he felt at having lied to Kate about how he'd come to be on the London train.

He had had an old dream again just a few nights ago, not long after the note with the plectrum had arrived. He was a young man. Hidden in the shadows, he had watched her, his first love, from the other side of the road. She was standing in front of a gate, as if she were waiting for someone. He had felt that same sense of relief as he turned away, and then a pang, as he remembered when he couldn't wait to see her. The memory had haunted him over the years and had never gone. What was it she had once said to him?

"The trouble with this life, Stephen, is that it's so easy to just drift away."

He hadn't understood that at the time, but he did now.

The train ran on through the dawn.

"Cheshire is considered the Surrey of the North, you know," said a woman behind him, in a voice that could only belong to someone who said things like that.

Stephen instinctively looked up from his book and out of the window. It was not yet light enough to see much, but he knew the landscape of where they were well enough. On a bright morning, you would indeed notice the manicured borders and the neat farmhouses, spread as far as the eye could see across the plain, but even then, he thought, this felt like the North, not the Home Counties. A long time ago, he had spent a brief time in a Surrey village and had never felt so out of place in his then short life.

'RED WINE DOESN'T GO IN THE FRIDGE!!'

Even now, he cringed at the memory of the note left on the kitchen table. He was only just nineteen, the furthest from home he'd ever been.

'I was only just nineteen, the furthest away I'd ever been.'

He hadn't picked up a guitar in years but often still found himself doing this, almost unintentionally. As the rhyming couplet took form in his head, and a melody began to wrap around it, he began to slip in and out of a doze. The saving grace of the early journeys he still took was the chance to recover the hours he'd lost during the night.

After a while, he sensed a slowing down, and then became

aware that this was the train, not just him.

They were approaching Crewe, and the time to himself was coming to an end, judging by the reservation cards left in the seats around him.

He knew that, in truth, his feelings about his privacy were conflicting. He had never stopped being the gauche nineteen-year-old – small talk with strangers was excruciating for him – but he was aware that time alone inevitably led his thoughts back to Surrey, and to other times and places.

"Loneliness still follows me," continued the song in his head, "and every place I'm going to be is always on the way to somewhere else."

*

Within the past month, Stephen had told Kate more than one lie. Individually, none of the lies came from the machinations of a man intent on deception, but collectively they troubled him.

He had not told her about the note (therefore not strictly a lie, he allowed himself). Had he done so, a difficult conversation would have followed, and one in which he would not have had ready answers to the inevitable questions about the sender, what the message meant, the plectrum, the inscription.

The second lie, and this was unequivocally a lie, was that the pre-retirement course scheduled for Birmingham was over-subscribed, and so he'd had to book a place with the same providers (Third Age Solutions), but in London. When he had checked the list of venues and available dates, and realised that he could be in London today for a plausible reason, he had nevertheless circled the room several times before sitting back down and, with a resolve he began to regret minutes later, sent the confirmation email. Any satisfaction he'd felt at the success of this plan had ebbed away days ago, as the time to decide finally where he was going once he had reached London loomed larger than he had imagined it would. He turned the plectrum over and over in his left hand.

The third lie, and at this realisation he began to see biblical overtones to the betrayal of his wife's trust, was the pretence that he was still on medication. He had not been for several weeks, in fact.

The train began to slow down again.

*

The handwriting on the envelope could have been Phil's, but it had been a long time since Stephen had seen anything written in his old friend's hand. It had been a long time since he'd seen anything handwritten, let alone receive it in the post.

The letter had been sent to his parents' address. Why would anyone write to me, a 59-year-old married man, at my parents' home, he wondered.

If it was Phil, he supposed that that was the only address he had, and that, being Phil, he probably still imagined Stevie boy tuning his guitar in his bedroom, while his mother made the tea and Mr Elijah complained about the racket. Phil probably still thought of himself in that way.

It was a surprise that Phil had kept any address, but there it was, in a familiar hurried scrawl. Typically for Phil, it was still the correct address, when nobody else would have imagined that to be realistic after all this time.

Tom Elijah had been lying in a churchyard in the hills of North East Wales for many years now, but his widow had refused to leave the home in which Stephen and his sister had been born, and she had handed the letter to him when he'd called at the house on one of his irregular duty visits.

"Don't worry, son, you're grand," was always Cathleen's response to the apology for not having been in touch. The Sligo accent was as broad as he could remember, like a reminder of how uncomfortable she still made him feel.

The letter had broken the routine and lightened the tone of the visit, and it was only when he got home that the handwriting registered with him, and he deliberately left it in his coat pocket, to open in the office in the morning.

Kate was marking essays when he went in, a pasta bake was in the oven, and all was calm, but he instinctively felt that nothing would be calm again after that night.

Now on the train, he looked again and again at the envelope and yes, of course it was Phil. He knew that from the moment he'd opened it. Only Phil would actually hold himself to an agreement made so long ago.

"But Stevie boy, we have to do this!"

That was what he would say now, as he had so many times in the deep past, and Stephen had swallowed his reservations. Not only Phil would hold himself to the agreement they'd all made. A few days after receiving the plectrum and note, he'd sealed an identical delivery, marked 'FAO Martin Rogers' and sent to a PO Box address in Manchester.

It occurred to him that you could not describe people you hadn't seen in decades as 'old friends', however close you'd been. Even if the three of them were still alive, the young men they'd been had gone. The past was gone, wasn't it?

He gripped the plectrum tighter and looked up, to see somebody walking out of that past, and towards him.

*

The train had been slowing down indefinitely, and now jerked to a halt.

Where were they? Buckinghamshire? Hertfordshire? He thought maybe twenty minutes from London, given the folding of laptops and checking of watches in the quiet carriage, but it could be almost anywhere in England, looking outside.

The level fields and hedgerows gave no indication, but the sun was rising, and the mist was beginning to thin. The early spring morning stretched out ahead, like the hues of green fading into the horizon.

Since she had walked past him, then returned to her seat further down the carriage, he had leaned into the aisle several times for a longer look at the young woman, but all he could see was the turn of her neck, as she leaned into an unseen companion. She remained just on the edge of his vision.

There on the border between past and the present, a line came back to him.

'Her hair fell like rain down her shoulders...'

His line? Yes, he wrote that song, a long time ago. He wrote it about her.

He shivered, although it was April, and he was still in his winter coat.

An announcement of the delay, and the regret for the

inconvenience caused, broke the moment, and he found himself exchanging knowing grimaces with the man opposite, but he was no longer listening. He had to see her face again. He stood up and looked across the seats.

Through an open window, Stephen Elijah thought he could hear the high, whistling call of a red kite, stooping over the track. He was walking down the sunlit streets of a long-gone world, that was unfolding around him: the Broadway on a Saturday morning, the 134 bus, Phil's friend driving them to The Flask in Highgate, the Salvation Army selling their newspaper there, full grants, cockle sellers, independent record shops, cross-legged on the floor at a party at that Dutch girl's flat, Phil, Martin, The Clash, his first electric guitar, his friends, his beloved friends, the very heaven that was North London in the nineteen seventies. He was looking into those eyes he had last seen forty years ago, and thinking it could not be her, but it was.

Emma.

PART TWO

STEPHEN ELIJAH

1975-1980

"Stephen! Come on, Stephen!"

He jerked back his head and opened his eyes, convinced for a moment that his father was on the train, and that actually they weren't on a train but were back home, that he hadn't started packing, that he'd lost the new pen set, that the taxi was here. Doctor McFadden had warned him about possible sleep disturbances and bad dreams when he was prescribed Elavil a few months earlier.

"Mrs Elijah, I was on the Normandy beaches when I wasn't much older than this lad, and I got over all that unpleasant business without drugs. Fresh air, plenty of exercise. Have you ever played rugby, Stephen?"

The family GP's usual outlook notwithstanding, both Stephen and Cathleen had been impressed by the young consultant who had advocated the antidepressant, Cathleen because he was from Donegal, Stephen because of the Led Zeppelin T-shirt under his white coat.

"It's an illness, Steve, just like any other, and this medicine will sort it out."

Cathleen hadn't even corrected the impertinent shortening of her son's saint's name, and came away from the hospital convinced that God, perhaps assisted by this wonderful new invention, had answered her prayers. The appointment with Doctor McFadden, made at Cathleen's insistence that the boy needed a thorough health check before exposing himself to life in London, was therefore like a cold shower for both of them. In answer to his blunt questions, Stephen assured the GP that he had noted no changes to either his bowel movements or his libido. He had closed his ears and averted his eyes from his mother at that point, but the realisation that he still liked to imagine Janice Edwards undressing had been a relief, and he thought that that was more or less what Doctor McFadden was getting at.

The sleeping had been a problem, however. Nights of insomnia were followed by waves of exhaustion during the day. More than once, he had been woken at the end of his lunch break by one of the other temps at the supermarket, and his dreams were becoming so vivid that it would sometimes take him a minute or two to readjust to where and when he was. Mostly, it irked him that old McFadden's warning had been borne out, and that the young psychiatrist had perhaps not been candid about all of the drug's side-effects. Occasionally, it now occurred to him that he might have a long-term problem, and that this wasn't going to evaporate just yet, drugs or no drugs. In the meantime, having convinced his parents that he was feeling fine, and happy, and able to cope with university, he now relived the mortification of them seeing him to his seat in the carriage and making sure that his case was properly stowed. Cathleen had told the couple opposite about her boy going off to college, and how nervous he was, and, as he came to, he realised that the smartly dressed woman was smiling at him.

"Feeling better for a nap?"

He smiled back and nodded and leaned his forearm across the journal in which he'd been writing, imagining that she'd tried to read the poem he'd left unfinished.

He had drifted off while weighing up alternatives to

'death' as the rhyme. Mister James, his English teacher, had encouraged his writing, but Stephen was struggling with the exhortation to find his own voice and 'stop rewriting T S Eliot'. Besides, his father had memorably vilified Eliot's poetry as 'like a fart in a jam jar' after picking up his homework one night.

"*Iesu mawr*, call that poetry?"

It was difficult to follow Mister James' advice when it seemed to dovetail with Tom Elijah's more robust assessment. Besides, Bob Dylan liked Eliot.

The couple had assured Cathleen that they would make sure that Stephen was heading in the right direction once they reached Euston, and the woman smiled to think of how visibly excruciating this had been for the boy. He has such dark, sad eyes, she thought, reminded of the fiancé she had lost in the war. Her husband, a kind and good-humoured man, had hooted with laughter when Jim Elcoat and Peter Maguire ran along the platform, waving off their childhood friend.

Stephen discreetly closed his journal. Gazing up into the clear autumn sky, he picked out what looked like a large bird of prey, hovering on the currents above but effortlessly keeping pace with the train.

THE JOURNAL OF STEPHEN ELIJAH

Mister Kirwan (is he a doctor?) suggested that I keep a journal of my thoughts and feelings, even my poems, and that we could chat about them when I see him. Little does he know that I've been keeping a journal since I was fifteen! Anyway, he seems alright, although I wish CE would stop ogling him and saying 'Yes, doctor' every time he speaks. A pair of Paddies together, as TE said. CE says that we're allowed to say that (and Julie) but not him, although he's the only one who does, especially when he's been in the front room with Dave Jones, who always brings a bottle of Scotch round. CE says Dave is unhappy at home, but he and TE are always laughing in the front room. Maybe Dave should write a journal. I tried whisky once, it was Peter's dad's, and it was horrible.

Mister Kirwan says that free time at weekends is a 'potential tipping point' for me, and that I should think about other activities that would get me out of my room. I couldn't tell him that my room is where I write my poems and play guitar, especially with CE sitting there. Anyway, TE has banned me from practising anywhere else in the house.

I spent Sunday helping CE with housework and cutting the grass. TE has just about come around to me giving up chapel, although he says that damnation is my choice. CE says that really I'm a Catholic anyway, and you never stop being a Catholic. I felt better after all the physical work, and watched the serialised Great Expectations *in the evening.*

Life was simpler back then!

I keep making lists of things I have to do. TE noticed me doing this. 'People who make lists never get anything done'. Mister Kirwan says this is fine if it helps me to worry less, but not to use it as a way of avoiding decisions. He says that sometimes you have to decide to do something that not everyone will be happy with. He doesn't have to live with my parents, though.

The exams are only a few weeks away. I made a revision timetable, but everyone does that, don't they? Even Mister James said we should. Peter asked if I'd allowed time for 'gentleman's relaxation'. He'd read somewhere (probably in one of his dad's magazines) that this eased stress. I told him to keep those thoughts to himself. He told me not to be such a homo, he'd noticed me staring at Janice's legs in English. She is very beautiful but she is a really nice person too. Anyway, I doubt she stares at me.

Mister Kirwan wanted to read the journal today, but he allowed me to read selected excerpts out loud to him instead. I didn't want him to read everything! He compared me to a car circling a roundabout, and said I was unable to decide which exit to take. He started asking me about CE and TE, which must be why he asked CE to wait outside today. She didn't like that, but Mr K told her that I was now an adult and that he had to think about patient confidentiality. Anyway, he can do no wrong in her eyes, according to TE, and I think he's right.

I'm writing this after midnight, by the bedside lamp. This evening was the Leavers' Dance. Mr K told me I should go, and ask 'that girl' to dance. How did he know about that?? 'Why shouldn't we dance, Steve? Why shouldn't we?' Except

I can't dance, not like the tall boy in purple velvet trousers who danced with Janice.

I got caught up in a terrible row between my parents today. TE was late back from the pub, and we'd started on dinner without him. CE was crying when he came in, Julie and I could hear her from upstairs. The front door slammed, and I went back down. CE told me he'd thrown his Sunday roast in the bin, and asked me to swear to God and the angels that I would never take strong drink, and wasn't that a sinful waste of good food? I suppose I sort of agreed, because TE later accused me of always siding with her, like a typical Irish Mammy's boy, when all he'd done was to stay for another half hour to listen to the landlord's new Frank Sinatra record.

Mr K has given me a 'strategy' to use, which makes my life sound like a battle. 'Follow the plan, Steve, follow the plan, and not the mood'. The next time I have a choice to make, I should make a decision and follow that plan, and ignore any second thoughts, otherwise I'll be stuck on that roundabout for ever. Mr K likes this driver image.

Follow the plan, not the mood. Follow the plan, not the mood. Follow the plan, not the mood.

First entry for three weeks. The exams are over. Hard to believe. A lot of us finished today. People hung their ties around the school gates and wrote on each other's shirts, although not me (CE would kill me). A group headed off towards the Red Cow, and Janice's boyfriend called 'Are you lot coming?' to Peter, Jim and me. I think he was just being polite. At least I did make a decision, not to go.

Mr K thinks I've done well to cope with the exams but that they weren't really my problem. He says I need to prepare for university, because no one sets out schedules and gives you as much guidance there, and that I need to work on the strategy. He told me to write out a list of my 'bad words', then screw up the list and throw it away.

Church, chapel, Sunday, Irish, Welsh, parents, girls, career. Those are the words I wrote down, but I don't think I understood what he meant.

Last session with Mr K, so of course CE had to come along. She'll miss these trips to hospital more than I will, although she later complained to TE that it was inappropriate to make a joke out of sending a kid off to college with a free supply of drugs. Mr K told me to remember to breathe!

London next week. TE has gone very quiet, and today he brought home a smart new pen set and told me my grandfather would be proud of me. CE never talks much about the other grandfather, I wonder why? She just keeps saying there's so much to think about and to buy. This evening I remembered the last thing Mr K said to me: "Stephen, just be here now. It's the only place you can ever be."

*

He had lost the new pen set. Two nights earlier, he had met Jim and Peter for a farewell drink at the Red Cow, or a 'snifter or two', as Peter described it. Peter lived alone with his father. Stephen had taken the silver Parker cartridge pen and matching biro to the pub in order to write out his halls of residence address for his friends. He had held out the unfounded hope of Janice being there and asking him to do the same for her.

Jim was impressed by Tom Elijah's largesse.

"My parents just got me an umbrella!"

He told them how General Eisenhower had used a Parker to accept Germany's surrender, and briefly wondered whether the set was a special edition, brought out after the moon landings a few years earlier, as he'd read that they each had a speck of moon dust built into the design. Stephen's immediate suspicion the following morning was that Jim had been sufficiently jealous to have pocketed the pens, but he was careful to avoid accusations when he phoned.

"Sorry, Stevie, I just remember you putting them down on the table. You know what you're like after a sniff of the barmaid's apron."

While his parents were out at the morning service, he had time to try the pub, but nothing had been handed in. The dawning realisation made him feel sick: that he would be telling his father that the expensive pen set, bought to commemorate his son's golden future, had been left in a bar. He wasn't sure which was greater at that moment, fear of Tom's unpredictable rages or the overwhelming guilt. He tried to think what Mister Kirwan might advise but couldn't begin to imagine, and so in the end he fell back on his own tried and tested strategy. He told his mother when his father was out of earshot.

The agreement with Cathleen that the loss of the pens should be kept to themselves, so long as Stephen promised to go to Mass during his first week away from home, had held for the rest of Sunday and until he was on the train. Tom would have been equally infuriated by the thought of his son 'blabbing to a damn priest', but the uneasy truce between his parents over their children's religious upbringing stayed in place. Tom had even come home early from the pub, 'for the boy's last day'. At the thought of that, Stephen's eyes now began to sting, to his surprise and horror.

"Wembley!"

The jovial man opposite was pointing out of the window, and Stephen took the opportunity to crane his neck around so that the nice woman couldn't see the tears he immediately rubbed away.

"Wembley Stadium! That's where it happened, young man, that's where we won the World Cup! You remember that, don't you? I bet you do!"

Stephen had a hazy memory of another argument between his parents, after his father's edict that no one in the house should be supporting 'bloody England'.

"They oppressed my people and my culture, and yours too, Kate! I'm not having our kids betray their forebears!"

Cathleen had ignored the reduction of her name to the more English-sounding variant, and waited until Tom left for his shift at the fire station before producing the two Saint George's cross pennants from behind a cushion and turning on the television just as extra time began.

"I do remember", said Stephen, "I do".

LONDON

My first entry for more than a week. Thought I would start a new chapter, under a new heading. This is where I live now.

Journey down was fine except for the nosey old couple opposite. I wish CE hadn't spoken to them. I got a taxi, but the money TE had given me wasn't enough! When I arrived at halls, the warden told me I'd have been quicker walking. When he saw the guitar, he reminded me about the rules on noise. He wasn't very friendly, but he seemed to be like that with everyone in the queue to register. There was another lad with a guitar case just behind me, and he got the same lecture. My room is nicer than my bedroom at home, but I have to share the baths and showers with everyone on the corridor. I unpacked, then I looked out of the window (I couldn't see any of the famous sights TE had told me to look out for), then I sat on the bed. I made another list of the things I needed to do – register with doctor, see personal tutor, collect timetable, go to English Department cheese and wine evening (what will TE think?!), phone home – and then it was dinner time. The refectory was scary, because you had to decide to which table to take your tray, and there were no unoccupied tables. Everyone seemed to be talking, as if they already knew each other. Then I caught sight of the boy with the guitar. He stood out, as he had bright red hair, and he wasn't talking to anyone. I took a deep breath, just like Mr K told me, and went to sit opposite him. I smiled but he ignored me. He could barely draw breath, he was eating so fast, and then he went to fetch seconds. When he sat down again, he started talking to the girl next to him, who was very pretty. How can you do that? I was at school with Janice for seven years, and I never spoke to her more than half-a-dozen times. She laughed at something he said, then he looked at me and asked me what my guitar was. So he had noticed, although I had to ask him to repeat himself, as his accent (Cockney, I suppose) was very strong. He said 'Nice', then got up and left, before I could say anything else. The pretty girl also went, and I had the table to myself, and could think.

I met my personal tutor, Doctor Friedman, who is American. She also sounds German when she speaks, like Henry Kissinger. She has also invited her tutor group to a cheese and wine evening. These appear to be common social events at university.

Doctor Friedman left Germany when she was a girl, because her family were worried about the future. She came to London first, then went to America. She told us this at her evening. Her life seems so exciting and exotic, compared to mine, although I didn't like to ask her whether all her family managed to get out of Germany. She asked me about Liverpool but I couldn't think of much to say, except something bland about The Beatles. She said that her son was in the music business, but I think she was just being polite. Everyone there sounded about ten years older than me. How do you learn about drinking wine and holding interesting conversations with academic emigres before you're even nineteen?

*

"Stephen! Come on!"

Mister James was standing on his desk, glaring down at him.

"How do I get there, Stephen? How do I get to Little Gidding?"

He had the answer, it was there, but stuck in the back of his throat, and it would not come.

He came to on the back row of the Senate House lecture theatre.

"We must ask ourselves that question. How did Eliot get from 'The Wasteland' to 'Little Gidding'?"

His sleeping patterns had begun to settle again, as his brain adjusted to the drug, but the daily strangeness of everything in his new life had often left him turning things over in the early hours. In any event, he could see at least two other people in the hall who had been unable to resist the dry and strangely soothing tones of the lecturer, and were still gently nodding.

I don't blame them, thought Stephen, as he leaned over to retrieve the pen he'd dropped during Mister James' visitation, just as the person on the row in front of him turned round to hand it back.

"Oh my God, isn't this awful? Oh, hello!"

It took a moment for him to recognise her, wearing glasses and wrapped in an enormous scarf, as the red-haired guitarist's friend.

"Hi!" was all he could whisper in reply anxious not to be heard around the hall.

Ten minutes later, with T S Eliot left wandering the metaphorical highway until next week's lecture, she turned back to him.

"We were just going for a coffee. Fancy joining us?"

He expected to see the unfriendly boy next to her, but her companion was a gaunt youth in a corduroy jacket, which came as a relief.

"I think we all need one!" he said.

"Quite. I'm Caroline, this is Hugh."

They sat in the Students' Union and continued the shared joke about the sleep-inducing lecturer. Stephen remembered Hugh from Doctor Friedman's gathering.

"An awfully nice woman," he drawled, in a manner that brooked no disagreement. Stephen nevertheless liked him immediately, even more so when he left for a tutorial soon afterwards.

Caroline was still wearing glasses, and he'd noticed that her hair was up. Perhaps this was her undergraduate persona, perhaps back in her room she took off the glasses and unpinned her hair.

"Stephen?"

"Sorry! Sorry, I just drifted off for a moment. Yes, I agree, it's all about Anglo-Catholicism."

He had opted for the module on Eliot's later works, expecting more of the rock 'n' roll poetry of 'The Wasteland', as Mister James had disdainfully described it. He'd had enough of the Bible at home, and *The Four Quartets*, with its references to Julian of Norwich, was not what he'd imagined. Caroline really was pretty, though.

Bukowski said that we should live our lives so well that Death would tremble to take us.

Mister James said that Bukowski, Ferlinghetti and Kerouac were just drunks who couldn't write, but anyway, I'm never going to be able to live like that.

Caroline asked me back me back to her flat (she has a flat!), to show me her Beat Poets collection, and so I could tell her all about The Mersey Sound, which I've never heard of. She clearly went to a more progressive school than me, and she is from the South, after all (she said the Hampshire-Wiltshire border?). I had to get back to halls for dinner, so she told me to come to their party on Saturday, and she wrote the address and phone number (!) on my hand. I didn't like to ask her where Kentish Town was. Her hand felt nice, and she was so chatty, although she probably doesn't think that about me.

Caroline Bloxham. Kentish Town. Hampshire-Wiltshire. The Mersey Sound.

Sunday. I didn't go to the party. How would I begin to find out where Kentish Town is, and how to get there? Mr K would have known. Anyway, I didn't go to Mass this morning either, although I told CE I did when I phoned home (or is that home now?), so maybe Death will tremble to take me.

I sat in the same place for the Eliot lecture as last week, with a copy of 'The Mersey Sound' sticking out of my pocket, so you could just make out the title. Hugh was in front of me again, but I couldn't see Caroline anywhere. He told me all about the party (Hugh went?!), a lot of the year were there. Caroline's ex-boyfriend had turned up unexpectedly, and there'd been some trouble. She'd now gone home, Hugh said, to 'sort her head out'. He raised his eyebrows when he said this. He also told me that the red-haired guitarist had been there (does anyone know his name?) but not with Caroline. One of the few, he said.

*

"A true Celt, Mister Elijah, all highs and lows, no even keel. Wouldn't you agree?"

"Sorry?"

"Beckett. You know of him? The raison d'etre of our class?"

Stephen liked Doctor Friedman, but she had the reputation for taking no prisoners in her tutorials, and why would she? She had him in her sights now, and would not let go, and all the while Philip was making grimaces at him from over her shoulder.

"Mister Elijah, if you come to my classes to catch up on your sleep, I suggest you save your time and ours and simply remain in bed. Now, since you are here, may I invite your thoughts on Beckett and his Irish psyche?"

Philip later suggested Beckett and The Irish Psyche as a name for his band, to general amusement, but all Stephen could think of now was his mother, and how she would have responded to this question, and how she would never have heard of Beckett.

"God, Stephen, will you look at him. That face would

97

drive rats from a barn!"

"Well," he stuttered, "I'm half-Irish, and there's something to that."

"Mister Elijah, I am Jewish, but I do not claim to understand Kafka any better because I am. You have clearly not done the reading that I explained was essential to today's discussion. Miss Devereux?"

Burning, he silently cursed Cathleen.

Doctor Friedman gestured for him to wait behind, as the other students left her room a few minutes later.

"Stephen, is everything alright?"

She thought of her son, living with a demanding WASP girl in Brooklyn, and wondered at the darkness in this boy's eyes.

"I'm fine, Doctor Friedman. Sorry about earlier."

"I'm sure Beckett will get over it, but you seem to be constantly sleep-deprived. As your personal tutor, that is my other concern. Tell me, are you the first in your family to go to university?"

"I think so. My mother lost touch with her relatives."

"Ah, so she's the Irish parent?"

How did she know that?

"Stephen, let me tell you something. We are all of us only ever a grandmother's whisper away from a ditch at the side of a road. Now. Phone home this evening, go and have a beer, get a good night's sleep, and get back to Mister Beckett tomorrow. All will be well."

All will be well. Judith Friedman sat in the fading afternoon light for some time after Stephen had left, wondering whether she believed that about anybody or anything.

98

Two hundred miles away, Cathleen was meanwhile puzzling over her discovery of Stephen's lost pens in her husband's sock drawer.

PHILIP

So the red-haired guitarist has a name. I haven't seen much of him since he was talking to Caroline that day in the refectory, but I keep hearing about him from other people, mostly stories involving parties and drinking. Then he turned up in Dr F's Modernism tutorial, after missing the first three. She asked all of us if we agreed that he should be allowed to join the group late (she does things like that), and of course no one objected as he stood there grinning, wearing a red and white striped waistcoat. CE would say he was charming.

Yesterday, when Dr F had finished with me, he was still just down the corridor, rolling a cigarette.

"Still with us, mate?" was all he said when I walked past him. Later on, he was holding court in the Union. TE would have said he was 'full of cachu'.

He is in a band already! We've only been in London for two months! Actually, I think he is from London, although his accent keeps changing.

I need to get back to the poetry, I've been spending too much time writing songs, which all sound like Bob Dylan rejects. Follow the plan, not the mood.

*

By the end of his first term, Stephen had worked out how to get to Kentish Town, not that he wanted to go there now. He had made a couple of friends in his block, although none on the course, and had found a couple of record shops where he liked to spend Saturday afternoons. He had colonised a square mile or two of central London. He had not seen a doctor at the university practice, as Mister Kirwan had advised, because he hadn't felt overly anxious since the first couple of weeks. He supposed that the pills were working, maybe even curing him. Any thoughts he might have had about this improvement being connected with being away from home were quickly suppressed, but he made no weekend visits, although he wrote to everyone regularly, even Julie, and made a reverse charges call each Sunday night.

As to the work, he would often reflect with disbelief on the idea of being kept, and given money for records, so that he could read literature for three long years.

Stephen Elijah might even have been said to have found the elusive even keel.

The next year, everything changed, and was never the same again.

In the years to come, Stephen would look back on this night, and wonder that it was Hugh, of all people, who persuaded him to go with him to the monthly Rock Society evening. The two were by no means friends – the self-assurance and the gentleman farmer outfits intimidated him – but he was flattered by Hugh evidently regarding him as one of his circle of acquaintances, and so was easily persuaded. Hugh would later become a suffragan bishop, as was his father, but he remained a lifelong devotee of the blues, and there was a band on that night he was keen to see.

Stephen had been to one of the evenings just before Christmas, along with Johnny Delaney, who was in the room opposite, and who fancied himself as a singer. With no idea what he would do with them, he had crammed a sheaf of lyrics into his inside pocket, and spent the night listening to performers not short on confidence but with even less talent than Johnny. He didn't expect his second visit to be any more worthwhile, although Hugh had been at pains to point out that the blues band had actually been booked, and that the part of the evening reserved for 'the deluded hopefuls' was therefore curtailed. Nevertheless, he once again carefully folded several sheets of scribble to pocket size before he left his room.

The Rock Society was based in the Union building, in the performance area adjoining the bar. The sign over the connecting door advised that this was the Woolf Theatre, and that only plastic glasses could be taken in there. Stephen wandered aimlessly around the gloomy, cavernous space, and thought that he had never seen anywhere less like a theatre. Hugh had arrived with several other people whom he didn't know – the circle of acquaintances appeared to be endless – and was now talking intently to a man who was sitting on the edge of the tiny stage at the far end of the hall. Stephen guessed that he was in the band. If he was, he seemed to be unconcerned by the small groups of stragglers making up the audience, most of whom sounded like they were on first name terms with him.

Feeling increasingly out of place, Stephen paused at the table at the back of the hall, where he feigned interest in the piles of T-shirts on sale.

"Fucking stupid name, eh?"

He didn't immediately realise that the figure in the shadows behind the table was talking to him, although there was no one else anywhere near the two of them. He looked up. Looking back at him, behind sunglasses (what would Tom Elijah say?!), was a thin man in a vest. Stephen had no idea of how to reply.

"Aren't you in the band?"

The laugh was more of a rasp, which then became a raking cough. Stephen thought that he had never seen anyone less healthy-looking, not even the unfortunate Dave Jones, who was now in hospital and not visiting Tom anymore.

"Jesus, mate! No! I'm just selling T-shirts. What do you reckon?"

He held one up, and yes, the name was, well, fucking stupid (Stephen!) but there was something about the design, something fascinating. Was that an eye?

"Buñuel. *Un Chien Andalou*. Just before the blade slices it, you know?"

He didn't know, but he did know that this man came from somewhere else, somewhere he'd never been, somewhere more exciting than the Woolf Theatre that night.

The Rock Society secretary, an earnest-looking youth, had just come on stage to announce the support act. Hugh was still preoccupied, and two women were now checking the sizes of the T-shirts, so Stephen moved away and went back to the bar. As an older man, he would rely on a mobile phone as his prop to be able to sit on his own in a public place, but that night he had his lyrics with him. Tucked away in a corner, he read and reread them, avoiding eye contact with anybody who came too close.

"What you got there, mate?"

The Buñuel T-shirt seller was standing over him, pint in one hand, cigarette in the other. Stephen's reflexes took over, and he folded the sheets, but he heard himself reply, "Just some song lyrics," rather than the usual, 'Oh, nothing'

"Mind if I take a look? I'm Martin, by the way. I hate all that boring crap in there. Fat blokes playing music they stole from some poor black bastards and making it worse. Do you play?"

Having evidently lost interest in selling his designs to the blues crowd, he sat down, and took the crumpled pages from Stephen's loosened grip before he could answer.

"Stephen Elijah. Is that you? Cool name, man."

Martin read through every single lyric, nodding occasionally and pulling on his cigarette. In the light of the bar, he looked even thinner, and older, and his pony tail added to the raddled appearance. He looked both worn out and alert at the same time.

"Steve, man, some of these are good. Bloody good."

It is always easier for us to look back from the future and understand more clearly what was happening to us at a significant time in the past, but Stephen knew at that moment, as Martin started talking about situationism, that something of consequence was taking place. He had seen an exit, and he was coming off the roundabout.

MARTIN

At first, I was scared of him. Actually, I still am. Why did I agree to go to this rehearsal? I'm not even sure it is a rehearsal, he just said we needed to get together and see what happened. And I don't think he knows much about music. I had to explain what chords were when he asked me about 'the letters over the lyrics'. But he said he thought I might have something he'd been looking for, and that I looked right. He kept talking about art and philosophy, and about his 'Bonfire Club', which is a list of people who should be tied up and have their instruments burned in front of them! TE would be with him on that, except that I'd be on his list, so that makes me think I should go to Martin's flat next week. He lives in Kentish Town (why does everybody live there?), but this time I will turn up. Kentish Town is where everything is happening, so I have to go.

*

Stephen had begun to regret agreeing to take his guitar and his songs over to Martin's flat within minutes of leaving the Union bar. He shored up his determination with a firm declaration of intent in his journal that night, but he slept badly for the worry, and he dreamed of his father, who kept saying 'But why, Stephen, why?', in a hurt tone. He knew that it was irrational, but he phoned home the next morning. Tom was of course at work. He had been promoted a couple of years previously and was now on regular daytime hours, after all those years of Cathleen hissing at the children to remember that Daddy was asleep.

"Grand, son, we're grand. It's lovely to hear from you."

His dismay at the thought of a conversation with his mother was suddenly punctured by the realisation that he hadn't phoned at the weekend, and he pictured Cathleen alone in the house every day. He also remembered that he had forgotten to take his tablet yesterday. Mister Kirwan had told him not to worry if he did that occasionally, but he might as well not have, and Stephen duly braced himself for what was now sure to be a bad day. It was even raining.

By the evening, the rain had gone, and the world was brighter. On reflection, he had dealt with his unease over his father without having had to speak to him, and the course of the day steadily improved. His Beckett essay was in his pigeonhole, complete with an A- grade and the comment 'You know your compatriot better than you think', which puzzled but delighted him, and made him think of the warm tone of Judith Friedman's voice. The college librarian, an unsmiling man from Argentina, was handing out glasses of wine to students as they came in. Apparently, the President had been deposed. Stephen couldn't take more than a sip, but felt happy for the man, who had always seemed sad and lonely, and who was trying to explain to a colleague in heavily-accented English what had been happening in his homeland.

Back in his room, he sat with his guitar and notepad, and wrote 'Trying To Explain' at the top of a blank page. He tried to imagine the sad librarian explaining why he never smiled. The title was a start. It hadn't been a bad day, after all.

*

On the following Sunday morning, there was a note in his pigeonhole, addressed to 'Brother Elijah' and written in an ornate script he had never seen. How had Martin managed to deliver the note, and how did he know where Stephen lived? The thought unsettled him, as did the artistry of the handwriting, but not as much as the content did.

'Little brother, we start the revolution on Tuesday!'

A more prosaic reminder of the address had followed.

Two days later, to his amazement, he found himself plodding along Prince of Wales Road, past boarded up houses and sheets of corrugated iron emblazoned with 'Hands Off Camden Gestapo!' in red paint. Kentish Town was undoubtedly more exciting than the Woolf Theatre, but Stephen was conscious of the anorak his mother had bought for him, and of the guitar he was carrying, his sixteenth birthday present. If this was where everything was happening, everything looked bleak and unwelcoming. Should there have been a comma after 'Hands Off...'? What if Martin lived in a squat?

Martin did not live in a squat, but in a cared-for terraced villa house. With some relief, Stephen tried the doorbell, which appeared not to work, or did it? He thought maybe he could hear something like a gong, in the distance, but if so, nobody was coming to the door. He checked the number over the frosted glass panel against Martin's note, and had just reached for the brass knocker when the door swayed open, leaving him waving his arm towards the young woman who was standing there. His discomfiture was complete when he realised that she was wearing only an outsize T-shirt, one of the Buñuel designs. At least he must be at the right place.

"Um…"

The guitar case apparently conveyed all she needed to know, and she turned to the staircase behind her.

"Martin!"

Without a word to Stephen, she walked away back down the long hall, while he kept his eyes fixed on his feet. He had a memory of his father shouting down Julie, who was fifteen at the time, when she'd wanted to stay overnight at a friend's New Year's Eve party, and wondered whether Julie would in the end become like the unfriendly girl in the T-shirt, however much Tom yelled at her about self-respect.

"Steve! Welcome, brother!"

In the darkness of the stairs, Martin looked paler and even thinner than he remembered, and was still wearing his aviator sunglasses. He waved a cigarette in Stephen's direction.

"Come on up!"

By the time he'd reached the landing, Martin had disappeared, and no bedroom lights were on, but he could hear the wheezy laugh from the previous week just as he realised that a narrower staircase, back over his shoulder, led to another floor. There was a dim light up there, and there was another voice. He stopped halfway up. He had not thought that other people might be involved in this, whatever this was. He was wondering whether he could get back to the front door without being noticed when Martin half-opened the door directly above him.

"Come on, mate! Elijah went up by a whirlwind into heaven!"

Stephen had imagined what this moment would feel like,

as he finally pushed open the door, but not that the Old Testament would be quoted, or that someone else would be in the room, someone he knew.

At the opposite end of the long attic room, on one of the many cushions scattered across the floorboards, lay Philip Cross.

Stephen was not sure what was going on.

"Martin? What's going on?" said Philip.

"Phil, Phil, Phil, Phil, Phil…"

"Nothing against you, mate," he added, turning to Stephen and then back to Martin.

"You told me this would just be you and me. What's going on? Who else have you asked along?"

"Phil, Phil, brother…"

As he stood there helplessly, wondering if he could still make it down to the front door unnoticed, an image came to Stephen's mind of Mister Kirwan reminding him that here and now was the only place he could be. Philip was now walking around in circles, waving his arms about, and steadily raising his voice, while Martin repeated his name as if it were a sort of mantra, in that slurred way Stephen had noticed last week. He vaguely supposed it was an affectation, but it seemed to work, and Philip came to a halt. All eyes were on Martin.

"Right, so, okay, first of all, no one else is coming along. It's just you two and me. Phil, this is Steve, Steve…"

"We already know each other."

"Really, Steve? Wow! That's amazing. How come?"

"From college. I actually met Philip on our first day there."

"I don't remember that," muttered Philip, "I didn't even

know you played guitar."

"Right, okay, now then, apologies to you chaps. I seem to have got ahead of myself again."

Another wheezy laugh followed.

"Steve, I met Phil at a party a couple of weeks ago, just before I met you. I'd seen his band earlier that evening. Phil, thanks for the ten quid, by the way. I haven't forgotten about that. I met Steve at the union bar. He showed me some of his songs. I think maybe we might have something here, you two and me. Steve, Phil's band are a bunch of dull old musos, but Phil is dead good."

Philip opened his mouth and shut it again. Stephen wondered if he knew about the Bonfire Club.

"Can I say something?"

"Of course you can, our kid. This is what I wanted, a chat, a spliff, get to know each other. Phil's had his strop now."

"The thing is, I've never been in a band, not a proper one, and I'm not a great guitar player."

Philip sighed and shook his head, and Martin took off his sunglasses. Stephen had guessed he might be ten years older than him, but now he wondered. 'Like pissholes in the snow', he could hear Tom saying about the bloodshot eyes.

"I know you've never been in a band, little brother. Look at you! Of course you haven't. But that's what I want. You're pure, you're an artist, you even have a prophet's name. I had to rescue Phil from the bunch of old farts he was wasting his talent on, but you don't need saving, you're already saved."

"I'm making money, if you don't mind!"

"Phil, anyone can make money. We can make history!"

Martin was now jabbing his sunglasses as he spoke, and Stephen was transported back to the chapel he'd grown up in, and to the uncompromising sermons he'd heard there.

"And this man, this man, he has some great songs, or ideas for songs, and you'll love them."

Both of them looked at Stephen, still holding his guitar, still wearing his anorak, and an expectant silence settled over the attic.

TRYING TO EXPLAIN

I did it. I did it. I went there, and it was weird, and Phil Cross was there, but I did it. I felt like I was caught in the middle of an argument, an argument about me.

I don't know why Martin was so secretive. It was as if he thought neither one of us would turn up if we knew the other would be there. He's probably right. When I took out my guitar, Phil asked to see it. He played a few scales, really fast, and handed it back. When I started, my fingers were all over the place.

Martin said "Steve, Stevie, stop! Just play your newest song. Newest is always best."

So I played 'Trying To Explain', which I only finished last weekend. It felt easier because I was still feeling my way into it, if that makes sense. It isn't about the sad librarian anymore, I'm not sure what it's about, but it has a tune. I worried that I'd accidentally stolen it, but I think it really is mine, and it sounds like a new song, not just me trying to be someone else.

Phil was tapping his foot whenever I opened my eyes, and Martin was smiling, with his eyes closed. All he said was "Yeah!" Phil said "Nice song. I could do something with that." As if he's doing me a favour! Well, maybe he is. We're having a proper rehearsal next week.

Dream – I was with the girl in the T-shirt. She put a ring of pure light on my finger, and it turned into music. All the while, TE was banging on a window, shouting something at me, but I couldn't hear him.

*

"There are worse places to be than Russell Square on a warm summer evening. Eh, Steve?"

Philip lay on his back, chewing on a blade of grass. Stephen stood over him, constantly turning as he tried to keep a simultaneous eye on every entrance to the gardens.

"For God's sake, Steve, you don't even know what he looks like. It's not like he's going to miss us, the only two people here with guitar cases. Relax. You're making me nervous."

Stephen thought that he'd never met a less nervous person.

"Steve, he's my uncle. He's known me all my life, you know?"

"But he's not much older than you?"

"Nope. Well, ten years maybe."

Stephen thought of Uncle Evan, leading his donkeys along Rhyl beach, as worn down by his life as the lame animals were. He sat down.

"So you are from London?"

"Just about. Well beyond the North Circular. Over that way."

He waved his arm in the direction of the Senate House, rising over the square, but Stephen's boundaries were still around Prince of Wales Road and the graffiti there, and he couldn't begin to imagine some place beyond the North Circular, wherever that might be, that had produced Philip

114

Cross. Over the course of half a dozen rehearsals, he had complained about having to play bass guitar to accommodate Stephen, about lending an electric guitar to him, about Stephen playing it like a folk singer, about Martin not being able to play.

"You two make me feel like Paul McCartney must have done. I play everything better than anyone else in the band."

Stephen thought he was right, especially when it came to Martin. There had been a basic, neglected drum kit in the basement of his house, and Martin had evidently planned that he would play this.

"Long-term loan, brothers!"

However, he had no apparent ability to do so, although he also seemed spectacularly impervious to criticism. Stephen wondered if McCartney was in the Bonfire Club. Yes, of course he was.

"Phil, Phil, Phil. Now then. This is rebellion. This is existential! This is not jazz!"

"Ain't that the truth."

He smiled at the recollection. He realised that he was beginning to like them, and then he remembered why he was in Russell Square with Philip, and that Martin could barely keep the beat, and that he felt sick.

"Oy oy!"

Several of the many sunbathers in the garden turned to see a man striding from the far corner across the lawn.

"Here we go!" said Philip, sitting up.

"Does your mummy know you're here?"

"Does your sister?"

The man, who was as tall as Philip and at least as voluble, leaned over him and kissed the top of his head.

115

"Pat, Steve, Steve, Pat, who is a disreputable man, and a bad influence."

"He's always quoting his mother", said Pat, as he stretched out his hand.

Uncle Pat, thought Stephen, as he noticed a ring on every finger. Evan, with his shivering donkeys, was an uncle, but Pat looked more like a big brother, and he and Philip were clearly at ease with that.

"If you boys are ready, the van's parked just on the other side of the square."

Pat looked nothing like his nephew, but Stephen thought they were unmistakeably related. Cross family parties would be noisy. Or would that be Cross? Philip never mentioned his father. According to him, Pat had 'dabbled in the business', which Stephen thought probably meant that he'd driven people and their guitars around London, as he was doing now. In fact, Pat had bought Philip his first guitar, and had taught him some chords, but Philip never told anyone this.

"So you're about to lose your virginity tonight, young man?"

Stephen was concentrating on sitting upright in the back of the Bedford, along with various speakers and microphone stands, and by the time he realised that Pat was talking to him, Philip was giggling.

"Sorry, Steve, he brings shame to the family."

"Pat! You know me!"

Pat clipped his head as he drove on.

"Too right! Almost there."

Ten minutes later, the van was in the car park of a pub in Camden Town, although it could have been anywhere to Stephen, who had not spoken a word since Pat had arrived.

As the back doors swung open, he jumped out, almost knocking Pat over, and just made it to the gutter before heaving up his dinner. He felt someone gently rubbing his back.

Pat had only had older sisters, and had always indulged Philip like he was the missing younger brother. Maybe he shouldn't have, he sometimes thought, but this kid seemed so much younger, far from home, and terrified.

"Alright now, you're going to be fine, boy. Just take a few deep breaths. I'll bring everything in, you go in with Phil and have a look around."

Philip had already disappeared, and Stephen set off for the door, left swinging open. There was a poster on the window, next to the door, listing forthcoming attractions for 'Wednesday night – Live Music'. Somewhere in the middle was Philip's 'proper' band, as he still described it. Underneath, in barely legible black felt tip, was added 'Support – Bonfire Club'. Stephen thought he might be sick again, but he also felt a sense of exhilaration, which went hand-in-hand with the fear, like it would not be denied.

That sense receded as he walked through into the bar. It was gloomy and cavernous. The ceiling was stained yellow-brown and the wallpaper was peeling. A single barmaid gave him a disinterested glance and returned to her conversation with a man with a teddy boy quiff. The only other people in there were a couple of elderly men at a table, both wearing hats and drinking stout, one jabbing his finger at the other.

"Charlie! I'm fuckin' telling you!" he repeated.

Philip appeared from a side door marked 'WC', headed directly to the bar, and punched the man with the quiff on the shoulder.

An hour later, Philip was still at the bar with the teddy boy, and another, older man, who'd joined them. Pat had left two guitar cases and two amplifiers on the tiny stage at the far end of the room and had gone to fetch Martin and his drums. Stephen sat at a table in front of the stage and tried to look nonchalant, wondering if there was something he was meant to be doing. Philip had pointed in his direction during the lengthy conversation, and Stephen realised that, of course, the group at the bar were the 'proper' band, men with beards or sideburns, real musicians, people with whom Philip felt comfortable.

He was still unsure what to make of Philip. Martin routinely told him to stop being a 'mardy muso bastard', and Doctor Friedman had recently expressed her view that the study of European literature was 'not set in tablets of stone brought down from Mount Sinai by you, Mister Cross', but everything bounced off him, usually to the sound of his own booming laugh. When he stopped complaining about Martin's lack of professionalism (which seemed a pointless complaint to Stephen), he could be convivial and generous. He had happily lent an electric guitar to Stephen and taken the time to explain the various knobs and controls to him. The conviviality was more in evidence just now, as Stephen watched him empty another glass.

There was still nobody else in the pub. The aggressive old man and his friend had gone, and there was still no sign of Martin, which occurred to Philip at the same time.

"Where is the old hippy?"

He was waving his arms about as he walked from the bar.

"We need to sound check and he's not even got his kit set up yet! Jesus, I got him on the bill, I lent you a guitar, I arranged the lift for him. He lives ten minutes away!"

Philip's tirade was directed at Stephen, as if he were standing in front of Martin, hiding him.

"Shut up, you noisy little sod!"

Pat had pushed open the door with a bass drum, and Stephen closed his mouth and gave silent thanks. He wasn't entirely sure what a sound check comprised.

Pat was closely followed by the T-shirt girl from Martin's house and two other young women, each of them carrying a part of the drumkit.

"Hark at the pied piper! What happened?"

"That kit must have been standing in that basement for years. The stands were so rusted, it took forever to take it all down. Your mate was no help either. Sent his harem along and decided to walk. Said he needed the air. He looked like a strong breeze would blow him over."

None of the three women looked likely to accept Pat's description of them, but the T-shirt girl bore this out by telling him they were no one's harem but that he was 'a pathetic little eunuch'. Now that he had the chance to look at her, Stephen thought that she had hair the colour of buttercups, but that she was as intimidating as he'd imagined when she had opened the door to him.

Pat laughed and said, "Fair enough!"

One or two other people were drifting into the bar, the stage was taking shape, and still Stephen sat there, taking it all in, and wondering what Charlie's friend had been trying to tell him.

BONFIRE CLUB

I just got back. I had to write all this down while it's still in my head.

I followed the plan until I met Phil in Russell Square, but then I followed the mood. I was sick with nerves, and I could not speak.

Phil's uncle took us to the pub and helped with all the equipment. He seemed nice, but Phil ignored me once he was with the 'proper' band, and so did everyone else, except Martin, but he didn't arrive until just before we were due on stage. He just said he'd had to see someone. I thought for a minute Phil was going to hit him.

Phil lent me his guitar and he played bass, as agreed during the rehearsals. Just before we went on, there were twelve people in the bar, including the other two from the proper band. I counted them. It still felt like ten times that number. Martin did the talking.

"Good evening! This is like being back in Salford! We are Bonfire Club!"

We started with 'Trying To Explain'. I kept my eyes closed all the way through, and then we got applause, and someone shouted 'Woo!' Then we did half-a-dozen covers, and that was it. It went by so quickly. I forgot two lines, and played the wrong chord once, but no one seemed to care, except Phil.

Martin kept saying 'The new wave is breaking!' and told me I was a street genius from the suburbs. The barmaid told me she liked us better than 'those boring old farts', meaning the proper band, but they were ten times better, and made no mistakes, and looked like they were enjoying themselves.

Martin actually fell asleep in the pub. Pat said on the way back that we'd need to keep an eye on him.

The girl in the T-shirt is called Emma.

*

Less than two weeks after Bonfire Club's debut, Stephen went home for the rest of summer. He had not seen Martin or Philip since that night, nor had he sought them out. He had returned to his room in a state of ecstasy, having had a vision that felt as real as anything Cathleen's saints had had, but, by the end of the following day, his mood had flattened. He wondered how anyone could lead a daily life at the pitch the other two did, and was relieved when Philip failed to appear at Doctor Friedman's final tutorial of term. His efforts to restore equilibrium to his life, however, were thrown off balance by two events.

After the tutorial, as she wished her students a good summer, Doctor Friedman touched Stephen lightly on the arm.

"Mister Elijah, I think that you have been hiding your light under a bushel."

She smiled at the boy's uncertainty, and he blushed.

"Matthew, chapter 5, although I do not believe that the reference was to rock and roll."

He forced a polite laugh as he backed out of the room.

A few days later, he checked his pigeonhole for the last time, while taking a break from packing. There was another note addressed to 'Brother Elijah', in that script. How did anyone learn to write like that, let alone Martin? Then he wondered why he thought 'let alone Martin', and he put off opening the letter until he was safely on the train home the next morning.

"Steve. You were great. You will be even greater. See you in September. Love from Martin."

His sense of relief at not being summoned back to the revolution, and at Martin apparently understanding that he would be away from London for several weeks, was intertwined with the realisation that the night in Camden Town was not over. Doctor Friedman somehow knew about it, and Martin's fervour was unquenchable, as he would learn over the next few years. Stephen folded up the note and put it in his inside pocket, next to the plectrum he'd started carrying around with him.

Only Cathleen was at home when he got in, and he was immediately aware that his once weekly phone calls had steadily become less regular towards the end of his first year. He wondered how his mother could make him feel so guilty about that without actually saying anything, or anything directly.

"God, Stephen, all those bombs! All those poor souls at the, what was it, the Ideal Homes thing. We were so worried about you!"

"What would I have been doing at the Ideal Homes Exhibition?"

"You could have been in the area. Seventy people injured! Ah God, and all with families worrying about them. Wicked, those men, plain wicked!"

Cathleen's father, who had died long before Stephen was

born, had enlisted in the British Army and been decorated after the Somme. She had always held up the grandfather they had never known to her children as the role model of a decent God-fearing man.

"Anyone finds out where you're from, you get any trouble, just you tell them about Granda. Not all the Irish are murdering bombers!"

He thought of the numerous occasions since last year when people had asked him whether he lived near Lennon and McCartney rather than accuse him of terrorist sympathies, but said nothing more to her about bombs in London.

Julie was away on holiday with her boyfriend's family, and his father was at a retirement party, so Stephen ate dinner with his mother, and made light conversation. When did Julie get a boyfriend? How had her O-levels gone? How did she manage to get their father's permission for the holiday? 'God alone knows that' was the answer to most of his questions, but they were on safe territory, the shared amazement at Tom Elijah's uneven-handed treatment of his son and daughter.

Back in his bedroom, he unpacked, took out his notebook, and wrote 'I'm Telling You, Charlie' and underlined it. He put the notebook at the bottom of his wardrobe, transferred the plectrum and Martin's note to his new trench coat, and went to meet Peter at the Red Cow.

Much later, it must have been after midnight, he was woken by the familiar sound of Tom making his way up the stairs, very slowly but not quietly. The bedroom door opened and he listened to the approaching tread. He lay there in the dark, pretending to be asleep, even as his father leaned over him and gently stroked his hair.

123

HEATWAVE

TE complained that I've spent more of the last few weeks in the beer garden of the Red Cow than at home. When I am at home, he spends most of his time sitting in the front room on his own, especially since Dave's funeral. Anyway, it's still too hot in the evenings to stay in, and I get paid weekly at the Co-op, so I'm not relying on him for beer money, as he put it, although he'd question my masculinity if he knew I drank lager shandy. As did Peter, who is still at home, working for his dad's company. Jim is away in Spain with his family. TE and CE had their fortnight in Wales, which gave me a break, although I should not have mentioned it to anyone, as Peter invited a few people back from the pub on my behalf one night. I went along with it because Janice was among them, and without her boyfriend, but all that happened was that her friend was sick in the kitchen sink and Janice had to hold back her hair and take her home. Somebody broke a glass, but no one seemed to notice when they came back last weekend. Julie, however, somehow knew about the evening. She had two weeks of boredom and resentment inside her – TE would never allow her to stay at home with just me – so that's hanging over me.

I have written three more songs, and I want to go back to London. I want to see Martin and Phil, because I know something will be happening.

And Emma. I want to see Emma.

*

As agreed during the weeks leading up to the end of their first year, Stephen, Johnny Delaney and Rob Gifford, who had also lived on the same corridor, had found a flat to share for the second year. Tom and Cathleen had regarded this as Stephen taking yet another step away from home, and so did he, and it had been a difficult discussion when he'd asked for a loan for a deposit.

"You'd think I was planning to move to Cambodia," he said to Johnny, who'd moved in over the summer.

The flat was actually the top floor of a large Victorian house in Gospel Oak, owned by a young couple with a baby, who lived on the ground floor. Stephen had asked Johnny to repeat the address when he phoned him at home earlier in the summer. It had sounded like a small town in Texas rather than a North London suburb.

So here he was, on an early autumn afternoon, in his own room in a London flat, a long way from home, where his mother was still wiping her eyes.

Here he was, Stephen Elijah, resident of Gospel Oak.

He ought to go out and find a phone box. There had been riots at the Notting Hill Carnival on the weekend just past. Gospel Oak was now attached to the map of North London in his head, but it was still a small map. He did know, though, that he was nowhere near Notting Hill, but Cathleen would not hear that, and Tom would not hear of the boy upsetting his mother. That's your job, thought Stephen, but out he went.

It was beginning to rain, and a palpable sense of relief was in the air. Several people had come out onto their doorsteps with arms raised. Someone cheered. Perhaps the newly appointed government minister really had broken the drought, although Tom's view was that God was behind it, for reasons no one could know, and he would choose when to end it.

On his way back from the phone box, Stephen had just decided once and for all that God didn't exist, or at least Tom's God didn't, when a voice spoke to him. It wasn't a god, but it was a revelation.

A boy of his age was leaning out of a first-floor window, smoking, and from the room behind him a radio was at full volume. He'd never heard anything like it. Loud, uncomplicated drums, distorted guitar played at breakneck speed, an otherworldly vocal. The boy looked at him, and Stephen realised that he'd stopped in his tracks and turned to face the window.

"The Damned!" called out the boy.

He smiled at Stephen, waved his cigarette, and disappeared back into the room. He was wearing eyeliner, Stephen realised. Wearing eyeliner, smoking, surrounded by glorious noise. By the time he got back to the flat, he had synchronised the boy and the music into a memory that filled him with a thrilling excitement, a memory he never quite forgot.

Johnny was at the top of the stairs.

"Someone called while you were out. He left a note. Bit of a weirdo."

He handed Stephen the torn-off back of a cigarette packet.

"Brother Elijah, welcome to the future. Meeting at HQ on Friday."

HQ was the basement of the house in Kentish Town, which had been the rehearsal room for the weeks leading to Bonfire Club's debut. Those rehearsals had all been lit by two naked lightbulbs. In the daylight creeping in through two windows at ground level, the grime and the damp were all around them.

"Martin, this is a dump."

"Phil, this is for free, spiders and all!"

"And why is she here?"

Stephen had of course arrived at the house thirty minutes early, wearing the new trench coat. Martin had answered the door wearing just a pair of cut-off denim shorts.

"Little brother! Come in."

The sunglasses were in place, and Martin had waved him toward the stairs to the basement while talking to someone in the kitchen, at the end of the long hallway. He had sat down there, with his coat pulled around him, for several minutes, before he heard two people coming down. Martin, now wearing an ancient-looking parka over his shorts, was carrying a tray of mugs. Behind him came the T-shirt girl, Emma.

Stephen smiled at her. She did not return the smile. The embers of his adoration of Janice Edwards died in that moment.

"The chair she sat in, like a burnished throne..." he silently recited to himself.

By the time Philip arrived, thirty minutes late, Martin had outlined in great detail his plan to write and illustrate the definitive guide to British birds of prey.

"Magnificent, Steve! Survivors. Misunderstood

127

survivors."

He had said nothing about the show in summer, or anything about the future he had proclaimed in his note. Emma had said not a word, nor did Martin acknowledge her presence there. She could be a ghost, thought Stephen, and only I can see her. He could not stop himself from glancing at her while Martin talked, even though he felt sure that he should not. He dared not say anything to her, but took in the sunlight straining through the dirty window and catching her hair. Her lips remained pursed, and she stared into the distance or down to her hands, folded in her lap. She appeared indifferent to everyone in the room, and Stephen understood that this was not an affectation, even as he thought that she was the most unimaginably beautiful person he would ever see. He shivered and pulled his coat around him more tightly.

"Right, now then, so this is Emma."

"I remember, but what's she doing here? I thought this was a band meeting."

"Patience, young Philip, it is a band meeting, that's why Emma is here."

"I'm sorry?"

"She's going to change the world with us. She's in the band!"

In the silence that followed, Stephen heard what he thought was a mouse in the far corner. Emma raised her eyes and looked at him for what felt like a long time. Then she picked up a sheet of paper and began to speak, and they all listened, even Philip.

MANIFESTO

1. Camden gig. The first song was superb. Stephen has to write more as good as that, quickly. We will never gravitate beyond toilets like that if we carry on playing boring old men's songs.

2. The three of you looked terrible. Stephen looked like a kid whose mother buys his clothes. Philip dresses like a hippy. Martin needs to cut off his ridiculous ponytail, and never wear a vest on stage again – being the drummer is no excuse for not looking cool. None of you understands that how you look matters, but it does.

3. Bonfire Club is an unimaginative name for a band. Martin has explained the provenance but it makes you sound like a comedy group. The name of the band matters, as much as how you look on stage. From this day, we are Generation 27. If anyone knows anything about Lorca, they will understand. If not, they won't, but that doesn't matter. The name sounds dark and mysterious (like Lorca).

4. To burn with desire and keep quiet about it is the greatest punishment we can bring on ourselves. Generation 27 will burn. This life is evanescent. If we become rich from this, then we stop, because we are not here to become rich. We are here to burn.

5. I will play bass guitar. Philip can then switch to lead guitar. I have never played, but that doesn't matter. Philip must leave that awful band and commit to this one, as we all must.

6. We now begin work on original material only, to be played at all future events.

7. We record Stephen's song in six weeks' time. We will divide the expenses between us.

8. Generation 27 is born. Sign up to this or walk away now.

Emma Dehasse-Carter
8th September 1976

*

"Who the fuck is Lorca?"

Philip broke the silence two minutes after Emma had finished reading, handed the sheet of paper to Martin, and left the room without another word.

Stephen had been listening, but only intermittently to what she had said. Whenever he thought about Emma in the years to come, which would be often, he never forgot her voice: the honeyed tone, the cut glass accent, the slight lisp. The first thing she had said, as she looked at him, was in praise of his song. Nothing else had mattered as much after that.

"And who the fuck is she? Did you know she was going to do that?"

"Do what, little brother?"

"Stage a coup!"

Martin cackled and coughed, as he often did. Stephen remembered what Pat had said about keeping an eye on him.

"Now then, comrades. Emma and me, we have been talking over the summer."

130

"I bet you have. Anything else you've been doing over the summer?"

"This is not a Yoko situation, Phil. Okay, just listen,"

They both listened, to Martin's description of Emma as a 'sort of girlfriend', who shared his ideals about the new wave of music. She had pointed out that the phrase 'new wave' had originally been used by a revolutionary movement in French cinema. At that moment, Stephen had looked at Philip, expecting him to detonate, but he was actually reading the manifesto, as Martin went on.

"So, right, I really think she can bring something, you know? A vision, a bit of glamour, sophistication, an edge."

"Steve, you worry me."

"What?"

Philip had now folded the sheet into a paper plane, which he had aimed at Stephen's head.

"What are you thinking? You never say."

"Well, erm, I was thinking about a boy I saw a couple of days ago, the music he was playing. I think that's what Emma means. New wave, punk, you know. The idea of being uncompromising, doing it all yourself, keeping the music raw and exciting. You see, my life is just so, so… dull. Safe, but dull. And I want to burn."

"Jesus, I'm surrounded by artsie-fartsies. I suppose she's another painting school drop-out?"

Martin didn't reply, but walked across the room to where Stephen sat, enveloped in a coat too big for him, picked up and unfolded the plane, and leaned over to kiss him on the cheek.

"So, young Philip, are you in?"

"Where do I get better clothes?" asked Stephen, trying to

ignore the kiss, but feeling oddly moved.

"What's this about a record?" said Philip.

ANARCHY

It's not as glamorous as it sounded on the manifesto.

One of Martin's friends from art school part-owns a recording studio, just off Archway Road, and he let us book it for a few hours at 'mate's rates', as Martin put it. But it's been postponed twice, and it turns out that the few hours begin at 11.00pm. We're here now, which is where I'm writing this. We're all sitting around in our coats, waiting for the engineer to turn up. He's at the pub, apparently. The studio is an old church hall. Wonder what TE would say? Wonder what Mister K would say? Well, I am here now, but it doesn't feel like the only place I could ever be.

We have rehearsed every week since Day Zero, as Martin calls it. Emma is nothing like as bad a musician as she suggested. Martin said that her parents had paid for piano lessons, and a piano, so she at least knows the theory of what she's trying to do, although she and Martin would hate me mentioning theory. She also has her own bass guitar, which made Phil happier. Perhaps her parents bought that for her too.

I'm still using the guitar Phil lent me, but he seems less bothered now he can be the guitar hero in the band. He's not one to stand in the background, plucking a bass guitar. Neither is Emma, though. Since Day Zero, she has barely spoken to Phil or me. When she does speak, it's usually to remind us of something in the manifesto. Even Phil goes along with this. I think he just fancies her, but she has this aura about her. You feel that something is going to happen when she's there. The engineer has arrived.

Later. The engineer only came to take us over the road to the pub he'd been in. He sounded like he'd been in there a while. He was very apologetic and insisted on buying drinks for us all. Martin didn't seem to care, and he shared jokes with the engineer about their friend in common. Everyone in the pub seemed to be drinking Guinness. Phil thought that should make me feel at home, but CE would not have been happy about the 'Free Derry' poster above the bar.

We're back, and it's now after midnight, and Cosmo (the engineer) is wandering about with cables and microphone stands. The place is a total mess, and it's now freezing cold, but Cosmo is assuring us that he'll soon be ready and that you can't rush these things. Emma is sharing a joint with Martin. Phil, who looks baby-faced without his beard and with his haircut, sits in a rocking chair, muttering 'For fuck's sake'. Martin keeps reminding us that we're paying next to nothing for this. Emma has gone to sleep on the old leather sofa. Now Cosmo says he wants to play us something 'to get the blood up'.

'Anarchy in the UK' he shouts down a microphone.

Where was he? Not at home. Where was home? He could barely move his head toward the pale light around the curtains, and then he remembered the whisky, and then where he was.

"Oh God, God, God!" he said, also remembering why he was here. The last piece of wisdom imparted to him by Doctor McFadden had been about 'young men's excesses', specifically drinking. The old man, who had now retired and moved back to Scotland, had been thinking of pints in the club bar after the rugby matches he had advocated, but the principle was the same, Stephen thought ruefully.

"There is no cure for a hangover, my boy, no cure. Just get up, move around, and drink water. We've all been there!"

Cathleen had been happier about that advice to her son than Mister Kirwan's jokes about drugs.

"Ah, we'll miss him, so," she had said when he'd phoned his parents a few days earlier.

So he got up from an unfamiliar bed, slowly, in the darkness, in a room in a house he did not know, although he had a memory of Emma's mother having shown them around when they arrived, and of her accent.

Bearings. Open the curtains. This is not going to be good, Stephen.

It was not, the collision between a late night and the relentless light of the morning, just hours apart. But the view.

Across the fields, through the breaking mist, to the Surrey

135

Hills, and not a soul or a sound. For several minutes, he was transfixed. Was this what peace was? He did not want to move, but he needed to find a bathroom. Surely there were several in this house, but he had no idea how to find the one he'd staggered into last night.

Relief washed over him as he finally connected the urgency of his need with what he'd thought had been a cupboard. His own bathroom! Why had no one told him? He knelt before the toilet just in time, and immediately felt better and lighter of heart, and returned to the Surrey Hills, as the previous day gradually fell into place, in all its blurred glory.

He felt as certain as he could be that he had said or done nothing to cause embarrassment, although he had been flustered when Emma's father, upon learning that his 'people' came from the 'North country', asked him what the hunting was like up there.

The four of them had arrived in Pat's van in the early evening, when it was almost dark, and he'd had only an impression of a very unfamiliar landscape, involving narrow lanes, fields, expanses of woodland, and detached houses. Inside 'the pile' (Emma's father again) was an entire world, of casual entitlement and tasteful décor. Emma had made clear several times on the journey from London what she expected from them, and what they were not to say or do, much to Martin's amusement and Philip's impatience, but, from the moment he crossed the threshold, Stephen imagined himself to be at the head of a vast army of Elijah and Flaherty forebears, with a responsibility to keep them all quiet and well-behaved. Every step he took, through the panelled hallway into the drawing room, was cautious, as were his responses.

"Pa, Martin, Philip, Stephen."

"Mister C," said Martin.

"Hi," said Philip.

"Pleased to meet you," said Stephen, offering his hand.

Emma's mother, he assumed, was the voice from the next room, speaking loudly in French. A minute later, as the four men stood making awkward small talk and Emma stared at the floor, she appeared on a wave of perfume and with the rustle of a silk dress. She was the most exotic person Stephen had ever seen, an impression reinforced by her embracing her daughter and kissing both cheeks, and then doing the same to Martin, Philip and him. Her accent was less pronounced when she spoke in English, but it added to the fascination.

"So sorry, I was on the phone to my sister. Emma, you never call Tante Camille! My boys! Emma has told me all about you and your pop group. How marvellous!"

If either of her parents knew anything about Emma's unclear relationship with Martin, they said nothing. Philip had later said that he felt like he was in an episode of *Upstairs Downstairs*, but did not once smirk, and Stephen thought that Martin had toned down his accent (or maybe he normally toned it up), although the sunglasses stayed in place, as did the ponytail he'd refused to cut off.

The evening had thawed, particularly once Pa Carter, as Philip later referred to him, began handing out cans of strong Jamaican lager.

"One of the foreign correspondents came across it. Lovely stuff, bit of a kick to it. Any of you boys ever been to Jamaica?"

"Well," said Martin, but he was elbowed by Emma before he could add, 'sort of'.

"Pa, the boys don't want to hear all your journo stories."

"No, Richard, Emma is right. Boys, let me show you the house."

Stephen's recollections in the early morning became hazier from about that point, although he could remember stumbling over 'Thank you, Mrs Dehasse-Carter' when she leaned over him to pour more wine.

"Please call me Sophie!"

He also remembered how miserable Emma had seemed to be all night.

"Looks like we failed the test, mate," Philip had said, as the two of them made an attempt to tidy up the kitchen after everyone else had gone to bed, "and I don't rate the old hippie's chances tonight, eh? Not after the red wine on the rug! Anyway, Pa Carter probably has an armed guard outside her door all night."

Stephen had actually noticed Martin slipping out of the front door on his own a few minutes earlier but had said nothing. His headache was now getting worse, as he found his way back to the kitchen, in search of water. He wondered if Doctor McFadden had ever felt this unwell.

He thought at first that he and Philip had left the lights on, but then realised that someone had actually been up before him when he saw a note on the table.

'Red wine doesn't go in the fridge!!'

The note was propped against the offending half-empty bottle he remembered putting in the fridge. He would have done that if he'd been sober, and shame washed over him as he thought of Tom Elijah's annual bottle of Blue Nun with the Christmas dinner. At that moment, Emma walked in. He turned away from the table, but not soon enough.

"So who's the guilty man, you or Phillippe?"

She drifted past him, wearing a Che T-shirt. Stephen kept his eyes down as he flushed.

"Oh, don't worry. It's just Madame Sophie reminding her darling daughter how much they paid for her education."

"Erm, why was she up so early?"

"Her horse. She likes to ride as the sun comes up. God knows why."

He remembered Cathleen helping him up onto Poncho, the only one of his uncle's donkeys he would ride. Poncho was the oldest, and was arthritic, and Stephen had stroked his head all the way along the beach and back.

"Your dad doesn't go with her?"

"Ha! No. He's already left for the office. Angry editorials don't write themselves, you know."

"Did they meet in France?"

He felt himself on the point of running out of conversation just as Sophie came in, to his relief and to his horror. The note, the writer of it, and the guilty man were in the same room.

"Stephen thinks you're French, Maman."

"Belge," said Sophie, "Belgian. From Charleroi. In the French-speaking part. Oh, Emma!"

"What?"

"Smoking in the kitchen. Wandering around in next to nothing. I apologise, Stephen. And you have not made him coffee!"

"Pa smokes in the kitchen, the kettle is on, and he is capable of making his own coffee. He's more embarrassed by your bitchy note and by your ridiculous jodhpurs than by me in a T-shirt. Oh, and Stephen, just so you know, I am wearing pants."

"Don't slam the door!" called Sophie after her daughter. She smiled at Stephen and shrugged her shoulders, as the noise echoed throughout the house.

*

"I wanna riot of my own! Yeah!"

"Martin! Jesus! Stop shouting and stop drumming on the biscuit tin! Can't you ever just sit still and do nothing?"

"Sorry, little brother. Too much of Mister C's whisky, eh? But no, no, no! If you're sitting still and doing nothing, you're dead."

"I feel dead. And that song is crap. When are you ever going to riot? And don't start on another lecture about a bunch of art college wankers changing the world with three minutes of guitars a chimp could have played!"

It was mid-afternoon, and the four of them were in the kitchen, from where Stephen had barely moved since Emma had made her exit. To complete his earlier mortification, Sophie had proceeded to talk frankly about how she and her husband worried that their daughter was wasting her time, and their money.

"What problems can she have, Stephen? What problems? I had problems when I was young. I had real problems. I had the Germans take my father away, I didn't see him for three years. We had nothing to eat. Emma has had everything. Her father got her that job with the publishers, we even pay the rent on that house. And Emma is not her real name, you know that? Well, it is her middle name, but she was baptised Eloise, named after my mother, her grandmother that she never knew. But she will not answer to that. She told us when she was eighteen that she was now Emma. Of course, she had just read Madame Bovary. My poor mother."

She had sobbed dramatically. Stephen had wondered whether Sophie and her husband knew that Martin, among others, had taken up residence in Kentish Town. At that moment, he fervently hoped not. Martin would certainly not have concealed the fact. He understood now how he and Emma could afford to live in that house. Philip had told him that Martin had been a trainee draughtsman but was 'thinking of jacking it in'.

Meanwhile the two kept sniping at each other, Philip shouting for quiet as he watched two Aspirins dissolve in a mug of coffee, Martin proclaiming The Clash and Generation 27 as the future of rock and roll. Emma sat painting her toenails black, occasionally looking at Stephen.

"Sorry about my mother earlier," she said eventually.

Since Cosmo had recorded 'Trying To Explain', and the four of them had emerged into a winter dawn on Archway Road with two dozen copy tapes, the Generation 27 manifesto had remained nothing more than a statement of intent. The tapes had been left with the disinterested receptionists at several record company buildings, and given to a couple of promoters that Martin somehow knew ("For an art school drop-out, he knows a lot of people," Philip had observed), but not even a single rejection letter had come back. They had been offered a return to the Camden pub, as headliners, but as Bonfire Club, and on condition they played a few 'audience favourites'. Stephen had been surprised by how vehemently Philip had turned that down.

"This is the way to go, not back to toilets like that place.

If there's a new wave, we need to ride it."

He had looked at Emma as he said that, ruffling his auburn crop.

"A pugilist is our Phil," said Martin later, "but a realistic one. And malleable."

The familiar wheeze had followed a wink to Stephen.

When Richard Carter had suggested Emma's band for the twenty-first birthday party of a family friend's son, he had done so with good intentions but not the faintest glimmer of understanding of how badly received that idea could be. Nevertheless, they had done little more than rehearse for several weeks, and the vote was in favour of taking the booking, by three to one.

"I've almost forgotten how to play a show," said Philip. "We have to do this, it'll be easy, like being paid to rehearse."

"And it is good money," added Martin.

"We can try out the new material," said Stephen, "with maybe a few covers. Just a few."

Emma had said nothing, in the way she was now saying nothing, which was to say at an ear-splitting volume. She wished she had never passed on her father's offer.

"After all, home is where the heart is," Martin had continued, "and we get to meet your folks!"

As they had left the house in Kentish Town that evening, Stephen and Philip thought they could hear Emma from a long way down the road.

"Rather him than me, Stevie boy. He hasn't got the sense he was born with. Either that or he's high again. Or both. Pat was right, I need to stop lending him money."

*

They had dispersed, changed into their stage gear, and reassembled in the kitchen, where Richard had reappeared, in a purple velvet suit, and was handing out cans of lager again.

"Nice duds, Mister C."

"Thank you, Martin. Now when you boys are dressed, perhaps we could have a photo in the garden? It's almost like summer out there."

"Pa, for God's sake, we are dressed. What's your excuse for that outfit?"

"Emma! Your father wore that suit for our silver wedding anniversary, don't you remember?"

Stephen had caught the perfume before Sophie had sidled up to take his arm. He tried not to look at Philip.

"Anyway, you all look very striking in black. Don't you think, Richard? Come on!"

She led the way down some steps to a back door, and out into an expanse of lawn which appeared to have no bounds, and then stood back from the four of them, as they squinted into the sunlight.

"Now everyone, smile! Everyone, Emma!"

Emma looked away, hands in the pockets of her leather jacket.

"Should we put the beers down?" muttered Stephen.

"Nah! Cheers!" yelled Philip, grinning for posterity.

As he was gazing into the fields opposite the house, it seemed to Martin that, above the hillside, a dark speck was wavering against the sun, and then it suddenly fell towards the distant woods.

*

Of course, thought Stephen, they're going to the party. Who would wear a purple velvet suit for just hanging round the house, even here?

They were trundling along the lanes, following the silver Volvo, with Emma and Martin in the back. The van wasn't big enough for all four of them to sit in the front, but it was too big for their meagre equipment, and bodies wedged up against a bass drum and speakers were a necessity. Stephen was relieved to have his turn on the passenger seat for other reasons, however.

"She's sweet, and your dad!"

"Martin, she is not sweet. You don't know her. Just do not say anything else. She'll save it all up and use it against me. And my father is an idiot. She was all over Stephen and he didn't notice."

"Didn't care, more like!" whispered Philip, but not quietly enough.

"At least my father is still at home, you creep!" bawled Emma.

The conversation in the back continued in hushed tones, while Philip looked at the road ahead and said nothing for a while. They eventually turned into another lengthy driveway and pulled up behind the Volvo in front of an enormous marquee. Martin leaned over between the front seats.

"Fuck me! They live in a tent! Now then, have we been brought here under false pretences? Are we playing for a bunch of Home Counties paupers?"

"You idiot. They were hardly going to have a band playing in their house."

Emma pointed towards what Stephen guessed was the

'Mole Cottage' on the sign he'd noticed at the driveway entrance. The whole area seemed to comprise euphemistic cottages and lodges, each one bigger than the last. He echoed his father.

"*Iesu mawr* !"

"No need for that sort of language, young Stephen!" shouted Philip, seemingly back to normal, "Let's have a look in this tent then. And what was this kid's name?"

The boy's name was Ed. He was standing with his parents at the far end of the marquee when they walked in. Richard and Sophie clearly knew them well enough for air-kissing. They called Emma 'darling', but she hung back from the group, pulling at Martin's arm as she did. Ed sweated in his suit under the lights, and looked uneasy, and Stephen wondered if any rich people were happy. He imagined Tom putting his arm reassuringly around the boy and taking him off for a pint. He wondered what his parents were doing at that moment.

It was still early by the time they had set up on the low stage, and people were only just arriving.

"None of them will dance until they're pissed," said Emma, "we should go on late." So they sat in a corner, drinking Ed's parents' champagne, until Martin took a tin and a packet of Rizlas from his pocket.

"Careful, mate, not in here!"

"Phil, brother, don't worry. Look. They're all at it."

Sophie was openly sharing a suspiciously large roll-up with Ed's father. She giggled as he topped up her glass.

"You smoked enough last night, didn't you? And you were out late. Where did you get to?"

Stephen remembered seeing Martin leave the house but

had decided not to mention that. He knew that the champagne had loosened his tongue. This didn't seem to have worried Philip, but Martin moved on.

"Now then, can anyone tell me how Rizlas got their name?"

"No, but you're going to tell us, aren't you?"

"Indeed I am, Phil. The Lacroix family first made rolling papers, at the time of Napoleon. The paper was made from rice. *Riz*, in French. They added the 'la' bit of their name to 'riz'. *Et voila!*"

"Bullshit!"

"*Merde!*" added Stephen, before immediately regretting it when he noticed Emma raise her eyebrows.

"That's true, actually."

Ed had joined them, minus jacket and tie, and looking more at ease than earlier.

"How are you, Em?"

"I'm fine, and don't call me Em, or I'll call you Edward, and tell everyone why."

"We've known each other since we were kids," said Ed, unperturbed, "and I'm named after Burne-Jones."

"Who?"

"Oh Philip, my man! The Pre-Raphaelite painter. You know? The wan maidens, the flowing locks, the lowered eyes. And a fellow draughtsman. Did you go to art college, Eduardo?"

"God, no. I was never much good at that, that was just my mother. We're apparently distantly related to the man. No, I'm just reading PPE, I'm afraid. At Oxford."

Emma didn't bother to stifle her snort. Stephen had never heard of Burne-Jones either, but he watched her as she bowed her head. He now knew how to finish the song he was writing about her.

*

As Stephen crouched down to fasten his guitar case, he could see under one of the trestle tables the indistinct form of two people apparently the worse for wine. Then he realised that one pair of legs, in stilettos, was gradually draping itself over the other, and he stood up sharply.

"Jesus! Emma was right," said Philip next to him, reeling in a cable, "that was the most bombed audience I've ever played to, and that includes my relatives. I bet not one of them noticed any of the cock-ups. Easy money, Stevie boy!"

Emma, who'd left the clearing away to 'the plebs', as she'd taken to calling them since they'd arrived (Stephen wasn't sure whether seriously or humorously, or both), was meanwhile talking to a man who'd walked over to the stage just after they'd finished playing.

"Does any one of you have a tape? And has anyone seen my bloody mother? Pa is keen to get home."

"Bob! Is that you, pal? Glad you could make it," called Martin by way of a reply, and he left his partly-disassembled drum kit to join the conversation.

"Tape, anyone? Tape!"

"You have all the copies, Martin! And don't worry about the drumkit, I'll pack that away for you."

Philip was wrong. Stephen had one copy that he'd taken from the original batch before they'd left the Archway Road studio that day. He didn't know why, but he'd carried it with him ever since, even to his parents' and back over Christmas.

"I have one!"

"Fantastic! Bring it here, little brother. Quick!"

He reopened his guitar case and reached into the small compartment behind the neck, taking care not to look under the trestle again.

"Who is this geezer?" muttered Philip, "Let's go see."

The man turned to them as they stepped off the stage, and Stephen handed the tape to Martin, who immediately passed it on.

"Thanks. Bob Spendlove," he said, extending his hand. He was clearly not one of the party guests, was Stephen's immediate thought. Spiked peroxide hair, a vintage black suit that suggested a Dickensian villain, brothel creepers, and red tinted glasses.

"Right, so then, Steve, Phil. Bob has some contacts in the business. Me and Emma got talking to him, and he said he'd like to hear us. So, here he is!"

"Hang on!" said Philip, "Hang on! What contacts? Who is he? Where did you get talking to him? And when were you going to tell me and Steve?"

"Let me answer those perfectly understandable questions, seeing as they're mostly about me."

Stephen wanted to laugh at that, but the direct manner and the level gaze behind the tinted glasses was forbidding, as was the polite but curt tone.

"I vaguely knew Martin at art college, then we ran into each other again at a couple of markets, him with his silk screen T-shirts and me selling proper clobber and imported records. He and Emma told me all about Generation 27. I loved the name and the concept, and they asked me along tonight. I didn't realise they hadn't told you, but I'm glad I

148

came. You were so much better than I was expecting. You have something, and I'd like to help move things along. And I do have some contacts, and some favours to call in."

He examined the scrawl across the cassette case.

"Trying To Explain. I'm Telling You, Charlie. Bonfire Club. You played them all this evening, didn't you? To be honest, they could have sounded better, but they're decent songs, with tunes, and they sounded fresh and new. Better than all the clapped out old covers the posh boys were falling over to. Leave this with me. I'll call you, Martin. Gentlemen. Lady."

He winked at Emma and turned on his heel, without waiting for any response. Weaving around the bodies and debris of the evening, he seemed to Stephen like a departing visitor from another world. That's someone who noticed the cock-ups, he thought, but he likes my songs. He wondered what favours he meant to call in.

"Cheeky little sod, isn't he?" said Philip, "What sort of a name is Spendlove, anyway?"

*

"Her hair fell like rain down her shoulders
She was pale as the first morning light
And all of the things I never told her
Still keep me awake in the night."

"What?"

Philip was through the kitchen door and heading for the fridge before he knew it. The house was so big that you could hear no one approaching until they were upon you, thought

Stephen. Perhaps that's how people got away with all those literary country house murders.

"Just reading through some lyrics."

"Let me see."

Stephen snapped shut the notebook.

"Suit yourself. I don't get people who keep journals anyway."

"I don't, not anymore. I keep this for ideas."

He was sure that he had never told anyone that he had been keeping a journal, and he watched Philip carefully.

"There must be some of Pa's beer left in here. Did we finish it when we came back?"

It was almost midday, but Stephen had not seen any of them, or been seen, since he'd gone straight to bed when they got in. After Bob Spendlove had left, they hadn't been sure how to get back to Eaton Place, as Philip called it, once they realised how drunk their driver was. Martin had said he could drive, but Philip refused to give him the van keys.

"No, no, no, no, no! You'd kidnap us, and you and Bob Spendthrift, or whatever he's called, would sell us all into white slavery. Or even worse, you'd take us to Manchester!"

Within minutes, he was stretched out on the stage, snoring loudly. Martin was involved in a conversation in the far corner with Ed. There were a few stragglers still dancing in the space between the tables and the bar when the DJ announced the final record.

"God, I hate this. So cheesy," said Emma, looking over at Martin, who appeared to be giving Ed some money, "oh, come on."

She took Stephen's hand and pulled him after her, as the lights dimmed. Synthesised strings washed over the marquee, and an aching voice cut through, singing about not being in love, because big boys didn't fall in love.

While he was still wondering where to put his arms, she twined hers around his neck. His hands trembled as he rested them lightly on her waist. They began to sway in time.

As the music swelled to an orchestral climax, she rested her head on his shoulder. Stephen almost stopped breathing, for fear of breaking the moment. He wanted to enfold her, but he was acutely aware of his physical excitement and the shame of it.

"The trouble with this life, Stephen," she half-whispered into his ear, "is that it's so easy to just drift away."

Then she lifted her head and gently took his arms from her. The lights came back up, as a tear ran down her face. She leaned back to him, kissed him on the cheek, and turned away.

Stephen Elijah finished writing the new song in the early hours, alone in his bed, but he didn't play it to anyone for another forty years. By then, he would understand what Emma had said to him on that night when, just for a moment, he held her. For now, all he knew was that Mister Kirwan had asked why we shouldn't dance, and that he would tell him why if he ever saw him again.

"I am undone," he said out loud, and he closed the notebook.

*

"Valediction Records."

"Valediction Forbidding Mourning. Now then, my Dad used to read that out loud."

"Oh yeah. Donne."

"What in the name of God are you three talking about? I was asking about this record label."

Bob Spendlove sat at the end of a table in The Pillars of Hercules, a vodka and tonic and a sheaf of papers before him. He looked up at Philip.

"I don't know what those two are talking about," he said, waving at Martin and Emma on his left, "I just like the name. Anyway, Linda came up with it."

"I thought you chaps were the poetry scholars," said Martin, pointing across the table.

"I know who Donne bloody is," replied Philip, as he reached for another handful of crisps, "and I don't care that much what this label is going to be called, but I want to know how it's going to work, and how it helps us. And who's Linda?"

"Linda is my wife and my business partner. We'll run the label, we'll manage the band, you'll make the records, we'll all make some money. Happy days all round."

Stephen felt like he was sitting in a board meeting, or what he imagined a board meeting would be like, complete with a ruthless chairman.

"Brother Elijah!"

"Hmm?"

"You're drifting off again, Stevie. What do you think?"

Bob had asked them to meet him, and had immediately put the suggestion. Stephen suspected that it had already been made to Martin and Emma. Either that, or they seemed blasé and unquestioning about the proposal, although they often appeared to be like that. They already knew Bob, of course, and Martin had declared his 'implicit trust' in him as they drove back from Surrey the previous week. Philip had responded that he couldn't trust anyone called Spendlove.

"Well, I'm not sure. Shouldn't the four of us talk about this?"

He had not as yet spoken a word directly to Bob, and he looked across the table as he said this.

"Sure, of course," said Bob, "I'll leave this with you. Read through it, have a chat, get back to me. I've pitched my spiel. We'll meet again when you're ready."

An hour later, they were still in the pub, Bob having left what appeared to be some sort of contract on the table, at which they stared during moments of silence.

"He looks Jewish," said Philip suddenly. Stephen tried to picture Bob standing next to Doctor Friedman. The barrow boy, as Philip had also described him, alongside the stern academic.

"He sounds it too. What was that spiel bollocks?"

"Don't be a racist prick."

"Right, Emma, Phil. Enough now. We need to decide."

"I'm not yet convinced. He needs to get us, otherwise he won't fight for us."

"Fair point, Emma. Steve? Phil?"

"I don't care whether he gets us. Will he get us on the radio? Will he get us shows? Will we make records?"

"Brother Philip, those are fair questions," said Martin, ignoring Emma's raised eyebrows, "so how about this? He said the tape was with someone. I say we give him another couple of weeks. If something comes of the tape, we sign this deal. If not, we don't."

"Yes!" replied Philip, slamming down his empty pint glass as if to emphasise his agreement, "I knew there was a hard-nosed Lancashire mill-owner lurking in the hippie!"

Stephen thought that this had probably been Martin's plan for the last hour but said nothing other than "Okay."

"Three to one," added Philip, "my round."

While he was at the bar, Martin excused himself, and Stephen clasped his hands and stared resolutely at the floor. He did not look up, not even when Emma said "Coward."

*

Three days later, as Stephen was wondering about the point of studying a poem written in Middle English, he was disturbed by an increasingly familiar thunder of heavy feet up the stairs. He braced himself for the knock on his bedroom door.

Philip had taken to calling at the house once he had the address. There was a phone where he was living, and so the pretext was usually passing on messages from Martin, or messages from Emma via Martin, as Philip unfailingly put it. Often there was no message, and they would go to the pub.

"We're in a bar in Gospel Oak, Stevie! Gospel Oak! Clint Eastwood drinks here, you know."

The hammering on the door had duly begun.

"Steve! Steve! Come on!"

Eric and Jen were not much older than the three students who lived upstairs in their house, and were tolerant to a fault, or at least because they had a mortgage to pay, but they had a baby and a yappy dog, and Stephen knew better than to pretend that he was out, at least where Philip was concerned.

"Sorry, didn't hear the bell," he lied, although he hadn't been expecting anyone and had assumed the ringing was for

154

someone downstairs. He waited for the habitual launch across the room and onto the bed at the far side, but instead Philip stayed in the doorway, arms aloft.

"We got played! Spendthrift did it! Come on, get your shoes on. Martin and the Ice Queen are waiting for us!"

"What?"

"Put Chaucer down. Get your shoes on. We were played on Capital Radio last night. Come on!"

"Did you hear? Which song?"

"No idea, Martin just phoned. Let's get over there!"

Half an hour later, the two of them stood in the rehearsal room, Phil with his hands on his knees and complaining of a stitch.

"You ran here?"

Martin was incredulous and unable to stop laughing, gasping for breath more than either of them.

"You'll have a heart attack, Phil! The two of you just calm down now. Emma's making tea."

"But you told me to get straight over! You said we were on Capital!"

"Sit down, little brothers. Time for a chat. Tea's up."

Emma came in with a tray. Stephen didn't think he'd ever seen her in anything other than all black, since Philip had first pointed it out ("Even her knickers, mate, I bet."), but today her T-shirt proclaimed 'Generation 27. To Burn' in bright red letters across a yellow background.

"Jesus!" said Philip, but not about the shirt. She had had her previously shoulder-length hair cut to a sort of tousled bob just before the Surrey trip. If that had been done to provoke the comment from her mother, it had worked ("Oh Emma! Did you cut that yourself?") but evidently that had not been sufficient, and it looked like she might have really cut it herself this time.

"Ah yes," said Martin, "a platinum Jean Seberg, eh?"

"*Mademoiselle la gamine*," said Philip.

"*Enculez vous*," replied Emma.

Stephen followed none of that exchange. His only thought was that his new song had been torn to pieces, in front of his eyes.

"To business, then."

The usual slur in Martin's speech had gone, and he took off his sunglasses.

"Jesus!" said Philip again.

"Now then, young Philip, enough blasphemy. Right, so, it was the late-night show. Well, early hours of the morning, to be strictly accurate. I can't remember the name of the show, or the presenter, I was barely listening. Bob hadn't told me anything, so even he can't have known. I knew he knew someone at the station, that's all. Then, boom!"

"Which song?"

"What do you think, Brother Elijah? The classic, the single."

"He means 'Trying To Explain'."

"Thank you, Emma, I think he realised."

"I didn't. Did you hear it, Emma?"

"You must be joking. Why would I be listening to Capital Radio at that time of night? Or ever?"

"I wasn't listening, I keep saying, it was just on. Anyway, come on now, order. Bob got us on the radio, he kept his side of the deal."

"There was no deal he knew of," said Emma, "it was our decision, or rather yours. All two and a half of you."

"I thought it was your idea to bring him to the party?"

"No, Philip, it was Martin's idea, but he isn't the one Bob fancies."

"Harsh but true," agreed Martin, "but we are a democracy. We agreed to do this. Emma thinks Bob's had his roving eye on her since he first met her, which is probably true, knowing him, but she also suspects his other motives."

"What do you mean?"

"She insisted he read the manifesto, Phil. He was not enthusiastic."

"He fucking well laughed, Martin, and you said nothing."

Emma's unenthusiastic response to Bob Spendlove now became clearer, at least to Stephen, who decided he could now understand the accusation of cowardice, which had caused him anguish since they'd last met.

"He might have smirked to himself, but he didn't laugh!"

"He doesn't understand what Generation 27 is about. He doesn't take it seriously. It's all just about the money to him. What happened to your revolution? We agreed we were not here to become rich, all of us did!"

Emma never raised her voice, Stephen had noticed, but she could reduce a room to silence, as she did now. He heard himself breaking that silence.

"We did all sign up to the manifesto. We also agreed to have Bob as our manager if something came out of the tape. I don't see why we can't stick to both. Can't we?"

Philip shrugged and grunted what could have been taken as an assent. Emma looked at Martin.

"Little brother, you have youth, talent and wisdom. I, for one, am humbled. Phil?"

"I did sign up, Steve is right, and this is a good band, but that's why we need to be heard by more people, that's all I'm saying, and if Spendthrift can help us with that, well. There's something about him I don't trust, we'll have to keep an eye on him, and okay, he shouldn't have sneered, but Steve. We have to do this!"

"Well now," said Martin, putting his sunglasses back on, "I think we have a consensus. I haven't forgotten the revolution, darling, I haven't been into the office for weeks, I think I've been sacked, there's my commitment. But I can't keep on living off handouts. I have my expenses, like all of us. We need to be playing better places, making proper records, if we're going to do this full-time. If we're agreed, I can show this contract to a friend of a friend, who's in the business, sort of. If he says it's fine, I say we sign. Unintended rhyme there, by the way."

The wheezing laugh was cut short by Emma getting to her feet abruptly and heading for the stairs. Stephen couldn't tell if Martin had heard her mutter under her breath when he'd spoken about handouts and expenses.

"Emma?"

She stopped but did not turn around.

"Of course, I'm only the girl, the eye candy, but don't you ever call me 'darling' again, Martin. And Philip, try talking to me like I'm in the room. Stephen, just stop being so scared of everything."

Now she did turn around.

"Look at the three of you. Bob Spendlove would eat you for breakfast if he could. Luckily for you, you have me."

She turned back and disappeared upstairs. Fifteen minutes later she came back down to the basement, where the three were trying to decipher the contract.

"We're going to the pub," she said, zipping up the pocket in which she'd put a small knife.

IN BLOOD

Three in the morning.

Handkerchief still tied around my finger.

I had stopped keeping a journal but I had to record this. I doubt that Mister Kirwan would think this a good thing. Maybe he would.

We went to the pub around the corner from Martin and Emma's. Emma produced a sheet of paper and dictated what she called a 'real contract' to Martin, who wrote it down in his old-fashioned script (the only valuable thing he ever learned at art college, he says).

She said, "If I sign Bob Spendlove's contract, you all sign this."

Phil said it looked like a blood oath, and Emma said yes, that's what it was, a blood oath, and it would bind us forever, and outlive people like Bob.

She then took out four plectrums and handed us one each. They were dark blue and inscribed 'Valediction Records' in gold.

It turned out that Bob and Martin had already had these made, and I think Emma knew how Phil would react, especially after a drink. Phil called Martin a manipulative bastard and said that he'd sign a blood oath before he signed a bloodsucker's contract. Martin laughed, which made things worse, and we were asked to leave.

Phil said, "Ally Pally."

We have all been up there at night a few times recently.

Phil has a friend in Crouch End, and he said it was a good place to sit and think and look at the lights. You could even see St Paul's. Phil had the van and so we drove up there (he has Pat's van all the time now, as Pat is apparently ill).

Phil was right. It was where we needed to go.

We sat on the usual bench and Emma took out the oath, which we all signed. It means that if any one of us is in any sort of trouble, or needs to see the others urgently, then we meet right here. We keep the chain of communication we have now, so Phil might have to fly to New Zealand to kick my door in in ten years' time, but I didn't say this, not after Emma took out a knife. She said, "In blood, forever," and cut the tip of her finger, and smeared a drop of blood next to her signature. No one said a thing, and we all did the same, and said the same when we did it.

We sat in the darkness and looked out over the lights of London, in silence.

Stephen Elijah
5ᵗʰ May 1977

*

"Mister Elijah. Well now."

Professor Fordham was reading the papers handed to him by Doctor Friedman, who had not smiled as Stephen sat down. According to college rumour, Fordham had been shot down over the English Channel during the Battle of Britain, hence the scar running down the left side of his face from temple to chin, and the glass eye. Stephen thought it also an explanation for a brusque manner, which made the Head of

Department's end of year reviews with the students an intimidating experience for most of them.

"And how has our Mister Elijah been doing? Has he done himself justice, hmm?"

"I think he is honest enough to know the answer to that."

Fordham scared him but his tutor's words pierced him. Once again, he felt shame for having let her down. He wanted to apologise for her having been forced to leave her childhood home, only to have to deal with the likes of him some forty years later, an idle boy who frittered away his time. At his age, Fordham had flown a Spitfire against the dark forces who had murdered Judith Friedman's relatives. Stephen couldn't compete with that. His only recent injury was a self-inflicted one.

"Mister Elijah?"

"Sorry."

"I asked you, sir, if you were indeed honest enough."

"I do know that my grades have slipped."

"Mister Elijah, they have done more than slipped, it would appear. Two hand-in dates missed, absent from several tutorials, no apologies to the staff in question. Please consider this a rocket. There has to be an immediate improvement, sir, else we shall have a far less pleasant conversation come the Michaelmas term. I can be no clearer. I wish you a pleasant summer. Come back here a different man. Good morning."

He dared not look at either of the two people on the other side of the table as he left the room, and he walked miserably down Tottenham Court Road to the bus stop, wondering when and for how long he should go home. At about the same time, Tom Elijah, attending a committee meeting about a

Silver Jubilee street party, felt himself struggling for breath and in severe pain.

1978

Bob and Linda Spendlove appeared to Stephen to have manifested from one of the gothic novels he was reading that term. You wouldn't sit down for a cup of tea and a chat with either of them, he thought, but there was a seductively debauched glamour around them. His father was sufficiently recovered from his heart attack that summer to have pronounced them as 'bloody oddballs', had he ever met them, but Stephen had one foot in a world he would never attempt to explain to Tom and Cathleen.

Bob took out his fob watch.

"Come on then, people. What do we say?"

"A whole week?" said Philip, although Stephen knew that what they were all really thinking was "Northern Ireland?"

He had returned to London later than planned for his final year, a decision taken out of his hands by the need to stay and help Cathleen while Tom convalesced. Doctor Friedman had been insistent.

"There is no rush, Stephen. We'll talk when you get back. There will be plenty of time to catch up. Your family comes first."

There had also been plenty of time to catch up with Generation 27, and the three others had been similarly supportive.

"Now then, little brother. Get your dad sorted out. Don't worry about us."

He spent all summer worrying about them, about the final

year, about the future, possibly a future with a disabled father or a widowed mother, and he thought about Emma's comment that at least his father had a heart.

"I am too young for this," he said to himself often, but sometimes out loud.

In fact, Tom had only spent five days in hospital. It had been a minor attack, and he was discharged with a stern warning about lifestyle – a word he hated – and advice to take things easier.

"*Iesu mawr*, I'm not bloody fifty yet! What am I supposed to do? Sit in front of the TV until I die?"

Nevertheless, he gave up smoking completely and immediately, and the desk job at the station became permanent. In all other respects, he picked up where he had left off, for good or ill, although Cathleen appeared to have aged ten years in those few weeks, as she patiently changed sheets, made tea and listened to her husband and son bemoan their treatment by life.

Julie had left for Warwick University, where her boyfriend already was, and Stephen knew how quiet the house would be when his mother came in from her morning at the local school kitchen.

"We'll be fine, boy. You have to get back."

Tom had clasped his hand for a moment longer than usual and had smiled at his son.

"Stevie? Stevie!"

Philip had thrown half a digestive biscuit across the rehearsal room.

By the time Stephen had returned to Gospel Oak, Generation 27 had been played on the late night show on Capital Radio several times, and 'Trying To Explain'/'I'm

Telling You Charlie' was the first official release on Valediction Records. Martin had wanted the occasion marked by red vinyl – "Our debut and yours, Bob!" – but the idea had been firmly ruled out by Linda, whose role in the operation seemed to be to steer her husband away from possible bankruptcy. They had nevertheless paid for an initial run of a thousand copies and had spent the previous few weeks touring the record shops of North London. Philip had seen a copy in his favourite one, in Muswell Hill, and had returned there with a friend who had a camera. His constant misgivings about 'the undertakers', as he called Bob and Linda, had receded at that point. Even Emma had cautiously allowed that Bob had put his money where his mouth was. There was, however, no suggestion that the record was selling in significant numbers, and none of them in fact knew how they would learn that anyway. If Bob and Linda knew, they didn't say, and no one asked them. When they arrived at the rehearsal room that evening, then, none of the four was sure what to expect. Years later, Stephen would wonder why Martin had rarely been surprised by much that happened to them back then. With hindsight, he usually attributed this to the effects of the life Martin was then living, which at that time he was only beginning to suspect, but he also became increasingly certain that 'the Lancashire mill owner' often knew things before the other three did, even Emma.

"A tour. Just over a week. Scotland and Northern Ireland."

One of Bob's contacts had turned out to be a promoter in Glasgow. Stephen wondered how you got to know a promoter in Glasgow, but Bob had apparently persuaded the man to book Generation 27 at clubs in Paisley, Dundee and Edinburgh, so long as they also played shows in Belfast and

Derry ("Sometimes Londonderry. Check who you're talking to first!").

"This sounds like a quid pro quo to me. Be good sports and risk a bombing, and you can play some nice places in Scotland too. And the week after next? That's suspiciously short notice!"

Bob smiled: Stephen felt ill at ease, even vaguely threatened, whenever he did so.

"Nicely put, Phil. And close to the truth of it. The original booking pulled out at the last minute, that's why it's short notice. But come on. These kids in Ireland are starved of touring bands. They'll come out, even if they haven't heard of you. The Clash made their name over there!"

"Yeah, with all that posing against the barricades bollocks! Anyway, the punk thing is over. The Pistols have gone. Real music is coming back. Anyone heard that girl Kate Bush?"

They had been together long enough to know that it was often pointless to respond to Philip, such was the speed at which he moved during a diatribe, but Linda nevertheless did.

"You don't have to come if you'd rather stay at home, Philip."

"Well, I'm in," said Martin, before either Philip could reply or an oppressive silence settle over the group, "let's have a show of hands, comrades."

"Obviously we'll do it," said Emma, looking at Philip and not raising her hand.

"Brother Elijah?"

"You are not going to bloody Northern Ireland, boy. Over my dead body, you hear?"

167

"I don't care," replied Stephen, raising his hand high, "I'm going."

And so they were going.

Two days later, Philip came to Gospel Oak to tell him about a breaking news report that twelve people had been killed by a bomb in a Belfast restaurant, and Stephen decided that the rehearsed explanation to his parents for his absence from London would remain in his head.

"Makes you wonder why the other band pulled out, as if we didn't know," said Philip.

"Emma will still want to go," replied Stephen, which they both knew for certain, and which they understood was what mattered.

*

"My tights! Where are they? Em, you didn't take them by mistake, did you?"

Verity was Langford's girlfriend. Langford owned a campervan, out of which Verity was now leaning.

"I'm wearing jeans, so no," replied Emma, who was leaning against the side of the campervan, smoking.

"My new fishnets, the ripped ones, Vivienne originals. I only got them last week, especially for this. I can't find them anywhere."

Emma muttered to herself and turned to open the side door.

"Other side!" yelled Verity, "I'm not dressed!"

"Put the fag out!" shouted Langford after the disappearing Emma.

From a hundred yards or so up the hillside, Stephen and

Philip could hear the noise as they looked down at the car park, where Pat's van was parked next to Langford's.

"I don't want to know," said Philip, and they walked on a little further, slowing to a halt and turning to take in the view over Edinburgh and the bright blue Firth of Forth.

"You know this is an extinct volcano?"

"I know its entire history, mate, including the Camelot legend, and of course I also got the lecture on the wildlife from his nibs. Speaking of whom, I think I see the happy wanderer returning."

Philip pointed to a distant figure on the road to the car park.

"Where's he been all night?"

"Well now, that will be the first of many questions down there in the next few minutes, young Stephen. I suggest we stay up here a while."

"Oh God, yes. Why do you call me young Stephen?"

"Because you are."

Verity's suitcase had been emptied, and her clothes were scattered over every surface inside the van, but the brand-new fishnet tights were still missing. Langford opened the door.

"Martin's just coming up the road. Forget the tights, I'll buy you another pair. Put something else on and come out."

Langford was a tall, anxious man, who worked in publicity for the publishers where Emma also worked, according to Martin (although he couldn't tell the others exactly what Emma did there). Once Bob Spendlove had made it clear that he would not be going on the tour – "I only ever leave London under duress, and I have fish to fry, mostly yours" – and the idea of the four of them in Pat's van for a week had been vetoed by Emma, she had brought Langford and Verity to the pub one night.

"Martin and I will be in the campervan, you two can sleep in the jalopy."

No one was sure how Langford had been persuaded to offer his van, about which he talked constantly in the office, but his enthusiasm for the adventure had not dimmed after three days and two less than successful shows.

"But Edinburgh! That'll be great!" he'd said, after the tiny audience had drifted away from the back room of a Dundee bar.

The only price to pay, as far as Emma was concerned, was Verity, who had confided to her that she thought that Langford was in love with her. She had insisted that Emma promise to her not to take advantage of him. Emma had kept a straight face and made a solemn vow, and Verity had then apologised, and cried, and insisted on hugging her. And now the missing tights. And Martin adrift all night once more.

"Balls, they've spotted us and they're coming up," said Philip, "not that I blame them. Let battle commence."

Langford was striding towards them, grinning, Verity struggling to keep up with him.

"Slow down, Lan! Why the rush? I was talking to Em!"

"Park it here, mate," said Philip, "these are the best seats in the house."

"Sorry?" said Langford, as he had often done over the three previous days, but only Verity was taken by surprise by an eruption of shouting from below.

The four of them sat in a row on the hillside and watched two miniature figures approach each other, one faster than the other.

"Oh dear," said Verity.

"Wow! That was some punch, wasn't it, Stevie?"

From here, it was like watching ants after a kettle of hot water had been poured into their nest, the two of them scurrying around the car park in all directions. How unimportant everything could seem from a distance.

"What? Why would any of us have your tights?"

Verity's attention had only momentarily been distracted from her crisis, and she had resumed her interrogations, to Philip's astonishment. Then he remembered something.

"That reminds me of a party we once had. My uncle worked as a roadie, and he was with this blues band from Chicago who were touring over here. He brought them over to the house one night, after they'd done a London show, and we all had a few drinks. I guess I was about sixteen, but, you know. Anyway, one of them was trying to teach us how to speak in a proper Chicago accent. He said it was all front of your mouth, then back of your mouth, and he used this phrase to show what he meant. 'Smokin' hot pantyhose!' Try it!"

So they did, in unison.

"Smokin' hot pantyhose!"

"What has Verity lost?" called Philip.

"Smokin' hot pantyhose!" came the group response.

"What will Lan not see me in tonight?" joined in Verity.

"What will your first album be called?" added Langford.

"Smokin' hot pantyhose! Smokin' hot pantyhose!" resounded over the hillside, as Emma, having gashed open Martin's cheek with one of her rings, began to throw his clothes out of the campervan.

"Have you noticed?" Philip turned to Stephen. "When she gets angry, her lisp gets more pronounced. Quite alluring, in a way, I suppose. Not that Martin will be thinking that just now. Ooh, Martin, keep your guard up!"

*

Five hours later, the vans were parked outside the venue for that evening's show.

"'Clouds'?" said Philip, squinting through the early evening rain, "'Clouds'? That sounds more like a disco. Are we at the right place?"

Martin and Emma, reconciled after an explanation as to why he'd been unable to return from visiting friends until that morning, had disappeared into the building. Not for the first time since they had left London, Stephen felt thankful to be in Pat's van, his earlier misgivings about spending so much time alone with Philip now gone. He had even volunteered to sleep in the back of the van for the duration, rather than keep to a rota by which they swapped the comfort of the front seats. Whether or not it was true or exaggerated, Philip often complained of backache.

"Ten years of carrying speaker cabs around, mate."

The two of them were willing and able to tolerate each other, Stephen realised, and that was enough in the circumstances. Perhaps that was what friendship boiled down to in the end. He certainly did not want to think about the different dynamics in the campervan. Philip said what they were both thinking anyway.

"A nest of vipers, Stevie. The hippie, her ladyship, the drip and the deb. Temerity Verity. Sincerity Verity. All of them playing at being fucking rebels. All of them with their little secrets and lies."

After a few minutes, Martin and Emma reappeared. Martin waved at them and pointed to the campervan, before getting in.

"Now what?" asked Stephen.

"It'll be a problem with cash or the licence. It's always one or the other."

Reluctantly, they got out and ran through the rain.

"Right, now then," began Martin, a large plaster protruding from under his sunglasses, "problem, amigos."

"God, he's actually turning into Lorca!"

"Who's Lorca?" asked Verity, "Is that your father, Martin?"

"More his father-in-law," replied Philip, winking at Stephen.

"Shut up, you moron."

"Now then, Emma, Phil. So, Bob had left a message with the guy here. He's the one who's running the tour, sort of Bob's pal. So I phoned Bob, just now. You know that bomb that went off in the restaurant the other week? It turns out that this guy's partner, who sorts out their bookings over there, was one of the victims. They only found out for sure yesterday. There's no one who can step in and take charge, or no one wants to anyway. Apparently, it's all a bit, you know, hairy. They want to shut down for a bit, out of respect, or something like that. So, brothers and sisters, the bad news is that the shows over there are off. We're not going to Ireland. What can I say?"

There was briefly silence, and Stephen wondered if the sense of relief he felt, along with guilt at that relief, was shared by any of the others. Philip answered that, although he didn't sound burdened by guilt.

"Thank God for that!"

"Tell them the rest," said Emma.

"Oh yeah, we have to go straight back to London after tonight's show."

Stephen had just begun to wonder whether there was a sting in the tail, but he noticed that Martin and Emma were trying to suppress smiles, unsuccessfully in Martin's case.

"What? Why?" he said.

"Yeah, what's going on?" added Philip.

"I'm sorry? Four hundred miles overnight?" Langford sounded on the verge of tears.

"Comrades!" Martin spread out his arms, as if he were about to announce the triumph of his revolution, which in a way he was.

*

"De la Croix. De la Croix. What do you think? Classy, eh?"

For a moment, Stephen had slipped into a dream, and he came to with a start, aware that Philip had been talking to him. He had no idea where they were, but it was almost three o'clock, so they must surely be in England now?

"Well I saw signs for Leeds a few minutes ago, so we can't be far from the M1. Anyway, what do you think?"

Properly awake now, he realised that he'd actually asked the question.

"Think of what?"

"The name! Have you been listening to a word?"

"Sorry. Go on, tell me again."

"Jesus! Do you remember the bit about the Huguenot ancestry? Or are you still thinking about that wee lassie?"

The unpromising show in Edinburgh had turned out to be, by common consent, their best so far. The club was almost full, they had played an encore, and had sold all the copies of the single they had brought with them. Philip declared that they had now become 'a decent live band', Stephen was smothered in the arms of a young woman who had asked him to autograph her record, and the promoter promised to have them back any time, although his arm had been around Emma's waist for some time when he said this.

The world was now quiet, as Philip explained about the story handed down to him, about the father he could only dimly remember.

"Mum wanted me to have her surname but, you know, he was my Dad, it is my heritage."

"So that was originally the family name?"

"It must have been. Stands to reason, doesn't it? They must have anglicised it to fit in. The Huguenots often did that, you know."

"And you definitely have Huguenot ancestry?"

"I just told you! That's what he told Mum."

Stephen glanced sideways and said nothing.

"I've not heard from him for years. I think he's dead," said Philip.

The van rattled on, down the motorway and under the lights, and Philip talked about his childhood on the estate, about his mother's large family, how they'd supported her after Terry Cross had gone, how he was never going back there.

"I scraped the grades but I made it out of there. Don't care about the degree. This was always the plan. This. And now we're going on Radio One! And I am Philip de la Croix! This is me! Philip de la Croix!"

He was almost shouting, but Stephen's eyelids were too heavy, and his head was sinking to his chest, jerking in time with rattle of the van. He suddenly found himself walking out of Bethel, a voice from inside the chapel calling to him to never return. He was holding hands with someone he couldn't see properly. Surging with an indescribable joy, he turned to kiss her, and another voice, a quieter one, said 'This is never going to work out. She's going to die, and you're going to wake up'.

Chesterfield. Nottingham. Leicester. Rattle, rattle.

Back on an unlit stretch, he watched Philip, who was rigid and silent. He briefly worried that he might be sleeping at the wheel, until he heard one of the familiar heavy sighs. Why was he changing his name? Well, why not?

Many years later, Stephen wrote a poem, published in an anthology, in which he described everyone's life as a palimpsest, over which they constantly rewrote those lives. That night on the motorway, he was twenty years old, and had not yet even heard of that word, but he recalled his childhood friend, Jim, telling him about a new theory.

"This is incredible, Steve. They now think that most of the universe is made up of undiscovered particles we can't see. We can only actually see about 4% of the universe!"

Jim was now studying astronomy, and Stephen hadn't fully understood what he'd said at the time, but he now looked out into the blackness over the middle of England and back at Philip de la Croix, hidden in the half-shadow, and wondered about what he could not see.

The eastern horizon was beginning to glint as they passed Luton, and he remembered why they had done this overnight drive.

"Oh God! Tonight!" he said.

Philip whooped.

"Stevie, we have to do this! Tonight, Maida Vale, tomorrow, immortality!"

Stephen wondered whether Janice Edwards would have been impressed by him playing on a famous DJ's show, and whether he would tell his parents. All of them felt far away and long ago.

*

The set was to be pre-recorded, and so it didn't matter that Stephen hadn't decided whether to tell anyone about it. Who would he tell anyway? The thought niggled away through his four hours of broken sleep.

Philip had left him outside the house, as a milk float passed on the other side of the road.

Johnny and Pam were already up and in the kitchen. Rob had not wanted to renew the lease for their final year, following a furious argument with Johnny about orange juice that had disappeared from the fridge, and Pam had appeared from nowhere to take on the share of the rent. Stephen knew her vaguely from a tutorial class, but hadn't known that she had just started going out with Johnny until she moved in. His now sharing a flat with an unmarried couple was another thing not to tell his parents. Straight out of the lexicon of London depravity.

"What ho! It's the rock star!" said Johnny, sounding cheerful and whatever the opposite of depraved was.

Stephen set his alarm clock but hadn't needed it. He

returned to an empty kitchen. After several minutes, as he sat drinking coffee and tuning his guitar, he realised that the note left on the table was for him.

"Steve, meant to tell you before you crashed, the finals timetables are out. Check your pigeonhole. And Doc F was asking after you."

Martin, Emma and Bob were already at the studios when he and Philip arrived, led by a stern-faced security guard to a dingy waiting room. Bob was wearing a red beret.

"Easy, easy, easy," he said.

Stephen felt foolish and relieved to understand that they would not be playing live to thousands of listeners, but he also now wondered how long they would be there. It had taken all night to record a tape in a church hall – 'I'm not sure about the girl bass player, Martin', 'Your tuning has slipped again, Steve', 'You lost the tempo, Martin' – and this was the BBC.

"Generation 27, I presume!"

After several minutes of sitting around, the five of them had been asking each other if they were supposed to be doing something, but now a bald man in a Fair Isle sleeveless jumper was standing in the doorway.

"Bob Spendlove, manager."

"Nice to meet you, Bob, I'm Lionel. I'll be looking after you all this evening. You've got plenty of time, so just relax. Let me show you round."

Stephen's suspicions about the night ahead increased: he did not want to relax. An hour later, they were back in the waiting room, drinking more coffee and tuning up again.

"Well, who knew? A former skating palace! Incredible!"

"Now then, Phil, the man was being friendly, and

personally, I enjoyed the guided tour. What an amazing building, all that history, back to before the war."

"Lionel's been here since then, I bet. Did you notice those two blokes in long brown coats, just scurrying about, carrying boxes? And there was a poster of Noel Coward just down the corridor! We've gone back in time, I'm telling you!"

Stephen had half-expected the Maida Vale studios to be filled with famous people, casually wandering about, but the building appeared to be almost deserted, apart from Lionel, the security guard and the men in the brown coats. The half-lit corridors had reduced them to whispers, as if they feared to disturb the ghosts there.

"What about the archive of field recordings, eh? All those bird calls!"

"Here we go!"

"Don't mock, Phil. Some of those birds are in decline, you know. The Red Kite was common over London in Shakespeare's day, now it's endangered. Weeeoo we-oo we-oo we-oo!"

"Martin, for God's sake! You made me smudge my mascara!"

"Sorry, Em. Anyhow, why the mascara? We're just recording three songs. Unless Lionel and his jumper have caught your eye."

"Prick. And do not call me Em. I had quite enough of that with that stupid girl."

"Children!" said Bob, "Uncle Robert will take you all for drinks afterwards, and Martin can do his bird impressions, and Emma can flirt with the barman, but first. First, you have a shot. This show has made some big names. I got you this chance. Now take it."

He had barely raised his voice, but the room was now silent. Bob walked out.

Lionel reappeared.

"Come on then, chums! We're ready for you!"

They picked up guitars and drumsticks and followed him back into the dim passage. Stephen could barely see in front of him, but there was a faint light up ahead.

*

"Died. I can't believe it."

How could anyone have died, anyone they knew, that is?

It was late spring, and light and warmth filled Russell Square, and there were fledglings and red tulips, and a newly clipped sheepdog out walking. How could anyone they knew not be seeing this, not be feeling the approach of summer? It was beyond the imagination of two young men.

"I only saw her last week."

"Apparently she didn't want any of us to know. She was only diagnosed a couple of months ago. She wanted to carry on working until, you know, she couldn't. Mrs H was telling me."

"How come Mrs H knew and we didn't?"

"Secretaries know everything."

The sheepdog had pulled its owner away from the footpath around the gardens, and paused to look quizzically at them, both cross-legged on the grass, as if it too couldn't believe what it was hearing, before raising a leg and moving on.

"I have an essay to hand in. Well I did. It was overdue,

she gave me an extension. What happens now?"

"My birthday."

"What?"

"My twenty-first. A week on Friday, remember? We were all going to the pub after her final tutorial. I asked her along, she said she'd try to make it."

"God. She must have known she probably wouldn't."

"I know. That really was her final tutorial."

Stephen would forget much about these years, as we do, and would come to regret some of what he did remember. One of his deepest regrets was that he never handed in his overdue essay to Judith Friedman. Another was that he never told her how important she had been to him, how wonderful he thought she was, not that he would ever have done so at the time.

*

Within two weeks of that day, Philip and Stephen both had their twenty-first birthdays, Judith Friedman was cremated, in contravention of the faith she had long ago rejected, and Generation 27's live performance was broadcast on BBC Radio.

Stephen's birthday was the day after Philip's, but he didn't tell him, or anyone. He caught the train on that Friday afternoon and returned home for a family party, attended by numerous uncles and aunts from North Wales and most of his father's workmates.

He stood in the kitchen, a bottle of pale ale in his hand, set his face into a smile, and felt completely alone.

"I am two people," he thought, "two different people.

When can I just be one?"

Julie and Dennis sidled up to him. Dennis was the new college boyfriend, Cathleen had warned him, and there had been a disagreement over sleeping arrangements for the weekend.

"Not in my house," Tom had said, and so Dennis was on the floor in Stephen's room. He wondered if his mother expected him to enforce propriety and defend his sister's honour, like a good Catholic brother. Not for the first time, it occurred to him that his parents had probably got the measure of him but knew nothing about their daughter, and he decided not to mention any of this to Julie. She would not have seen the humour in it.

"This little birthday boy has a secret!" she said, sotto voce.

"Wow, man! Amazing!" said Dennis, to whom Stephen had taken an immediate dislike. He had briefly cautioned himself about turning into his father, but Dennis was wearing a Mickey Mouse T-shirt, and Phil would have openly laughed at that.

"What?" he replied, in his most disdainful tone, which had not worked on his sister for a long time.

"Your little band! Next Generation or whatever you're called. On that late show on Radio One next week! Dennis heard about it."

"Yeah, he was just saying what's on next week, and the name rang a bell. Very nice!"

Stephen understood that Julie had spoken about him to other people, and he felt both flattered and agitated.

"Don't tell them!"

"Why not?"

"Just don't!"

His vehemence brought the conversation to an end, but in the early hours Dennis turned over in his sleeping bag.

"Steve," came the voice from below his bed, "we won't tell, but you should. Why are you worried about what your folks might think about your band?"

He lay awake for what remained of the night, and left the next morning, with the excuse of finals revision.

"Ah, never mind," said his mother, "we can have a nice roast another day."

*

By the autumn, Stephen and Philip were the sheepish possessors of second-class degrees ("How did we do that, mate?") and were sharing a flat in Crouch End, which Philip had ordained the new centre of North London.

"*Sic transit gloria* Kentish Town, eh?" Martin had said, in a pointed tone, Stephen thought, but for no reason he could imagine.

"He thinks we'll talk about him," said Philip, "and he's right. Paranoid but right."

Stephen had found it unimaginably easy to tell his parents about the new move, or rather not have to broach the matter with Tom.

"I imagine you won't be coming home for now, then, boy," he had said to him as they sat in the Red Cow on the day the results had come out, "you being settled down there, is it?"

Unless Julie had gone back on her promise, all he still thought Tom and Cathleen knew was that he played his guitar with some friends, as a hobby, but he knew that the story about signing up for agency work while he considered his career options was not fooling his father.

"Don't worry, I'll talk to your mother. I know you don't want to be a bank manager. Just don't drift around. Don't lose your way back."

Tom's hand was on his shoulder.

"I won't, Dad."

He wondered why they had never been down to visit him since his first year away, but that was a conversation he thought that none of them would want to have. The next few telephone conversations with Cathleen were in any event dominated by the loss of two Popes within a month.

"God, son, they're saying now the Holy Father was murdered! What's to become of us?"

In Stephen Elijah's other life, Generation 27's BBC session had an impact none of them had foreseen. Within weeks, the Spendloves had paid for the pressing of a further ten thousand copies of the record, and Bob had moved the Valediction Records office from a lock-up to a rented top floor flat in Soho, complete with dedicated phone.

"Great deal," he said, "he owed me a favour."

"I thought he might," muttered Philip.

"Oh, and don't worry about the neighbours when you come by. They're harmless."

1979

Anyone who had seen the original poster and its message, and that was almost everyone in the country by then, let alone the commuters of East Finchley, could make it out underneath the defacement.

'Labour Isn't Working' had been painted over with 'Tory Scum'. More inventively, one of the imaginary unemployed people in the queue below the slogan now had a speech bubble filling the space above them, proclaiming 'Generation 27' in large red letters. Underneath the billboard, on the Great North Road, opposite the station, Stephen and Philip stood, appraising their handiwork. Somewhere close by, a car horn sounded, and again.

"Yeah, yeah, hold your horses," said Philip, "I don't know, will that do?"

It was almost midnight, but traffic was still roaring by, and Stephen was sure that an unmarked police car was on their tail. This was the third billboard of the night, after all.

"It's loud and clear. Come on, Mark's getting impatient."

He was more concerned about the spray can in Philip's hand should the inevitable blue light appear right now than he was about Mark, safely hiding down the side road, but the honking was straining his nerves. Philip chuckled as they walked back to the car.

"What? That wasn't funny, it was risky! We should have left it at one, like I said."

"I was just imagining Martin doing it, with Emma

directing him. We'd have been there all night. Situationist art, brothers!"

Stephen laughed at the image and the cruelly accurate impression. "Cruelly accurate" described much of Philip's way of seeing things, he thought, a little enviously.

It was a Sunday night, which had become 'Flask Night'. Mark would pick the two of them up in his Mini and drive up to The Flask in Highgate, where his girlfriend worked behind the bar. Waitress service and the occasional free round had turned this into a routine, an important one for two young men constantly about to run out of money.

"Fame and fortune don't come cheap, Stevie!", as Philip was fond of saying at that time.

They also regarded Flask Night as time off from Martin and Emma. Philip knew Mark from school. He was studying for the Bar, although he was nothing like any barrister Stephen had ever seen on television. Floppy blonde hair and a cavalier moustache added to a rakish mien. He smoked furiously and said, "Mmm, yes…" a lot, and the billboards had been his idea earlier that evening, after he had asked them how the band was doing. Stephen prepared himself for what he knew was coming in response to the question.

"Bob and Linda, Linda and Bob, they share a bed, they share a job,

They spend their love on money and song, how glad they are we came along."

Philip stretched out the final syllable for dramatic effect. He looked as pleased with his rhyme as he had each time he'd recited it over the weekend.

"The band is doing great," he added, when Mark simply looked bemused, "but we aren't. We've been on Capital and

Radio One, we're onto the third pressing of the single, we have our first full tour next month, and we've been interviewed for two magazines, but we're still doing cleaning jobs for an agency and cadging transport and beer off you! We haven't seen a penny from Generation 27 since the undertakers took over."

Stephen felt sure that the situation was far less simple than that, and was considering saying something along those lines when Mark responded.

"Publicity!"

"What?"

"Publicity. Think about it. Okay, you've been on the radio, your single is in the, what, the Top One Hundred? How many people will that register with? A few thousand? And how many people will see you playing at some dump in Hemel Hempstead, or wherever? More to the point, my dear, how many of those people will have forgotten all about you by next week? You have to keep on top of all this. You have to promote yourselves, every day."

Philip looked crestfallen. Stephen wondered if he'd been hoping for some free legal advice on how to access the money hidden in an imaginary safe in the Soho office. Sure enough.

"But what about our money? And stop calling me dear, I have told you."

"Philip, we've been over this. You showed me the contract. You signed it freely, no one made you. It looks fairly standard to me. This guy is in charge, leave him to it, at least for now. I don't know much about the business but it doesn't sound to me like he can be making anything yet. It takes a while for sales and royalties to come through, doesn't it? No, what I think you need to concentrate on is raising your profile, at least around London."

That was when Mark had brought up the idea of the billboards.

"They're everywhere. One on Hornsey Road, one at East Finchley Station. Think of it. Someone has already paid for the prime locations. You can scrub out the Tory lies and promote the band at the same time. All for the price of a couple of spray cans, which actually I can let you have for free."

Stephen wondered why a trainee barrister would have had spray cans in the boot of his car, but so it was that they were now walking back to the Mini with an empty one.

"Ha! Red Mark! That's what we called him at school. Still, he had a point. Good fun, eh, Stevie?"

As Mark drove them home, Stephen occasionally checked behind for the blue light, and wondered whether his father would think of their night as 'drifting around' rather than good fun. As soon as he was back in his bedroom, he picked up his guitar, then began to write down some lyrics. It was so easy sometimes, compared with everything else.

*

He was the last to arrive. Martin had called the previous evening.

"We have been summoned, brethren. Meeting at HQ."

By then it was too late to get out of the job he'd signed up for, clearing out a disused warehouse at the Isle of Dogs. What on earth would anyone do with a crumbling Victorian building on the river, he thought, as he swept out a century of grime.

The buzzer at the ground floor entrance now had a proper blue and gold 'Valediction Records' sign next to it. Perhaps Bob had tired of Philip drawing across the makeshift one to leave just the letters VD.

"More in keeping with the rest of the building!"

Perhaps also Philip might after all have had a point about the money. A smart sign like that couldn't have been cheap.

"Come on up," crackled a voice, Bob's by the brusque tone.

"Brother Elijah! How did you like the handiwork?"

"And he doesn't mean you stopped off for a massage on the way up."

"Now then, Phil!"

"He means the new sign," said Bob.

Stephen realised that of course Martin was the artist responsible for the Valediction Records upgrade.

"Thanks for coming, people," Bob continued, as they huddled in the tiny room, "I'll get straight to it. First of all, finalised tour schedules for everyone, there we go."

Stephen was relieved to see that Hemel Hempstead did not feature among the ten dates but did wonder where at least two places on the list were.

"Most venues have thrown in accommodation and food as part of the fee. We'll have to book a couple of B and Bs. Martin has printed off a hundred T-shirts. Okay, onto another matter, the visit I had yesterday from two of the Met's finest."

Bob paused. Stephen glanced at Philip, who was staring intently at the threadbare carpet.

"Go on, Roberto," said Martin.

"Three defaced billboards at locations around North London. All paid for by Her Majesty's Opposition, all with abuse scrawled on, and 'Generation 27' in big red letters."

Everyone in the room was now looking at Philip, including Bob. He went on.

"Would you believe? The sergeant at Muswell Hill Police Station mentioned the name to his son, who recognised it. He showed his dad the chart in Melody Maker, with the label name included. A quick look in the phone book and here they were, asking me if I knew anything about some incidents of criminal damage. Criminal damage! What could I say?"

"What?" said Philip, and Martin cackled.

"Phil, it's just as well you weren't here at the time, little brother. You look shifty at the best of times!"

"What did you say?" repeated Philip.

Even Bob was now smiling. Stephen recalled Philip's advice to watch his back 'when the undertaker smiles' and instinctively straightened up.

"Let's just say", said Bob, "that our friends in blue went away happy with my aggrieved denials and a couple of free records. Let me add that whoever committed these acts of vandalism, not that I have any clue, gave me an idea."

In the pub later, Philip was seething.

"That smarmy bastard, winding me up like that and then stealing my idea! Who are these kids he's paying anyway? And paying with our money! I'd have carried on for free!"

"Now then, Phil, calm down. You could hardly jump out of the van as soon as we got into town, go and deface a poster, then turn up to play the show with red hands. Ha! Caught red-handed! Red-handed!"

"Jesus, Martin, it's not that funny," said Emma.

Bob had paid two students – 'They're lodgers of ours, they need the money' – to drive the route of the Generation

190

27 tour and make sure that a billboard near each venue had been suitably defaced a couple of days before the show.

"Okay, fair point, but he's getting on my nerves. I'm making no money, and I get no credit for anything."

Stephen wanted to say that the idea had been Mark's, and he wondered why no one at the meeting had imagined that he could have had anything to do with events that night on the Great North Road, as the traffic had swept by and his heart had skipped several beats.

*

"In the midst of life, we are in death."

"Are you high?"

"The Book of Common Prayer, my love, 1662. And still it talks to us."

"To you maybe, and don't forget you're driving, and that this is Langford's van."

"Sid Vicious. That MP in the underground car park. Another girl in Yorkshire. Now this anti-Nazi protester, the guy from New Zealand. Here, then gone. It just makes you think."

"I'm turning the radio off, Martin. Will you please just concentrate on the road!"

Emma shouted the final injunction, as if Stephen were not there. He sat behind them in the campervan, pretending to be asleep, a tactic he had clearly exhausted.

"Stop pretending to be asleep, Stephen, for God's sake. Talk to me, just to shut him up."

They were returning to London from the last show of the tour, in Brighton. Pat's van was still visible in the rear-view

191

mirror. No one had been sure how Langford had been persuaded to loan the van when he'd been unable to join them, nor why Verity had nevertheless come along but had barely spoken to Emma. She was now in Pat's van. Stephen dipped a toe in the water.

"Last night was great, wasn't it?"

"Dull, dull, dull, dull, dull."

"What? Why? They liked us, didn't they?"

"They would have liked Cliff Richard. They were boring old men and they didn't care about the music. I thought we'd agreed never to play covers just to keep an audience happy."

Stephen could hear Philip saying that keeping an audience happy was the job.

"And about boring old men, that's what you three are becoming. You all looked just as bad as when I first saw you, even worse. You in a tartan shirt, Philip in that stupid hat, and him still with that ratty ponytail! It's like being on stage with three social workers!"

Since Verity had forced the change in the travel arrangements, Stephen had been transported around the south of England constantly feeling like a spectator at the Coliseum, watching in horror as the contestants hacked at each other with bloody intent, or at least one of them did.

"Martin, you let her sit next to you. She was doing it to wind me up, and you just let her. And I saw her hand on your leg."

"Where did you get to after the sound check? You promised me you'd stay clean."

"So Bob told me he lent you more money. How many times now? Is that the only reason you started this band, Martin?"

Now one of the contestants was trying to involve the spectator.

"Stephen. You're an amazing songwriter. I don't know how you do that. But please, tell me what you think about what I just said. Even tell me to shut up, but just tell me. What are you thinking?"

He did not reply that he wanted to put his arms around her again, or that he wanted to protect her from something he sensed was waiting for her further down the road she was on, and of course he never did.

"I'm sorry," he said, "I'll get rid of the shirt."

"The years will claim us all," came the voice from behind the steering wheel, as if he hadn't heard any of the conversation since he'd recited the Burial of the Dead.

*

"Come on, Stevie! You know me! A vintage 1957 model. I had to!"

Bob Spendlove was unreservedly happy with how the tour had gone. The venues had not been big, but they had mostly been filled, and the promoter was talking about a more extensive schedule in the autumn, possibly opening for a big name. 'Trying To Explain' had been licensed to a major distributor for a re-release, this time backed by 'Drifting Around' as a double A-side. Bob wanted to plan the recording of an album.

"The boy genius keeps producing the goods. Let's do it."

For Martin, the greatest triumph was selling every one of the yellow T-shirts he'd designed.

For Philip, it was banking his first cheque as a working

musician, handed to him in a Valediction Records envelope by Tracy, Bob's newly acquired P.A.

He was now explaining to Stephen why most of that money had already gone on a new guitar, although they were behind on the rent. They were on their way to a party, to which Bob had invited them.

"A distant cousin of mine, she's actually Dutch, works here in advertising. I'm hoping to get her interested. You'll like her. She's keen to meet you."

Neither of them cared to spend more time in the company of the Spendloves than was necessary, but free food and the chance to meet young women with exotic backgrounds who made money doing glamorous things was too enticing. Anyway, Martin and Emma would also be there, not that either much wanted to see Martin after his behaviour on the tour.

"He's getting worse," said Philip, "you must have noticed. Look at him, Steve, he's disintegrating. I get all the artsy-fartsy stuff, the concept, revolutions and whatever, but I wonder now if he only ever saw a band as a route to people who could meet his needs, if you catch my drift."

"I think Emma is wondering that. I had a grandstand view for most of last week."

"Sorry about that, young Stephen, but you saw what happened. Verity was most insistent on travelling with me, or at least not with Emma. She's actually okay, you know, once you get past the Sloane Ranger image. Anyway, she'll be here in a minute."

They were in a pub at the top of the road rising from Crouch End into Muswell Hill, its aloof neighbour.

"I thought you needed a refreshment break, as you put it?"

194

"I do! That is not just a road, it's an ascent! But I had anticipated that, I admit, and arranged for us to meet her here."

"For you to meet her here, you mean. And I suppose I'm buying her a drink too?"

"Come on, Steve, vintage guitars don't come cheap! Anyway, she's good fun."

They don't and she is, sort of, Stephen accepted, and he looked out from his window seat onto the North London streets washed in the watery light of a spring evening. The time and the place would come to feel like a dreamscape he had once inhabited, with a soundtrack in his memory of plangent guitars and lyrical melancholy. Everyone was thin and hungry, and the possibilities seemed to be without end. Philip might turn to Verity, and Emma might give up on Martin, at that moment he could think of no reason why everything for all their lives could not shimmer like gold.

Bliss indeed was it in that dawn.

*

"Steve! Steve!"

His father was shaking him as he yelled, and he never called him Steve. Then he opened his eyes to Philip in a pink dressing gown.

"Please, stop shouting."

"Who is that on the sofa?"

Stephen wanted to ask him about the dressing gown first, and then realised that he was slumped in an armchair in the living room, fully dressed. Oh God, not a Surrey Special.

Philip had used the term since their visit to the Carters'

two years previously, but no, to his thankful relief, he was able to move his head without feeling nauseous. Stephen was not in for a Surrey Special today, although he avoided looking at the open bottle of red wine on the coffee table.

"Why are you wearing a pink dressing gown?"

"It's Verity's."

"She brought her dressing gown to a party?"

"It's her coat! Jesus! Don't you remember?"

Yes, he remembered the bright pink fur jacket now, he remembered Emma stubbing out her cigarette on it while she looked down at him, sitting on the floor with Bob's cousin. He remembered Bob and Martin talking intently and quietly, and him wondering what about while he exhausted his small talk about the differences between living in London and Amsterdam. Amsterdam! Of course!

"Felix. That guy on the sofa is Felix."

"Yes. Good morning."

The guy on the sofa was evidently awake.

"Good morning, one and all. Anyone seen my fags?"

So was Martin.

"Oh Jesus, yes. We all came back in the taxi. I thought you were nailed on with that Dutch girl. Where did she get to?"

"She didn't get anywhere, that was Bob's cousin, it was her flat, it was her party. I was only talking to her."

"Actually," said Felix, who had sat up, "she is my girlfriend back home. Or was."

"Sorry, mate, no offence," said Philip, "but we're all worried about young Stephen's non-existent sex life."

A noise combining a raking cough with a throaty chuckle came out of the darkness under the window, where Martin

196

appeared to have spent the night.

"And how come you came back here with us if your girlfriend has a flat?" he asked.

"He just said, ex-girlfriend. More to the point, how come you did?" said Philip.

"Ah, now then. A fair question, brother."

The pause as he lit a cigarette continued, until they all realised that Martin had finished speaking.

"Excuse me," said Felix, "but where are we, and is it far to Victoria Station?"

As if by way of a reply, Philip picked his way across the room and pulled open the curtains.

"My God, Phil, where did you get that dressing gown?"

"Hilarious. You heard me a minute ago. At least I didn't spend the night with two other sweaty blokes. I'm making coffee, but not for you lot, well maybe for Felix. I love the way you say Victoria Station!"

He did not reappear, however, and the giggles from down the hall suggested that he would not be doing so.

"Young love, eh? Right then, comrades, coffee's on me. Come on. Oh, Steve, can you lend me a tenner?"

In the café at the end of the road, Felix told them how he had met Anika at university, how she was the love of his life, for sure, how he understood that she had to follow her career to London, how he had heard about the party from friends, and taken four trains and the ferry to win her back.

"I have failed, I think. Why did Phil say he loved the way I said Victoria Station?"

Stephen now remembered him lingering on the fringes of conversations, and felt profoundly sorry for their unexpected guest, especially when he realised that Anika had kept him engaged in endless chatter to avoid Felix.

"Come on now," said Martin, "I bet there are plenty of pretty blondes back home, strapping young lad like you."

"What do you do?" added Stephen.

"I work for NOS, our public radio. I am an electronic engineer, but I want to develop the music side of things. You know, maybe a producer, or a DJ."

Stephen looked at Martin, who said "Aha. Good for you, sir. Hmm."

After they had collected his rucksack – Anika was not there, to the relief of all of them – they had left Felix at East Finchley Station, with directions to Victoria and a dozen copies of 'Trying To Explain'.

"Love to Amsterdam!" Martin had shouted as they waved him off.

"Have you been there?"

"No, Steve, never, but if our pal can get us on the radio over there, who knows, eh?"

They ambled past the still defaced billboard, which looked much less impressive to Stephen in daylight, and on into another lovely evening.

"Listen to that!"

"What?"

Martin had stopped dead and raised a finger to the overhanging lime trees.

"Ssh! Listen!" he whispered, "Hear that sort of squeaking call? That's a sparrow hawk."

"I can't see anything."

"That's the idea, my friend. But he can see you."

They walked on.

"So have you always been a bird watcher?"

"God, no!" came the scratchy cackle, "My Dad used to take me out, but I've not done that since I was a kid."

"But I thought you were going to write a book about birds of prey?"

"I am writing it, little brother, or I intend to. Every call, every sighting is another page. Birdsong, Steve, it takes us to the glory of existence, the wonder of every moment. It reminds us that paradise is here on earth, every day. You ever heard of Stanley Spencer?"

"Oh, yes, the painter."

"Indeed, the painter. He imagined the resurrection happening in Cookham, his home village. Can you believe that? People thought him mad, but why not? That's what my book is about, paradise here on earth. Even the mundane can be mystical. We waste our lives wondering what it all means, and we don't see that, but a bird knows. So that's what I'm doing, remembering the mystical, like Spencer. You see?"

"I see."

They continued along Fortis Green, in silence.

"Steve?"

"Mm?"

"I know Phil's your friend, but don't believe everything he says. About me. About Emma. Things aren't that simple, you know? Nothing is that simple. You follow me?"

"I follow you."

It was to be many years before he did, however, thinking back to the evening he heard the call of the sparrow hawk.

*

It wasn't so easy to write a song about Margaret Thatcher's newly elected government. Stephen had felt that he ought to try, given that almost everyone he knew was fearful or angry or both, but he could not do it.

"I just can't write a political song," he announced to everyone.

They were all meeting with Bob and Linda to plan the schedule for recording the album. There were plenty of songs to consider for inclusion, most of them Stephen's, but Bob had asked him to write one about the volatile climate of that early summer.

"It's okay, Stephen, don't sweat it. Anyway, all songs are political. Yours are just different."

Bob was the only one there who called him Stephen, although Emma did when she was angry, which seemed to be more often now.

No one had disputed Bob's unequivocal assertion that Stephen would be the main contributor to the record, possibly the only contributor. They had by now all accepted that he had a talent that no amount of effort by any of them could match. Philip had played them a couple of half-completed ideas, but he didn't object to Bob's dismissal, or even the manner of it.

"Not good enough. Any more?"

There were no more. Stephen was the writer.

"His songs, they just catch fire," said Emma.

"Jesus," muttered Philip.

Bob continued as if no one else had spoken.

"A week in the studio booked, likewise an engineer. So you have two weeks to rehearse everything. You've been playing at least half the material for long enough now anyway. Marty will take care of the artwork; he has some amazing ideas."

"I'll bet Marty has."

Emma had been staring at Philip since his previous comment, and now stood up in front of him. How glorious she is, thought Stephen, although he suddenly wished he were elsewhere.

"Can you ever. Stop. Being. A. Cunt?"

Was that the moment, Stephen would later wonder, the exact moment when their roads all separated and began different courses into the future? He never forgot the look in Philip's eyes as everyone in the room caught their breath, a look of embarrassment and disbelieving shock.

"Ooh!" said Martin, wincing.

Stephen looked down at his feet and recalled his father telling his sister that 'young women don't use language like that' over something laughably mild.

"Time out, everyone!"

Bob, unperturbed, had raised both arms. Stephen glanced at Linda, who appeared to be equally calm.

"Philip," he went on, after the longest silence Stephen had ever endured, "Martin went to art school and he trained as a draughtsman. That's why he's doing the artwork. You're the most experienced musician, so we want you to produce the record. That okay?"

Philip cleared his throat.

"Erm, sure. I can do that."

Emma had not taken her eyes off him but now she turned to Bob and Martin, sitting together on the battered leather sofa.

"And I'll just look pretty and make the tea, shall I?"

"Em! Now then!"

"I haven't seen you for two days, Martin. Off around White City again, were you? Now you just turn up with your chum and the decisions have all been made, without talking to me. You've carved up the jobs between the boys. Well fine, you can go ahead and do it all without me, and without the name, the name I came up with, remember? The band I came up with. My idea. Before then, Stephen just wrote songs in his bedroom, and Monsieur de la Croix played in a pub with a bunch of old has-beens. My French name is real, by the way, Phillippe."

She was by now walking to the top of the stairs.

"I'm not coming back. And don't you come back to my house, Martin."

"Em!"

Martin showed no inclination to get up from the sofa. Linda followed Emma down the stairs, not before sighing heavily and raising her eyebrows at her husband. Bob adjusted his glasses and resumed talking.

In the following days, Martin made light-hearted references to 'the dropping of the C-bomb' but no one else ever mentioned it, although Philip did ask him why he hadn't followed Emma down the stairs.

"Not worth it, Phil," he replied sadly, "she always means what she says."

SO I'LL BURN – GENERATION 27
(VALEDICTION RECORDS)

Into the wasteland of post-New Wave steps a genuine contender. The London four-piece have promised much with the classic sleeper 'Trying To Explain' (included here as a re-recorded version) and a string of sold-out shows around fair England, and here they deliver. The debut album can be a tricky business since the summer of '76. We all want to spend our dole money and student grants on proper records, but we still want them to sound like the band is on the stage of a tiny club, right in front of us, warts and all. Few have managed this. Mostly, Generation 27 do.

Their roots are firmly in Ladbroke Grove, evidenced by the uncomplicated rhythm work of Emma Dehasse-Carter and Marty Rogers, but the songs of Stephen Elijah have a timeless quality, and guitarist Philip de la Croix weaves shimmering textures around them. He produced the album and shares the vocals with Elijah.

Personal highlights include the woebegone 'Judith', the effortlessly melodic 'Why Shouldn't We Dance?', the killer title track, and the throwaway instrumental 'Go Go Huguenot', de la Croix's sole contribution.

A very British take on Television might be a useful comparison, but the sound – by turns ethereal and insistent – is their own, and this is their time.

Side 1: Trying To Explain; Judith; Drifting Around; Why Shouldn't We Dance?; Broken Circle; Losing My Way.

Side 2: God Loves North London; A Jukebox In My Head (An Aching In My Heart); Amitriptyline; Song For Federico; So I'll Burn; Go Go Huguenot.

Frankie Blue
N.M.E.
September 1979

*

Emma never came back, not to the Valediction Records office. She turned up on time for rehearsals and for shows, sometimes with Martin and often not, and she complied with all the requests for interviews, of which there were several following the release of *So I'll Burn*. Most of the interviewers, and all the photographers, were only really interested in her anyway, and of course she knew that. Requests for autographed photos, and requests of a less wholesome nature, were passed on to her by Tracy via Martin, or Marty, as he was now insisting.

As the promoter had promised earlier that year, Generation 27 were booked for an autumn tour of student unions and full-sized concert halls, opening for a well-known American band. It was another step up, and it took Stephen back to the nerves of that night in a Camden pub. He lost these as soon as he realised that the stage lighting in the bigger venues meant that he barely saw the audiences. In any event, Emma, more than ever a magnetic presence on stage, carried the shows, as even Philip admitted.

"She still can't play, and I haven't forgiven her, but, well, she adds something."

She adds glamour, thought Stephen, and sex, and coolness, and darkness, that's what Phil means. She brings darkness. Some people just do.

No one said so but the meetings in the Soho flat became less fraught, although Philip seemingly felt less constrained about raising his voice.

"Look, Bob. And... Marty." He deliberately emphasised the latter. "I've been talking to people."

That means Verity, thought Stephen.

"Philip," interrupted Linda before he could continue, "if you're about to raise an issue with Valediction Records, which you do every time you're here, can you please remember that I co-own it, not Martin."

"Sorry! Sorry, sorry, sorry! No offence but that's how he comes across. You should tell him, not me. I love that purple eyeshadow, by the way."

"Now then, Phil, that was a bit below the belt."

Bob raised a hand.

"Phil, just so we're all clear. The record label is Linda and me, no one else. Your drummer is an old friend of mine, whose ideas I always find interesting, and yes, we talk a lot, but I am the manager. Okay? Now, who are these people to whom you've been talking, and what have they suggested you say to us?"

It was about money, of course, it always was. Verity would urge Philip to 'have it out with that dreadful little man', as if Stephen wasn't sitting in the same room at the time.

In his considered, yet always slightly unnerving tone, Bob explained again that he and Linda were nowhere near recovering what they had put into Valediction Records and Generation 27, and asked if Philip understood that. The new album might be selling well, but not enough for them to pay out advances while they waited for the money to come through. In the meantime, he pointed out, the tour had gone well, further shows were in the offing, and their television debut was coming up.

"Uh-huh," said Philip, "uh-huh," nodding along, and within five minutes his weekly rebellion had been spiked, although Stephen had to bear the aftermath on the way home.

"Thick as thieves, those two. Don't tell me that the undertakers don't sub him. How else could he get his hits, eh? You and I couldn't afford his lifestyle! I bet the Ice Queen has come to the same conclusion. When was the last time they turned up anywhere together?"

Philip was never going to raise his real concern about Martin with the Spendloves, but Stephen did also wonder about it. He had always shied away from admitting to himself that Martin was more than a casual drug user, and even people who were evidently well aware of this only referred to it obliquely, as if it were impolite to do otherwise. As to Emma, each time he saw her now, he found himself wondering if it might be the last. She was beginning to disappear into that darkness, and he couldn't explain why he imagined this, nor did he know what to do about it.

"Phil, go on home without me. I have to go somewhere else first."

*

What had he thought that he was going to do, that night in Kentish Town?

The television debut, on a late-night arts programme on ITV, had so far followed a similar course to their adventures in Maida Vale the previous year, involving a dingy 'hospitality suite', underlit corridors and endless cups of coffee. The only difference this evening was that neither Martin nor Emma had arrived, together or separately. The floor manager, a harassed-looking young man and the opposite of the BBC's unflappable Lionel, was chewing his fingernails and shouting a lot.

"Don't worry," said Philip, "they'll be here. They're not what you'd call routinely punctual people."

"I'll tell you what," yelled the floor manager, "if you start worrying, I'll stop!"

That seemed fair to Stephen, although it was of course wasted on Philip, who was even more distracted than usual.

"Phil! Stop being naughty! You'll embarrass Steve!"

Verity was sitting on his lap, making token efforts at removing his hands from under her coat.

"I'm just keeping them warm! I am a guitarist, you know."

Stephen was not embarrassed. Verity had been a flatmate for a few weeks now, and he had previously shared with Johnny and Pam, and so he was used to hiding behind a book in the armchair when discretion demanded. He had actually begun to like her.

"She gets on my nerves, too," Philip had conceded, "but she has a good heart. And fabulous legs!" Stephen did not dispute those assertions but, at this moment, he wanted to talk to Philip alone. Then Verity went in search of 'the little girls' room'. Phil was reading through the list of questions they were going to be asked by an interviewer in between playing two songs in the studio.

"Phil."

"Hmm? Oh, look at number four: where do you see yourselves in five years' time? They're not getting any more original."

"Phil, you know when we were coming back from the meeting a couple of weeks ago, and I went off on my own?"

He looked up.

"Yeah? I assumed a girl?"

"No. Well yes, but not in that way."

He put down the list of questions and wrapped his coat around him. Why were these places always cold and why were they always in them late at night?

"All ears, young Stephen."

"I went to see Emma."

"Why? She doesn't want to see us."

Just when I was trying to avoid asking myself that, he thought, Phil asks.

"I don't really know, I still don't. Something's wrong, though. I suppose I thought that if I could see her, I could talk to her. I just had this bad feeling. I can't explain it any better than that."

He imagined for a moment that Philip was about to say something, and then he went on, about his courage failing at the corner of Emma's road, about standing there against a privet hedge, looking across at the house for a long time, or at least until two figures emerged through the front gate. He had pressed back into the hedge, thankful for the streetlight close to the gate and the shadow over where he was crouched.

"I can hear someone coming. Hurry up. What happened?"

"She was kissing this man, arms around him and kissing him."

"Who?"

"Phil, it was Emma, and the man wasn't Martin."

"Oh dear! Who was it then?"

Verity came back into the room.

"What? It's like the piano player has stopped! I could hear the two of you stage whispering from down the corridor."

No, Stephen immediately realised, she hadn't heard anything, but Philip briefly raised a finger to his lips as she walked past them to the coffee machine.

"Oh," added Verity, "they're here, by the way, and someone else is with them."

"You mean Bob? Or Linda? But you've met them, haven't you?"

"Of course I have, at that Dutch girl's party. Silly Philly! No, this was a bloke I've never seen before."

They all turned expectantly to the door, as Martin's wheezes became louder.

"Who'd have thought it?" he said as he walked in, "The green room has a green door! Comrades, we have truly arrived!"

Emma was shrouded in an outsize tweed coat, and her lipstick matched her newly-dyed magenta hair. Behind her stood a tall man in a fedora, grinning.

"Brothers. Oh, and Verity, fantastic. Brothers, remember that first big album review? In the NME? Allow me to introduce that man of impeccable taste, the one and only Mister Frankie Blue!"

The tall man tipped his hat and performed a mock bow.

"At your service."

He was American.

"Cheers, mate! Really appreciated what you said about my playing, I thought you nailed it."

Philip was on his feet and pumping Frankie Blue's hand, wide-eyed with enthusiasm. He would never have noticed that Stephen was staring at Frankie, then at him, then Emma, almost by turns, and it was several minutes before Stephen could catch his eye and mouth: "That's him! That's him!"

*

Stephen walked from Euston Station to Soho. His thoughts became no clearer in the fresh December morning, except for the certainty that he would not be talking to either of his parents for the foreseeable future. He put his head down and stomped along Tottenham Court Road, heading for Bob and Linda's meeting and the welcome distraction from the past weekend. This could be a good morning, he thought. They hadn't seen the Spendloves since the TV show the previous week, but they all felt that it had gone better than they had expected.

"Man, we are actually good, Stevie!"

A cameraman had smiled and applauded as Philip strode off the set, arm around Stephen.

We actually are, we really are, he allowed himself to admit, and then said so.

Playing live on television had not affected any of them, although as Martin pointed out back in the hospitality room, the reality was that they had played two songs to an audience of half a dozen people, surrounded by equipment and cables. But yes, Generation 27 were actually good, they were all certain of this on that night.

The next morning, Stephen had heard 'London Calling' on prime-time radio while he was packing his rucksack, and had sat down heavily on his bed, and sighed.

It was impossible to tell with Bob, he reflected, as he neared the office. He could easily imagine him opening cheap champagne, but he might just as easily ask Stephen why he wasn't writing songs as compelling and catchy as that one.

"But I can only be me!" he said out loud on Oxford Street, and then turned into Berwick Street, where Bob almost collided with him. For a moment, he imagined that Bob had materialised on the street in a supernatural response to his declamation, then worried about whether he'd heard him, and finally that he'd come looking for him, even though he wasn't late. Bob, however, was equally surprised, as much as he ever was by anything.

"Stephen."

An unnerving sight in his black astrakhan coat, he gestured with a cigar in the direction of the office.

"Stephen, you need to decide. Me or him. I don't work with Nazis. Go."

Without a further word, he swept by, trailing smoke.

Philip was pacing the floor, flinging his arms around, when Stephen came in.

"I never thought! I mean, is it really a big deal, after all this time? You see loads of this stuff on the street! How was I to know he'd react like that?"

Martin sat impassively, staring ahead.

"Oh, Phil. Phil. Steve, we have a little crisis."

"I just saw Bob. What's happened? Oh."

Philip had turned towards him. He was wearing a military-looking cap, black, with the unmistakeable death's head insignia of the S.S.

"It's just fashion, Steve! I only bought it to wear on stage. I'm not a Nazi sympathiser!"

"Oh, Phil. He's an old friend of mine. And our manager. Bloody hell."

Stephen added the obvious unsaid.

"He's Jewish, Phil. Bob's Jewish. You knew that."

"I know, I know! Look, I'm sorry, okay?"

"Don't you think you should take it off if you're sorry? Bob might come back in at any moment. And what about Doc Friedman? What would she have said?"

"Well, not much these days!" bawled Philip.

Later, Stephen replayed that precise moment in his memory, when a long fuse finally blew and he swung a fist, catching Philip in the side of his head. The cap fell to the floor as he stumbled.

"My God, Steve!" said Martin, uncertainly getting to his feet.

Philip put his hand to his ear and Stephen stared at his unclenched hand, amazed at how much pain he was in.

*

"So, how have you been doing with the medication?"

"The same as last time. Tired, bad dreams, finding it hard to concentrate."

"They're just side effects. But do you think it's helping your mood?"

"It's, it's taken the edge off."

"Okay, that sounds positive, taken the edge off. You

212

talked about your difficult domestic situation last week. Any change there?"

"Not really, it's not too bad, we're talking again. Anyway, I've nowhere to go. The two of them do everything together, they keep out of my way. It's fine."

"And home?"

"No."

"I can see you're upset, but what do you mean by no?"

"Sorry."

"It's fine, don't apologise."

"I mean that I found it very hard, and it took so long, to get away from there, and I'm not going back. The last time I was there, I found that my mother had been lying to me all my life."

"About what?"

"Her father, my grandfather. She'd always told us he was a war hero; he was at the Somme. Then she had a terrible argument with my father, when he came in late one night. He called her a stupid Paddy, and she said something like at least her family had fought for their country, not been drinking for it, and he asked her which side and told her to tell me. Sorry, I'm rambling."

"I want you to talk."

"So it turns out that he was never in the army, not the British Army anyway. He was in the IRA and he was in prison when the Great War was on."

"She told you this?"

"Yes, after my father had stormed off. But even worse, she'd always told us that he died before I was born, but he didn't. My grandmother did, but he was still alive, in Ireland. He only died about ten years ago."

"So you're still only in your early twenties? It sounds like your mother might have had a difficult early life. She might have wanted to forget about it, and to protect her children from information they might struggle to comprehend. Parents will do that, for good or ill."

"She suffocates me."

"Hmm. Okay. How are things with the band? You're very good, by the way. My daughter has your record."

"Oh, well. Erm, thank you. So, like I told you, the one who shares with me upset our manager by wearing a Nazi cap."

"And you hit him."

"I know I shouldn't have."

"Why shouldn't you have?"

"Well, I don't believe in the use of violence."

"But you do. Self-evidently. And many people would say that your housemate was behaving appallingly and that he deserved a clip around the ear."

"Many wouldn't, though."

"Many wouldn't, but what are you going to do? You're never going to keep everyone happy with every decision you make. Punch the man who's being obnoxious, tell your mother to stop being over-protective. Tell that girl how you feel. Most of all, stop listening to that voice at your shoulder. You have to love yourself for who you are. Other people love you, why shouldn't you?"

"Yes."

"Stephen."

"Yes."

"Stephen. Your mother is your mother. Phil is Phil. You be Stephen. The only Stephen there will ever be. Nothing much else matters in the end. Just that."

1980

Stephen Elijah had walked from the psychiatrist's rooms in Highgate all the way back to Crouch End. He had passed The Flask, and had considered going in. It had only just opened but was already filling up with people dressed for New Year's Eve parties. New Decade's Eve, he reminded himself. In the midwinter dusk, the lights and laughter were appealing, but he knew that he would feel even lonelier if he went in, and so he had not. The flat had been cold and dark when he came in. Philip had been invited to meet Verity's family, somewhere in Hertfordshire, and he had heard from no one else connected to Generation 27 since the fraught meeting before Christmas. His parents had urged him to stay after Boxing Day, but it had been two years since he'd last exchanged letters with Jim, the only school friend with whom he'd maintained contact, and anyway, Cathleen had heard that he was now working in California – 'and doing very well, his mother says' – and this excused him from making an awkward phone call. Johnny had invited him to a party at Pam's friend's flat but he could not face the pity and the embarrassment, and so he had watched television until midnight, numbed to the charms of something called 'The 70s Stop Here!' by a Party Seven, and had woken up on the first day of 1980 feeling like the last person alive in London.

It became a pleasurable feeling on that morning. He made coffee and toast and sat reading at the kitchen table. He thought at moments like this that he could happily live on his own, and he stretched out and basked in the time to himself, the time to be Stephen.

"But who am I?"

His voice cut through the silence, and he waited for the answer.

Well, he thought, I am not the grandson of a hero of the Somme. Perhaps that man was meant to have died there. Perhaps I am the ghost of a child who was never meant to have been born, a disjunct in the years, like light from a dead star, lost in time.

He fetched his notebook and began to write down these thoughts, and they became the first draft of what would become his best-known poem, 'England Is Haunted'. Inevitably, he thought, he was interrupted by the slamming of the front door and voices coming up the stairs. "A person on business from Porlock," he muttered, and closed the book, tensing himself.

As far as Stephen knew, Philip had not spoken to Emma for several months, had made no attempt to apologise to Bob, and was avoiding Martin, who had telephoned the flat a couple of times before Christmas – 'I know he's there, Steve, we just need to sort things out, don't we?' – but Philip also appeared to be unaware of how this behaviour was affecting Stephen, or at least had decided not to think about it. He had even made no reference to his friend having punched him in the head since that day and, had it not been for Martin's phone calls, Stephen might have begun to doubt that that had ever really happened.

"Steve! Hippety-happity new year! Look at this! And this!"

With the kitchen door still swinging behind him, Philip

217

had thrown something to him and then tugged up his shirt sleeve, pointing at a red weal on his forearm. The something was a plastic block, composed of smaller blocks of different colours.

"It's Rubik's Cube! It's amazing! You have to match the colours on every side. Have a go! I couldn't do it all night. Only Hope."

"Hope what?"

"No, no, no, no! I mean Hope, her!"

Laughing uproariously, he stepped forward ahead of a young woman Stephen had assumed was Verity. He put the cube down.

"Look!" said Philip again, presenting his bare arm.

"A tattoo," said Stephen.

"Tadaa!"

"Verity," said Stephen, "you have her name on your arm. Bloody hell."

"Hi!" said Hope, "isn't it sweet?"

He's still drunk, thought Stephen, and where is Verity?

"I thought you were at a party with her parents? How did you get this done?"

"Me!" said Hope brightly.

"No, no, no, no! Not her parents, Stevie. They're abroad. We were at her brother's. Hope's brother. Verity's brother. You know?"

Of course. The resemblance was now clear.

"So Hope is Verity's sister, you were at their brother's home, and Hope tattooed your arm."

"Bingo, young Stephen! Now wipe that disapproving frown off your face, chapel boy. The lovely Verity has gone in search of more booze, we brought Hope with us to meet

218

you, and we intend to keep the party going!"

"Change of venue!" added Hope.

"The venue has been changed to protect the innocent!"

They both found this very amusing and were still laughing when the doorbell rang. Cursing the turn of events, Stephen left them to it and opened the door, not to Verity but to Martin, although it took him a few seconds to register this. The ponytail had gone, replaced by a severe crop, and he was clean-shaven. He was wearing prescription glasses instead of Aviators and was swathed in a long grey coat that was at least a size too big for him.

"New look for a new decade, little brother," he said, as if in response to the disquiet in Stephen's face, but he looked pale and drawn, and it was this that had made Stephen take a step back in the doorway.

"Steve, I know Phil's back, I found Verity's brother's number in Emma's diary. He told me. Can I come in, mate?"

He waved Martin in. Hippety-happity new year, he sighed, as he led the way up the stairs, then realised that he'd left his unguarded notebook in the kitchen and began to run.

*

"Where the hell is he?"

"Phil, he'll be here, brother. You should stop worrying at that arm, you'll make it worse."

"He's over an hour late. Does he know his way here?"

"Of course he does, Phil."

"Of course he does. Your buddy Bob."

Stephen wondered whether Martin had ever been able to detect acerbity. Perhaps that was how he maintained the relationship with Emma, whatever that relationship was. He had never been sure, but he no longer wanted to know. Since he'd last seen her, at the television studio, accompanied by Martin and the man who might be cuckolding him (cuckolding? What was it about an English degree that made him think like a Shakespeare character?), he had not spoken again to Philip about that, nor about much else. He had, of course, punched him.

They were now gathered in the rehearsal room in the house in Kentish Town, waiting for Bob and Linda to arrive. This had been Martin's idea.

"A chance to get things off our chests, comrades. You know, clear the air. Then we can move on."

By the day after New Year's Day, Philip had forgotten that he'd agreed to this, and Stephen was not confident that even Martin's enthusiasm and geniality would be enough to get things back to how they'd been. Perhaps what they needed was a Surrey Special, but then that reminded him of the night he had danced with Emma.

"More tea, gents?"

"Martin, I'm swimming in tea. He's an hour and a half late. How much longer do we give him?"

Kentish Town was considered a neutral place to meet. Philip would not go to the Spendloves' office, nor would he countenance Bob in the flat (nor would Stephen, but he hadn't needed to say so), and Martin had cast himself as a facilitator of peace talks.

"Just think of me as the U.N. Secretary-General with a Northern accent!"

Philip scratched his arm again. Hope had assured him that she had tattooed other people, using her brother's equipment, but 'Verity' was now spelt out in very bright, red, raised letters.

"But if their brother is a proper tattooist, why didn't you ask him to do it?"

"Steve, he would have charged! Anyway, he'd passed out by then."

Philip puffed out his cheeks and took out his Rubik's Cube. He had not asked whether Emma was going to be there, or even whether she was in the house, or living in the house at all, but Stephen was about to ask if she was coming when he heard her unmistakeable step. She walked in, smoking, brushed her hair from her eyes, and leaned over to kiss Stephen on the top of his head. He breathed in deeply and smiled at her. She looked at Philip.

"I'm sorry I called you that, even though you are one sometimes."

"I know I am. And I was asking for it when Steve fetched me one. You know me."

"My God! Sorted out in five minutes! Perhaps I should be the UN Secretary-General!"

"Martin, you didn't do anything! Except keep us sitting here all afternoon, waiting for the undertakers. And by the way, you have an enormous head. You should grow back your hair."

"Oh, now then, Phil," protested Martin, but they were all laughing, and he couldn't help but join in.

"Look," said Philip, "Stevie was right, I just didn't think. I've never pretended I like the man. I know he's your friend, Martin, but he and I, we just, you know. But I will apologise. If he ever turns up, that is."

"I think he's a creep," added Emma, "you all know that.

221

He doesn't care about Generation 27. It doesn't bother me if Phillippe offended him. He needs to be offended."

Martin just nodded and said "Hmm, well, okay then."

Stephen was by now hoping that Bob wouldn't turn up. Philip and Emma's shared antipathy toward him, even though it came from different places, was drawing them all back together, and he wasn't sure that this was the way to do it, or even that it was a good thing, a thought which came from nowhere and surprised him.

"I wonder why he didn't show up," he said, as the bus crept through the rush hour traffic on Junction Road.

"Well, we got by without the pair of them, young Stephen, wouldn't you say? Makes you think, doesn't it?"

Normally, their meetings had reconvened in the pub, but Martin had said he had work to do and Emma was seeing a friend, so they had agreed a date for an overdue rehearsal and a drink afterwards. *So I'll Burn* was still to be found at the lower end of the music weeklies' charts, and the last thing Martin had heard from Bob was that the agent for the American band they'd supported in the autumn was negotiating a further tour for late spring, and would they be interested?

Peace had seemingly broken out.

"What work was Martin doing?" Philip wondered aloud.

Stephen thought about the friend Emma was seeing.

*

"Sweet Jesus. You have to be kidding me, Martin."

The agreed rehearsal had been twice postponed, but now Martin, Philip and Stephen stood facing each other in the

222

basement in Kentish Town.

"You have got to be kidding," repeated Philip.

"Brothers, what could I do? You know how she gets."

Stephen put down his guitar – there would be no rehearsal today – and put his coat on. It was early spring outside but never down here.

"And you're also telling us that the Spendthrifts have disappeared?"

"Off the face of the earth. I've phoned the office, no one picks up. Same with the house. I've been round there twice, no one's there, no car. Nobody's seen or heard from either of them in weeks."

"So what about the tour?" asked Stephen, hands in pockets.

"God, Steve! Have you been listening? Where is she, anyway?"

Martin paused.

"Well, erm, I'm not sure."

Stephen imagined the scene, as described by Martin. How the American agent had turned up out of the blue two days ago, demanding answers about Bob, where he was, talking about contracts, money and lawyers. Martin had taken great care to recall Emma's exact words to the unwelcome caller.

"Fuck off out of my house, you fucking little accountant. You sleazy, corrupt shyster. Fuck off back to America and suck Reagan's dick. And if you see Bobby boy, take him with you."

Stephen wished he'd been there but was also glad he hadn't been.

"The man was throwing his weight around, he was very unpleasant," added Martin, in an apologetic tone.

"I'm not surprised, I don't blame him!" shouted Philip, as he aimed a kick at the open door, which slammed shut into Emma's face.

"Em! Oh heck, Phil!"

Martin ran to the door just as it reopened.

"We didn't even know you were here! Are you okay?"

"Oh crap! I'm sorry!" added Philip.

Emma was unhurt, having reflexively stopped as the door swung towards her, but they all fell silent as she pushed Martin's arm away.

"Go on, then. Why don't you blame him?"

"Because," began Philip, off his guard, "Look, I'm sorry, if I'd seen you there."

"Because?"

"Because obviously Bob has messed this man around, not to mention us. This tour was a step up, and better money. Why did you have to speak to him like that? We could have smoothed this out, he wasn't chasing us. But you just couldn't do that, could you? Let me guess. He was an enemy of the proletariat, he didn't understand."

Emma took a deep breath.

"He would not tell us how he got our address, and he thought we were hiding Bob. His attitude stank. Stank of male entitlement. And I should have been nice to him? Fluttered my eyelashes, hitched up my skirt? You're as bad as he was, Philip Cross. Huguenot, my arse."

"Now then, everyone."

"Shut up, Martin. If you hadn't been so lame, I wouldn't have had to step in."

Stephen thought that was probably accurate and fair, but Martin looked close to tears, and Philip was not going to let go, not this time.

"For God's sake, haven't you noticed in all the time we've been doing this? The music business is full of people like that! Our absentee manager is another. You know what I think?"

Philip threw up his arms in a typically melodramatic gesture, and paused for effect, but no one responded, and he continued.

"The undertakers have skipped, with our money and with his. We should be on his side, not throwing him out of the house. Why didn't you call me and Steve? I would've talked him round; I would've saved the tour. Now it's gone, along with a lot of money. I needed that money; I haven't got a daddy bailing me out while I play at being revolutionaries. Well done, you two. Fucking Lorca would be proud of you!"

He kicked the door again.

"I think we should stop, maybe."

Everyone turned to Stephen, who had wandered to the far end of the basement while Philip was yelling.

"What's that, Steve? I didn't catch that," he said.

"What did you say?" asked Emma, who had heard him.

"I think, I think maybe we should stop. Just stop."

"Yes, Steve, yes. This shouting at each other is getting us nowhere."

The shaven-headed Martin wiped his eyes and blew his nose.

"No. No. I mean stop all this. Stop being Generation 27."

*

225

"So, since we last met, what's been going on?"

"I've started writing poetry again."

"So, you used to write poetry, then you stopped, now you've started again?"

"Sort of. It was never much good."

"Did you show it to other people?"

"Only my old English teacher. He said I needed to find my own voice."

"And have you now?"

"I'm not sure. I think I might have stopped being T S Eliot but turned into Ernest Dowson."

"Ah. *Non Sum Qualis* something or other *Regno Cynarae*, yes? I did the Victorians for A-level. What about the band?"

"I, erm, I think that might be coming to an end."

"I see. You sound uncertain about that. Why might it be coming to an end?"

"The manager, I told you about him, and his wife, they've disappeared. The record label office is locked up. No one is in charge, no one's organising anything. Nobody much likes Bob, but everything is collapsing without him there. No Valediction Records, no Generation 27."

"And you want to prevent this collapse?"

"Actually, I was the first to suggest that we broke up. Just the night before last."

"But you want to prevent it, don't you? The tissues are there on the table."

"Yes, but I don't know how to."

"Stephen, maybe you can't. Maybe it's time for you all to move on. I understand how that might be upsetting for you, but you shouldn't feel guilty about making that suggestion. Remember what we've talked about, about not listening to that voice on your shoulder. If you want to let go, then let go."

"I don't know what I want, I don't think I ever have known."

"You do know, but only you. No one else can tell you. Not your mother, your father, not your friends, and not me. Only you, Stephen. Only you."

"But it's so hard."

"I know, I know. Just take a moment. It is hard. It's the hardest thing of all for most of us, facing ourselves."

*

Walking home from his session, Stephen felt a sudden burst of raindrops, and stood under a lime tree while the shower passed. As he looked up at the tower of Saint Michael's Church, a perfect rainbow arced into the pale sunlight of a late afternoon spring sky, and everywhere there was watery green. It felt as if he were in an Impressionist painting.

"I wish I could stay here forever," he said out loud, "here and now. Forever."

He no longer had any religious faith, or rather he now knew that he never had, but at this moment he would have welcomed the appearance of his father's judgemental god.

Stephen, I was here all along. Now what do you say, hmm?

When he got in, Philip, Verity and Hope were sitting around the kitchen table, on which stood two bottles of champagne, one opened.

"Stevie boy! Guess what?"

"Phil, about the other night. I need to talk to you,

227

privately."

They had spoken simultaneously.

"Me first, me first!"

He would have barely listened to Stephen anyway.

"Go on," he said, sitting down opposite the three of them. He felt as if he were about to be interviewed, but by people who couldn't stop laughing.

"So, Stevie, my man. We've been having a drink."

"Well, yes."

"Oh, he's so funny! Aren't you going to ask why?" piped up Hope, whom Stephen was beginning to dislike.

"No, no, no! No! I'll get to it! Leave young Stephen alone, my girl."

"Phil, stop calling me young Stephen. You're barely older than me."

"Ooh, touchy! Isn't he touchy?"

Philip reached for the unopened bottle.

"He's old enough to get married," added Hope, by way of reprimand.

"What?"

"Oh yes, Steve," said Verity, raising her hand as if to attract his attention, "you'll never believe this. I was clearing out my flat today and guess what I found? My Vivienne Westwood tights! Remember? In Edinburgh a couple of years ago? The smokin' hot pantyhose! They were at the back of a drawer, I never took them in the first place. Just think, if I had, Phil would never have told that story and I wouldn't have realised how funny he was!"

Just think, thought Stephen, now realising where this was all leading.

"I hate that word," said Hope, "it's creepy, don't you

think? They're tights. Pantyhose is what a dirty old man would say."

"And Americans," replied Verity, "don't be so narrow-minded. That American man who came round earlier to see Phil, he was nice. Phil has opened up my mind so much. That's why I'm marrying him."

The cork shot out of the second bottle and warm champagne spilt across the table. Hope screamed and dragged her chair back.

"I was going to tell him! Quick, pass me a glass, it's all going on the floor. Anyway, Steve, your turn. Spill! Like I just did, ha!"

Hang on, this is not the surprise. I knew this was going to happen soon, I could see this coming. But there's something else. What is it? Oh yes, what Verity just said.

"In private, Phil, please."

It took a further ten minutes of circular discussion about the sharing out of the remaining champagne, and Stephen twice refusing a glass, but finally he was alone with Philip in the living room.

"Sorry you had to find out like that, mate. Those two can't keep anything to themselves, not after a couple of glasses."

I bet they can, thought Stephen.

"Don't worry, it was hardly a shock. You're well-suited. Congratulations."

"Hmm. So, what is it?"

"I wanted to talk about the other night. You stayed after I left and I was wondering what you all said, but now something else has happened, hasn't it? Who was the American who came round earlier today, while I was out? It was the agent, wasn't it? Wasn't it, Phil?"

They faced each other in the gathering gloom, the silence only broken by the helpless laughter coming from the kitchen. Philip started to giggle.

"Hey, you know what? The tights? I got her those as replacements and sneaked them into her drawer, as a surprise. She spotted them in a place on the Kings Road the other week, so I went back and bought them. Well, I think they were the right ones, but it worked out, eh? Now she thinks she never lost them. I'll have to tell her; I don't want to lose the credit for that! What do you think, Steve? Steve? Oh yes, sorry, the agent. What did you want to know again?"

*

Stephen lay in bed until late the next morning. He had slept badly, and he could not bring himself to leave his room until he had navigated a route through the next few days, even though all was silent beyond his bedroom door.

Let me think, let me think. Let me get this straight in my mind.

So, three days ago there had been the row, the latest one, the biggest. Stop all this, was what I thought. Oh yes, of course, I said that. Then I left on my own and I walked all the way back here.

He got up and crept to the door. The flat was quiet and empty, and so he made his way to the kitchen, still on tiptoe, made coffee, and returned with it. The three of them had indeed gone, and even taken their empty bottles with them. He shut the door behind him.

Two days ago, he resumed, two days ago, although I only discovered this yesterday when he admitted it to me, Phil went back to Emma's house. He knew Emma wouldn't be there, I don't know how. He apologised to Martin for losing his temper – apparently he'd carried on shouting at them both after I'd left – and asked if he had the details of the agent, which Martin did.

Stephen broke off, to allow the events leading up to yesterday to settle into some sort of order that made sense. He sipped his coffee and watched a distant speck above Crouch End, as it circled and circled. What was that? Martin would know.

Yes, Martin. He gave the details to Phil, and Phil phoned the agent, who came here yesterday while I was out. Phil said that was not the intention and that he hadn't seen me to tell me, but I don't think that troubled him. He'd decided what he was going to do in any event. That's what he was really excited about last night, not getting married. That would all have been Verity's idea anyway. Phil would just see getting married as an excuse for a party. That's maybe a little harsh but it's still true.

"Steve, this agent, Jerry, he's okay, you know? He still wants to work with us. He was talking about us going to the States! But we need to sit down with the other two and smooth things over. What do you think? Come on, Steve, we can do this!"

*

"But I don't understand why Martin gave you the contact details for the agent. That sounds like he wasn't interested in talking to him again. And why would the agent…"

"Jerry."

231

"Jerry. Why would Jerry even consider talking to those two again, after Emma threw him out?"

"Steve, he's a businessman. He's prepared to be reasonable so long as we are. We can all make some proper money. Just think, New York, LA!"

"Hmm. Who decides on what is reasonable?"

Stephen had reluctantly agreed to accompany Philip on an unannounced visit to Kentish Town.

"She'll slam the phone down if I call ahead!"

He couldn't argue with that, and Martin never answered the phone.

"Hate phones, Steve. They disturb the vibe, you know?"

I have spent the last five years with three people who should be ahead of me in the queue for the psychiatrist, he thought. An epiphany on Fortess Road. He laughed.

"What's so funny?"

In the years ahead, Stephen would look back on this day, but he never laughed when he did.

As they walked from the bus stop, he was aware of Philip silently mouthing a prepared speech. I hope, I really hope that he's not going to tell them that Emma needs to apologise to the appalling Jerry.

It turned out that the speech was not needed. As always, they had to press their ears against the door to be certain that the sonorous bell was resounding deep within the house, but the brass knocker also went unanswered.

"I'm not even sure who actually lives here these days," said Philip, peering back at the street, "but anyway, there's a decent pub down the road."

"Okay, why not. Maybe we could discuss what exactly you're planning to say?"

"Yeah, sure, but there's something else I wanted to ask you."

When they arrived back that evening, Verity was standing in the kitchen, wringing a tissue between her hands.

"Where have you been?" she howled.

"Sweetness, what's the matter? Why are you crying? I told you, we went to see Martin and Emma. We had a couple of pints on the way home. Sorry we're a bit late."

"It's not that! You didn't see them, did you? I know you didn't, because they were here!"

"What? Why?"

Stephen had already seen the folded sheet of A4 to which Verity was now pointing, and he knew why.

"They were here for over an hour, waiting for you. That bitch, that bitch told me I'd corrupted you. She called me a whore! Why would she do that? How have I corrupted you? I don't understand, I just want everyone to be happy. Anyway, they've gone."

"Well, of course you do," said Philip, putting his arm around her heaving shoulders, while Stephen reached for the note, "and yes, they've gone, don't worry."

"No, I mean gone. Away. For good. And good riddance."

"Go on, Steve, open it."

And he did.

*

"Come on, Steve, this is me! I can't handle all that on my own, not in Rickmansworth. Rickmansworth, for God's sake! You know me. Come on!"

It was June, and they surveyed the haze over the distant

233

St Paul's from the usual bench outside Alexandra Palace.

"I don't know, Phil. I wouldn't be comfortable. I don't know your family. Are they all like you? Why not ask Pat? I thought you said he was out of hospital."

"He is but he's still struggling. They don't know what caused him to get pneumonia. He's only in his thirties, looks after himself, goes to the gym. Anyway, Malcolm said they might make it but that Pat didn't need extra stress just now."

"Red Mark, then?"

"No way! Can you imagine his speech? It would be the shortest marriage in history. Please, Steve. Verity likes you, you know. We can trust you."

Yes, everyone can trust me. Mister Reliable, always there. I rock audiences but I never rock the boat.

"You could always try Martin, and Emma could be chief bridesmaid."

They both laughed, a little harshly, but they both knew that Stephen would be Philip's best man on that September day, even though he would have left London by then. He had an agency job, neither cleaning nor a night shift, for once, that would keep him solvent for a few more weeks, following which he was going to meet Julie and Dennis in Paris. He had never been abroad. Then home. Home? The agency had offices around the country, at any rate, and he needed breathing space. For the first time, he understood what people meant by that.

"And obviously you can stop in the flat that night and collect the rest of your stuff," continued Philip. "But no rush," he added.

There was a rush, though. The house had been up for sale for several months, causing consternation for Philip, who had declared that he could never leave Crouch End. Some people, thought Stephen, when Verity's parents gave Philip and her the deposit as an early wedding present. Some people always get their timing just right, without any planning. By the time he was back from France, his and Philip's flat would have become Verity's and Philip's matrimonial home. Although he found it difficult to imagine this, Verity had reminded him often of late.

"It'll be lovely to have you as a guest, Steve."

In any case, Hope was moving in to help with the mortgage, and he detested Hope. She and Verity were both now working as temps.

"Regular incomes, mate, takes the pressure off me while I look at my options."

Jerry had evidently assured him of 'exciting opportunities', although Stephen suspected that Philip had not yet told him that Generation 27 had ceased to be.

It won't matter, it'll work out for him. Timing.

*

So it was that one Sunday in September, Stephen Elijah was to be found on a slow train, wearing an ill-fitting brown suit and with a bin bag of clothes at his feet. Everything else he owned had been moved to his parents' house before the wedding. He had dropped his key through the letterbox when he left the house that morning and had not turned around until Euston.

He recited the previous day's speech in his head, not that he'd had to memorise much. Verity had prohibited all but the most anodyne references to the band, and all references whatsoever to the absent members. Stephen's subject matter had effectively been limited to everything else he knew about the groom. When he realised how little that was, he was both startled and thankful. The speech would be short.

Neither Pat nor Mark made it to Rickmansworth – Stephen suspected that Mark hadn't been invited – but of course Philip's mother and numerous aunts, uncles and cousins were there, and were as raucous and as cheerful as he'd expected. Philip had clearly told them all about Stephen, and he found this touching. Verity's parents had spent the evening sitting in the corner of the hotel ballroom, watching over the increasingly dishevelled dancers and exchanging the occasional expressionless remark. The tattooist brother told Stephen that he was going to India to search for his soul, and Hope made a pass at him. Well, possibly.

"The best man has to dance with the bridesmaids, you know, especially when he's so handsome."

In his empty carriage, he remembered dancing with Emma one night, years ago. He took a crumpled piece of paper from his jacket and unfolded it. Since picking it up and reading it aloud to Philip several weeks ago, he had kept it with him at all times, although he wasn't sure why.

"Phil and Steve. Wanted to tell you to your faces but we missed each other. Not for the first time! So, the thing is I've been doing a bit of freelance work, designing record sleeves for a label in Manchester. An old friend roped me in. Now he wants me on board permanently. It's steady money and a great opportunity, so me and Em are moving up there, just to see how it goes. G27 was a glorious call to arms, now it's time to move on to do other things in the revolution. We're in the pub tomorrow night for a send-off if you can make it.

Remember Frankie Blue? He'll be there. Sorry this is so rushed but we have a lot to do before the weekend. I'll stop now, it's getting a bit tense here, if you understand me. Come and see us! We'll probably be back soon anyway, we can meet up then for a catch-up. If you want to rescue the drumkit from the basement, the neighbours have a spare key. The landlord will probably throw it out when he gets new tenants in. Have at it, little brothers! A truly magnificent pleasure! M."

Philip had sat down heavily and said nothing for several minutes, but Stephen had felt no shock at all. Everything made sense. He even felt a wave of relief, if he could admit it. By the next day, Philip had sufficiently readjusted his plans to declare that he would sooner go out for a drink with Lorca's corpse, and to ask Stephen if he wanted to stay in the band, or a band, with him. He could hear the relief in Philip's voice when he declined.

"Of course, Steve, I understand. You want a break. Time out. Of course."

They both knew that Stephen's time in London had come to an end, and that Philip now had plans to which he was incidental. Time out.

And now on this quiet Sunday morning, as the tints of green and brown went by the window, he thought of his failures. He had failed to save Generation 27, and he had failed to save Emma, whom he would never see again. He bowed his head and spoke to the carriage.

"Yea, I was desolate and bowed my head: I have been faithful to thee, Cynara! In my fashion."

And then he started and woke up.

PART THREE

THE VIEW FROM UP HERE

2017

KELLY

It had been typical of Grace, thought Kelly that evening. She had collected the post on Friday, barely looked at it before stuffing it into her bag, and gone straight to the pub for what turned out to be the rest of the evening. She had spent the next day in her pyjamas and in a haze, and had completely forgotten to check the bundle with the red elastic band around it.

"I wasn't snooping," her mother had said when she called her in from the garden, "I was just tidying your room."

Grace had sighed audibly.

"You are living here for next to nothing, Grace. I don't expect to have to clear up your mess. Anyway, they were virtually falling out of your bag. You might want to hang onto them until tomorrow before giving them to your father. He wouldn't be happy about you taking them out with you on Friday night."

"Sorry, Mum. I appreciate that."

She had flicked through the sheaf of letters, then caught her breath, before running back into the garden, where Kelly was wrapping her cardigan around herself. The sun was dipping, and long shadows crossed the lawn.

Sitting up in bed, Kelly was now regarding the note and plectrum before her. She had been craving this moment, the quiet and solitude, ever since Grace had urged her to open the envelope marked 'FAO Martin Rogers'.

"Your parents almost saw this! I'd have had some

explaining to do then, and I want to avoid that, remember? I'll open it when I get home. Anyway, there won't be much in it."

She was right in this, and had felt a deep sense of anti-climax before something thrilling occurred to her. Her note had not simply been returned to her by someone. The someone had written his or her own note. She examined the handwriting in wonderment. Neither was the plectrum the one she'd sent those weeks ago. The gold lettering was bright and clear. The someone had thought that important.

By now, however, everything had given way to panic and self-recrimination. Someone, and possibly all of them, had agreed to meet her in North London in just over two weeks' time. No, meet Martin. Meet an old man with dementia at a place she had no idea how to get to. She'd only been to London twice in her life, once on a school trip and once with Evangeline's father, to a football match, the details of which she had forgotten, except for the day-long drinking involved. She did not, then, consider herself prepared.

"Oh, Kelly. What were you thinking?"

No, no, no! Stop that! You are talking to yourself in your mother's voice. Not even your mother. Cathy and Ron Ackroyd are not your parents, they never were. That's her voice, her tone of constant disappointment, chipping away at an adopted child's sense of worth. But you are not theirs, you never were. Whoever you are, you are you, the girl who would not apologise on the night she left that house for good.

"Fuck you, Cathy Ackroyd. I am doing this."

So, on to practicalities, and there were many. That night, however, she fell asleep imagining one of the other people in Martin's photograph writing the note which now lay on her bed.

From the very next morning, Kelly was astonished at how quickly her plans took shape. Excited as she had been about the PO Box delivery, Grace made no mention of it at work. Kelly assumed that she would rather not know any more about it, and she was not going to disabuse her of the mistaken belief that the end of her temporary post collection duties was the end of the whole matter.

She probably doesn't really believe that, but she wants to, and I'll let her. She won't ask me anything when I ask her to take Evangeline that day.

She was examining the next fortnight's roster as she thought this, and chided herself for her cynicism, while at the same time acknowledging that there was no other way in which Martin could be in London on the third of April. Then her next piece of good fortune jumped out at her. Norah Flaherty was marked as absent on leave for that date, for several days on either side of it, in fact. The deputy manager had her spies at The Grange, no doubt about that, and the spiteful Irma, though loyal to no one, subscribed to her boss's philosophy and regime. Such was Norah's reluctance to delegate, however, that her occasional absences from the home invariably left a vacuum in place of authority. One of the more senior members of staff would be left in charge of the day-to-day care of the residents, but with strict instructions to phone the local surgery in the event of a problem, and Irma kept the administration of the home ticking over without being able to make any decisions herself. In short, Norah trusted nobody to maintain her standards, with the result that nobody did and nobody much cared. Here, then, was the window of opportunity, open wide at just the right time.

There was of course a steady flow of new residents into the home, replacing the departed, and there was temporarily a staff shortage, which Norah had proclaimed as an 'opportunity for career development'. For Kelly, this had meant her acquiring Carter Neville, who joined the three other old men for whom she had responsibility for waking, washing, dressing and putting to bed. She wondered why yet another 'abandoned grandpa', as Grace called them, had been given into her care, and she suspected that this was not coincidental. She was right to think this. Norah remained fixed on the idea that she and Martin were at the heart of a conspiracy against her, and her intention was to stifle the insolent girl by overloading her with the likes of Carter, a demanding and sprightly eighty-six-year-old. She had been working in care homes for a long time, and she knew very well the difficulties some of the younger women could have with their male charges. They're still men, Norah thought, they never change. There was something to this.

Carter was particularly troublesome for Kelly. Like most new arrivals, he had struggled with the sudden loss of his familiar surroundings (although his attempt to set fire to them had presaged his removal to The Grange) but, whereas for many their distress ebbed away with their memories, he remained alarmed and infuriated, mostly with his wife when she visited. Carter had been a solicitor, and he still insisted on wearing a tie every morning, even after he'd forgotten how to put one on. Each Friday evening, Mrs Neville would bring with her a half-bottle of white wine, two plastic glasses, and a bag of cheese and onion crisps.

"It was always our little ritual at the end of the week," she would say, before returning to the dark and empty pre-war semi where they had spent their married lives.

"Bitch!" shouted Carter, as she would cautiously approach across the lounge, clutching a carrier bag and smiling uncertainly, but the ritual did appear to strike a distant chord and calm him down, perhaps helped by the Pinot Grigio.

Grace had settled Carter into his room on his first night at The Grange and had warned Kelly about him.

"His hands! He's like an octopus! An old one."

That Friday, Kelly was getting Carter ready for the visit.

"Shall I smarten you up for your sweetheart, Carter?"

"Bitch!"

She was knotting a navy and white striped silk tie, the one he always insisted on to go with his blazer, when she felt his hand sliding up her leg, not for the first time.

"Carter! Gentlemen don't do that!"

She gently slapped his wrist and wondered how she'd forgotten her 'trousers on Friday' rule, and whether, really, it was time to report what had been a regular occurrence since Carter's arrival. Being old and ill shouldn't be a *carte blanche*, should it? But of course she knew exactly how Norah Flaherty would respond to a complaint. Oh well, and I bet the old bugger's snagged these tights. And then it came back to her, what she'd been trying to remember when Grace was talking to her in the garden. That night she had encountered a weeping Kalina in the dark corridors, her mind had only been set on finding Martin's guitar, but now she remembered. Sarah's tights had been taken. Just a couple of weeks ago, the same thing had happened to Grace. Carter had arrived at The Grange at about the same time as the disappearances began. She wondered. He had often been found roaming freely around the building, including the staff room.

You old devil, she thought, and made a mental note to look around his room when she was less preoccupied. For now, she needed to plan to be alone with Martin on the impending day, and not to be dealing with Carter Neville and his octopus hands.

*

The plan was simple, but it relied on an accurate weather forecast and somebody else coping with Carter on the day. On both counts, fortune smiled again. Once Norah was safely out of the way, Kelly had on the previous Friday completed a permission slip, authorising her to take Martin out on the following Monday. As she had expected, Irma had signed it without so much as checking it. Norah constantly advocated plenty of fresh air for the residents, and they were often taken out to the local shops, or the park, by carers desperate for a cigarette and a few hours away from the home, and no one would look twice at Kelly wheeling Martin out of the front door, especially on what was a perfect spring morning.

She had intended to ask Kalina to keep an eye on Carter, and felt bad about taking advantage of the poor girl's adoration of her, but the problem was solved by Carter's son and daughter-in-law arriving to take him out. They must be mad, thought Kelly, but she regarded it as a sort of miracle. Her huge sense of relief was tempered by increasing apprehension. This was all too easy, what was going to go wrong? Was she being led into a fiendish trap? As she was pushing Martin across the lounge to the door, constantly looking back over her shoulder as she did so, Irma appeared, coming directly towards her from the office.

"Having a nice little trip out, Roy? With your girlfriend?"

She winked at Kelly, who could have punched her there and then. That would have to wait. Actually, it would never happen, because today would be her last day at The Grange. For the moment she was unable to move, almost transfixed.

"Poor old sod, he hasn't had a visitor for almost a year now. I think his friend must have, you know, gone the way of all flesh. He looked even older than Roy."

"He had a friend?"

In spite of her desperation to get Martin out of the building in time for the taxi she had booked, Kelly was curious. She had always assumed that, if Martin had any living relatives, they'd long since relinquished any sense of duty to him and had left him to his fate, but she had never thought of friends coming to see him.

"Old chap, long white beard, always dressed very sharply, carried a silver-topped cane. He'd come about once a month, sit with Roy for an hour, have a word with Norah, then disappear until his next visit. Ah well, gone now. Have a nice time, Mister Roy!"

On she swept, but Kelly remained where she was, in thought for a moment. No, don't say that one of the young men in the photograph, one of the signatories, was visiting Martin until recently? And did this man live nearby? Had he now died? She was again struck with doubt about the wisdom and the point of what she was about to do.

No, think about it, Kelly. An old chap with a white beard. The young men from forty years ago were in their early twenties. They couldn't be more than sixty, sixty-one now. They would no longer be fresh-faced, but Martin's visitor sounded a good deal older than that. Martin, after all, was surely well into his seventies. And, she reminded herself, her note had gone to an address in London and had found its way back, so one of them must still be down there.

"Yes, of course," she said, and Martin looked up at her from his wheelchair.

"Come on, Martin. It's time."

She looked around the lounge one last time, turned to the door, and together they went out into a glorious April morning.

*

Norah Flaherty was on the case. That was how she liked to think of herself that morning. She knew perfectly well that mice would play while cats were away; that much was evident whenever she returned from an absence to find The Grange in a state of unholy chaos, as her father would have said. She had been thinking gloomily about this while wondering what to do with her overdue leave, and then the idea had come to her. They would all have their guard down that Monday, and she could use that to her advantage. Before anyone could hide anything or cover anything up, she would be there, unannounced and unexpected. Let's see how Kelly Ackroyd, or anybody else, likes that.

Norah was in the mood to take action. It was high time to re-establish order and control. She slapped the steering wheel with her left hand to emphasise the point, just as she was turning into the road where lay the entrance to the home, and almost swerved into the path of a taxi coming the other way. The driver sounded his horn.

"Bugger off!" yelled Norah, as the taxi pulled in to avoid her and passed by. This was going to be a good day.

As she locked her car, however, nothing untoward jumped out at her. Someone had left one of the home's wheelchairs near the gates, which irked her but was not unusual. A few residents were being guided slowly around the grounds, a practice of which she thoroughly approved, and none of the carers accompanying them appeared to be smoking. She went inside. All was quiet as she opened the door to the office. Irma was on the phone – she raised her eyebrows and waved – but she was clearly talking to someone about an overdue laundry collection, not to her husband, whom Norah regarded as a workshy hypochondriac. She went on into her office, took off her coat, sat down, and wondered what to do first.

"Mrs F?"

Irma had finished her call and was standing in the doorway.

"We can't get rid of you!"

Ha, thought Norah, no, you can't.

"Just a few odds and sods to clear up. Any chance of a brew?"

Irma disappeared off to the kitchen, leaving both doors ajar behind her. It was early to mid-morning, the breakfast dishes had been cleared away, and the lounge was full of dozing residents. Again, all normal. Then Norah remembered her intention to inspect those parts of the home into which she did not routinely venture. Now was the perfect time to do it, and she knew the perfect place to start.

The weird old man, little Miss Ackroyd's pal. Rogers, that

was it. She rarely remembered residents' names but this one stuck. Even before Kelly had come to the home, there had been the oddity of his arrival with that strange friend and the mysterious payment of the fees.

He would not be in his room at this time of day. As Irma came back in with a mug of tea, Norah brushed past her and made for the stairs, master key in hand. Room 27 was open, however. One of the larger rooms, it was nevertheless sparsely furnished. She remembered that he'd brought no furniture with him, and so there was only the standard bed, wardrobe, chest of drawers, table and chairs. There were also few personal effects. A guitar was propped up in the corner: Norah was certain that had been packed away years ago and was not happy to see it there. There was a black and white photograph on the table, with an empty frame lying next to it. Were those his kids? The only other item that was clearly Roy's was a Bible, and she remembered Kelly telling her how Roy liked her to read from it. She picked it up and flicked through the pages. It was old, and she put it down before she tore one, but not before noticing an inscription on the yellowing flyleaf.

'Martin. Christmas 1954. Always remember Psalm 121. Your loving father.'

She shrugged and looked around the sun-filled room. There was something under the bed. She knelt down, wincing as her arthritic hip grumbled, and pulled out a stack of books and magazines, which were all to do with... birdwatching? No pornography, just *The Happy Twitcher*, *Birds of Prey of The British Isles*, back issues of *Birdwatching Monthly*. Another strange hobby, thought Norah, baffled, but innocuous, and she began to wonder if this had been a waste of time. If Roy, Kelly and the little Polish girl had sat up here reading the Bible, discussing blackbirds and strumming the guitar, she reluctantly conceded that this did not amount to any sort of conspiracy that needed to be suppressed. She stood up, grunted, and sighed.

A quick check of the drawers and wardrobe, then back to square one. Maybe next a late-night inspection of the staff room. Neatly folded and ironed clothes filled the drawers and wardrobe, although there was another photograph underneath a pile of handkerchiefs, of a baby on a rug. As she was about to close the wardrobe doors, something at the back caught her eye. She reached over and pulled out an old, battered and bulging briefcase, of soft leather. Whatever was in it, and it clearly wasn't papers, did not resist her squeezing and prodding. To hell with it, she thought, I'm entitled to know. The briefcase was not locked and opened easily. She thrust in her hand, then withdrew it. Surely not? She turned it upside down and shook it. Onto the carpet cascaded perhaps thirty, maybe more, pairs of tights and stockings, of all styles and colours, settling into a tangled pile of gossamer. Norah's eyes widened and she opened her mouth, then closed it.

"Now I've got you!" she whispered.

PHILIP

"Stan, come on, help me out."

"Theo, I've never heard of Philip what's his name, or the band he was in, so you can be sure that most of our students won't have either."

Stan had been on the same course as Theo but had taken a year's sabbatical to be the union's entertainments officer. As such, he was responsible for booking all the acts who performed at the college. He was what Theo aspired to be: effortlessly knowledgeable, much admired by many female students, and, in Theo's eyes, lucky. Theo rationalised the successes of most people as mostly good fortune, and his own shortcomings as a lack of the same. Stan's help was therefore crucial to him.

"Look, I'm not asking the union for money, or any help. I just want the use of the performance space and someone on the bar. I'd promote it, I'd take care of everything, and you'd sell a lot of booze. There's no downside for you."

"You'd have to indemnify the union for the insurance."

"No problem," replied Theo, not understanding what Stan was talking about but sensing a shift from his initial dismissal of the idea. Half an hour later, he left the union office with an agreement finalised. He cared for neither Philip de la Croix nor his old man's music, but his new career as a promoter was up and running. Time to call Charlotte.

*

"Yes, yes, yes. Okay. Okay, honey. Sorry, Lottie, I mean Charlotte. I will call him. I have a surprise visitor, I got distracted. I'll call him today, promise. What's his name again? I'll tell him to stop pestering you. You don't want me to? Jesus, okay, I thought that's what dads did. Alright, promise. When will you be home? Oh, she's gone. Where was I?"

Felix was chuckling.

"What?"

"Oh my God, Philip, what will become of you once both your daughters are gone? I shouldn't laugh. I worry about you. Do you drink that much every night?"

"I was only being sociable, same as you. Stop being such an old granny."

Felix took his doctor's advice seriously, and he regretted the previous night's beers, but he had not been drinking wine and whisky chasers, nor had he eaten an entire naan bread with two starters. He gave up and changed the subject, or reverted to the conversation they'd been having before Lottie phoned.

"So, the plectrum and the note. You were explaining."

"I was explaining last night but you kept dozing off."

It occurred to Felix that his friend not only looked rumpled and unhealthy, which he often did, but also worried, unnerved perhaps. For as long as he'd known him, almost forty years now, Philip had seemed to bounce through life with abandon, heedless of the people who were left to clear up after his many unwise choices. It could be an endearing part of him, at least to some of those people, but exhausting to those who'd known him longest, and it had been too much

251

in the end for several women. As far as Felix could tell, those women now numbered Philip's elder daughter, and maybe soon the younger one. This was new, though. He was troubled by something.

"I'm sorry, I'm wide awake now. Go on."

So Philip told him about all that happened in the last few days, and it astonished him in the telling that it had really been little more than a week ago that the cub reporter, Leo or whatever his name was, had shown him that old photograph.

"Phil, the fact you saw an old band photo just before the note and plectrum arrived is a complete coincidence. You know that, right?"

"Hmm," said Philip, passing the note across the kitchen table, as he had the previous night.

"Phil, you showed me this already. April 3, London. A PO Box number. I think you're meant to reply to this?"

"I know, I worked that out."

"And this agreement you all signed, it was to come to the aid of whichever of you needed it, yes?"

"I'd almost forgotten about it. I don't know who sent this, or why."

"Does it matter? One of them did, because they need to see you. Why not just accept that?"

Felix knew why. He might as well have asked Philip to reconsider his refusal to perform old Generation 27 songs.

"Phil, no one should live in the past, but these people were your friends, maybe even closer than that. You wanted my advice?"

"I did not ask for advice."

"I think you did. My advice is send the note on to that address, and go to, Alexandra Palace did you say? Go there on that date. What do you have to lose? It's not like you have far to travel."

"Hmm."

Philip picked up the sheet of paper and examined it again, as if he might have missed something. Then he realised that he had.

"Wait a minute. No, that can't be right."

Before Felix could ask, he pushed back his chair and headed for the stairs, moving faster than he had all morning. After several minutes of drawers being slammed shut, he reappeared with an old address book, which he waved at Felix.

"I knew it. Look."

"What am I looking at?"

"There. Martin Rogers."

"But there's no address for him, only… ah!"

"Yes, only a PO Box number. He gave me this when we last spoke, when, you know."

Philip stared into the middle distance for a moment.

"Are you alright?"

"Sorry. Yes. Anyway, the point is that Martin never used a normal address. I remember him explaining to me that he didn't trust them. Don't ask me why. This was Martin."

"That was many years ago."

"But this has come from him, Felix. If he were dead, then it could only have come from Steve, right? And Steve would never use a PO Box."

"Okay, but the address you have is not the same as on the note."

"No, but both the numbers are Manchester. I'm telling you, Martin sent this."

Felix couldn't help but wonder to himself why on earth Martin could not have simply phoned Phil, as he had on that day in 1990, or at least sent him an actual letter, instead of leaving the two of them to decipher a mystery. At least Philip was beginning to think rationally rather than imagine that a ghost was haunting him.

"So," he went on, "I'm meant to pass this on to Steve. I do remember that much about the bloody oath. He came after me. Then, well, then he returns it to Martin, at that number. Martin knows that, that's why he added the PO Box."

An understanding dawned on Felix. The buried young men of a shared history were coming to life. 'Should one need the others'. Martin had decided he needed the others and he had gone back to the oath. No phone, no letter, no email; those things were for old, conventional people, which they had decided long ago never to be. Phil was the fearless boy of Felix's youth. It did not matter that there might have been more practical ways to round up the band. This was how they had sworn to do it and, now they were in the future they had barely imagined back then, it was what they were going to do. It was that simple, he realised, and he smiled at Philip.

"What?"

"Nothing. I think I might stay in London a while longer, if that's alright."

"Great! You can come to the college show."

"Ah," said Felix.

*

He didn't have any old Valediction Records picks, he couldn't remember the last time he'd seen one, so he'd just have to send this one on. And there was no point in rewriting the note, so the one he'd received also went in the envelope. He traced the faded lettering on the plectrum before he dropped it in and sealed the package. Whereas there was no doubt in his mind that Martin had contacted him, he was less sure about writing to someone in late middle age care of their parents' address, but there were of course no alternatives. He had no idea where in the world Steve might be, and he had never had a phone number for him. He supposed he could ask Lottie to do a search on her laptop, but that would be pointless. The surname was sufficiently unusual to turn up something, but he knew that Stephen Elijah would have no online presence beyond a couple of old features on Generation 27. He was wrong about this, but, in any event, he didn't want to wait around for his daughter to come home. He had to get this done and then focus on the forthcoming show. Off went the forwarded message.

In his appointments diary, he wrote next to Monday 3 April 'Ally Pally'. After a moment's thought, he added a question mark.

*

"Anything I can do?"

"Phil, I told you, no. Just sit there, take it easy, talk to me."

Philip drained his bottle of beer and leaned back on his chair to fetch another from the fridge. Felix looked at him, then went on with chopping peppers.

"Jesus, Felix, give it a rest. A couple of stubbies before dinner never hurt anyone. You've gone a bit holier than thou these days. I remember some nights out in Amsterdam. What was the bar we used to go to all the time?"

"We went in a lot of bars, Phil. Many are now gone, or are full of English boys in football shirts."

"God, this is like having my mother making the dinner, lecturing me while she did. What are we having anyway?"

Felix had offered to cook not because he was good at it, but he was going to stay for the next month and he suspected that Philip only ate healthily when Lottie was at home.

"*Sate Ayam*. Where are your herbs and spices?"

"Don't ask me. Feel free to rummage. That doesn't sound very Dutch."

"You might remember the bars of Amsterdam, my friend, but you've forgotten some fantastic Indonesian restaurants."

He remembered that Hannah had given him the recipe. He wondered where she was right now. He wanted to stop wondering and changed the subject.

"So, Philip. Tell me about this booking."

Wrong subject, Felix!

"I'm glad you asked me. I sensed a lack of enthusiasm when I told you about it. It was like talking to Maria."

Maria had left the previous year, shortly before Philip's admission to hospital, upon being told of which she did not return to London. Felix had never met her but felt an empathy, indeed felt that he was dangerously close to stepping into her vacated role as amanuensis and nursemaid.

"I am not Maria."

There was of course very little to tell, as Philip admitted.

"That reminds me, I must phone this guy."

"Phil."

"I know what you're going to say."

Philip held up the flattened palm of his hand between

them, as if to deflect what was coming.

"But you must still hear it. We are business partners. We are going to reissue the Generation 27 back catalogue. Maybe only one album, a couple of singles and an out-takes collection, but there will be interest around Europe, I know it. I could get you a dozen shows by the end of this week: Netherlands, Belgium, Sweden, Germany. You would sell CDs at these shows, there would be radio interest, interviews. We might double our sales. But you turn all that down for a college show. And who will come to this show? We are also friends, Phil. I don't want you to waste your time, to waste a great opportunity."

But Philip was already levering himself out of the chair and reaching for the phone in his pocket.

"A friend would support and respect my creative impulse."

And with bottle in one hand, phone in the other, he raised both arms, then turned and left the kitchen. In a cupboard, Felix found a box full of herbs and spices, none past their use-by date. He silently thanked Lottie and hoped that she might appear at the house soon. He didn't know her but thought she might be an ally. His radio shows for the next month were all pre-recorded, he would ask a friend to check the flat and his mail, and there was nothing requiring his physical presence in Amsterdam for a while. Someone needed to be here, to navigate Phil away from the wreckage of another terrible idea and towards a more realistic future, a better one for both of them. He also wanted to go to Alexandra Palace with him on the third of April. Whether he could do all this on his own was the question. What if Lottie never came home? What if he were confined here, alone with a deluded egomaniac, for the next month? He was helplessly fond of the man but had only ever managed to spend time with him in concentrated bursts. Then he had an idea. Then he dismissed it. Then he said to himself "Why not? *Godverdomme, ja.* Why not?" He began to stir in coriander powder. That might just work.

*

When Theo's phone rang, only a number showed on the screen, no name, and so he answered accordingly.

"Hello. Ransom Promotions."

"What?" said an unfamiliar voice.

"Ransom Promotions. Can I help you?"

"Who is this? I was after Leo."

"Ah, is that Phil de la Croix?"

Theo had prepared his script for the call but breathed a sigh of relief that he had remembered not to call him Cross, a touchy point according to Charlotte. He decided that a correction of his own name might be pushing his luck.

"So this is Leo, yeah?"

"It is. How are you, Phil?"

"Lottie, Charlotte, whatever she calls herself at college, tells me you're keen to put me on. I might be interested. What are you offering?"

Theo had managed to scribble down a few notes as Stan had been listing the dos and don'ts of promoting a show, and the very last thing he'd said to him now rang true.

"They're all arseholes, Theo. All bands, all performers. Every single one of them. Self-important, deluded, narcissistic arseholes. Be nice, be reasonable, but never give them an inch."

He cleared his throat.

"Well, whatever we make on the night, minus the overheads."

"I meant the guarantee. What is the guarantee? I normally ask for five hundred but I suppose it could be negotiated, this being my daughter's place. Oh, and I'll bring my own sound man, so I'll need the details of your PA system to pass on to him."

"Erm, of course."

Theo had not even thought about the PA and was relieved to realise that he would not have to. Phil's guarantee was another matter. Be nice, be reasonable, but do not give an inch.

"How about four hundred. That okay with you, Phil?"

"Four fifty. Plus dinner and drinks. The tight schedule bothers me, you see. I'll get photos and a bio over to you tomorrow, and I'll want to see the posters before they go out. Happy with that, mate? Send me the contract. Talk to you soon."

"Erm," said Theo again, two minutes after Philip had ended the call. He might need to talk to Stan again.

Back in Crouch End, Philip was pleased with himself.

"Who needs an agent? Five minutes, that's all it took. He agreed a higher guarantee than I'd have settled for, plus free bar. To think I was paying Jez all those years, just to do this."

Felix had once met Jez, Philip's last agent, not long before Jez had decided that his client was not only committing career suicide but was in the process damaging the relationships Jez had cultivated with some reliable promoters. Philip would tell anyone who asked that he'd had to get rid of yet another useless agent, but Felix knew that was untrue.

"I know you're his friend, Felix, and I do like the man, but this is my reputation at stake, not to mention my living. People I deal with regularly will not have him back. He might not care about that, but a couple of people have stopped taking my phone calls."

Once Felix had assured Jez that there was no longer anyone who could change Philip's mind, about more or less anything, and certainly neither of them, then he knew that the rupture was inevitable, and what Philip's version of events would be. Since the end of Generation 27, Philip had had at least half a dozen agents. He knew this because Philip had quite happily told him. Now he was about to tell him that he'd been right all along.

"I was right all along, Felix."

"Uh-huh," said Felix, head bent over the pan he was grimly stirring.

"These people are not artists, they're leeches. All they care about is milking all they can out of the artists. We're just cash cows to them."

Felix weighed up the assortment of metaphors.

"But is it not a symbiotic, rather than a parasitic, relationship?"

Philip giggled.

"Not the damn letter s thing again? You found that amusing when we were kids, but now?"

"Felix, you know me! Come on, it's just an affectionate joke. Anyway, your English is better than my Dutch. What the hell does symbiotic mean?"

"It means, Philip, that everyone has bills to pay, even the

wonderful, amazing artists, and I don't know how you think this show is going to pay your bills, even if you booked it all by yourself."

But Philip had moved on.

"Oh yes, I meant to add, I told him you'd be doing the sound. That alright?"

Felix stopped stirring and turned round.

"They have their own PA, of course, but I didn't want to waste money on some clueless kid at the desk."

He folded his arms and scrutinised Philip, as if taking stock. He knew how difficult he found silences. He pointed the wooden spoon at him.

"Now who is the leech, Phil? Hmm?"

"Felix, I just thought…"

"You thought you didn't need to ask. I would have agreed to do this if you'd asked me first, of course. You are letting me stay here, I cook dinner, I do your sound, no problem. But you should have asked. This is how you are, as you would no doubt say. But how you are is sometimes not good enough, Phil."

He turned back to the Aga and went back to stirring.

"Sorry, Felix."

"Okay."

*

At last, Theo had thought, I have learned something useful. I have finally picked up a transferrable skill from this dead-end course.

He and Philip had omitted to exchange email addresses, and he had had to call Charlotte for the information. For some reason, her phone kept going to voicemail, but she texted the address. Philip had responded several days later, despite his professed concern about the show coming up so soon, with several publicity photos and a biography. Theo thought that the photos reflected the man's conceitedness, even briefly wondering if the moody stares were ironic. They were also surely at least twenty years old. As for the biography, there was nothing in there he couldn't have invented himself, although he wondered why more hadn't been made of the briefly famous band he'd been in.

No matter, he had referred to his second-year course notes on layout and had drafted what he considered to be an eye-catching poster. He had duly sent it to Philip for approval. Now he dejectedly reread the email that had arrived that morning.

"Leo! No! I am not 'Philip de la Croix, ex-Generation 27 (Trying To Explain)'! I am Philip de la Croix! Please remove all this cheesy nostalgia bullshit before the posters go up. And I'm still waiting for the contract."

God! Now he tells me! Now he tells me! Only three weeks to go, no posters up yet, what do I do?

What he did not do was call Stan, whose patience with him had worn thin but who would have told him to ignore Philip and put the posters up as they were, because not to do so would be preposterous. Instead, Theo made the alterations. The contract was easy, just small print, you could cut and paste that from anywhere, and so he did. He doubted that Philip had ever read a contract, and on this at least he was right.

There we go! All done, easy.

The posters were on social media and every website he

could access by the end of the day, and he printed off sufficient to fly-post. He could ask Charlotte to help him with that. Ransom Promotions was up and running.

*

There was plenty to keep Felix occupied in the weeks before Philip's show, mostly to do with the impending release of the Generation 27 material, but, as he had feared, that was not the case for Philip.

"Phil! You would not believe how much still has to be done before the release date! Can you please leave me alone. And you still haven't given me the details of the college's PA system. I need to know what I'll be working with if you want me to do your sound. And shouldn't you be rehearsing?"

Philip was leaning over him as he sat before his laptop.

"Wow! Do these guys all speak English?"

"Yes, of course they do. Why would they have agreed to do promotional interviews with you if they didn't? Everyone speaks English and the Brits only speak English. Always this is how it is. These guys will all be able to ask you in perfect English when you are playing in their town, and they will all understand you when you say that you have better things to do."

"Give it up, Felix, for God's sake!"

He stomped off, muttering. Moments later, Felix heard the front door slam. Out of cigarettes, he thought, and picked up his phone. Hannah? No, he'd left two voicemail messages. Maybe that really was that. Time to let go, Felix. No, he needed to make another call, one he couldn't put off any longer. By the time Philip returned with his Dunhills (Felix had attempted one brief conversation about switching to vaping), he had set in motion the thought that had come to him as he had been making *Sate Ayam*.

They sat in the kitchen that evening after dinner, a routine into which they'd fallen quite happily.

"She is a charming young woman, Phil, you must be very proud."

Lottie had returned to the house that afternoon, done some washing, cooked a vegetable stew, and left just as abruptly, not before telling Phil that she'd seen a poster for his show, which had pleased him immensely. He was quickly brought back down to earth when she went on to express her relief that they used different surnames, so no one could connect her with something so lame. Felix had stifled his laughter.

"Hmm. She'll be gone soon. Like her sister, like her mother."

Felix saw the tidal wave of maudlin nonsense coming his way and changed course.

"So, the show at her college. The first of April. A Saturday, yes? And we go to meet Martin, or someone, on the Monday."

"We? I haven't decided to go yet."

"Okay, fine, but I wondered if we might go out for dinner on that Friday? I liked that restaurant in Muswell Hill. Maybe we could ask Lottie and her young man along? It would be a nice start to an important few days."

"Sure, why not? Lottie won't come, I can tell you now, and if she does, I'd rather she didn't bring that drippy boy with her."

"And you wonder why all these women leave you, Philip."

He reached across the table for the cigarettes.

"I thought you'd given up?"

"Ah well, mostly. I just felt like one."

"You look pleased with yourself. What are you up to? Felix the grouch, suggesting having fun. It's like you've reverted to your carefree youth."

In a way I have, thought Felix, as he blew out a smoke ring.

"I am up to nothing. Old friends going out to dinner, that's all."

He leaned back in his chair and smiled. That's all.

*

He had had to go back to Stan. He did not want to tell him anything about Ransom Promotions that he did not need to, fearing that Stan would point out something he should or shouldn't have done. For Theo, it was always folly to be wise. He had done what he had done, and he wanted no interventions to unsettle his certainty that everything was set fair and would work out. Except tickets.

"What? You're kidding me!"

Stan's response to the revelation that Theo had omitted to advertise sources of tickets for the show was not reassuring. Theo had clung to the hope that he might instead have chuckled, said it wasn't a big problem, leave it with him, he'd sort it out.

"You idiot!"

No, that was not going to happen.

"Okay, listen. It's not quite the disaster it would have been a few years ago, but you need to fix this today. The show's in just over a week. No one comes here to collect tickets anymore; they do everything on their phones. We all do, right? So you need to contact an online platform. They'll sell your tickets for you and take commission. Here's a list of the ones we use, they're all much of a muchness. But Theo, you need to do this right now, and you need to get the links up on your posters. You might already have lost some punters."

"Thanks, Stan. I owe you one."

"You'll owe me more than that if the bar doesn't make money."

But Theo was already out of the door.

*

"Why have you shaved off your beard?"

It was Friday afternoon, the day before the college show. Felix had immersed himself in what had turned out to be a vast amount of administrative work for the whole of that week. Having spent his adult life in radio, he knew enough about the music industry not to be surprised by how much went into the release of a record, but he was of course doing it all on his own, with no direct experience of running a record label. Centrum Records was him, just him. Even as a non-native English speaker, Felix hated clichés, but this really did feel like a steep learning curve. Why had he ever started this?

"It makes me look younger," replied Philip.

Felix looked hard at him.

"It doesn't," he eventually said.

"You're just jealous, you old fart. Fancy a beer?"

"Phil, I'm working. Please. Shouldn't you be rehearsing?"

"I rarely bother these days. You wouldn't believe the number of shows I've winged. No one ever notices."

Oh, I would believe, thought Felix, but you're probably right about no one noticing.

"I should maybe check in with Leo," he went on, "I didn't see anything in the *Guardian* or *Time Out* listings."

"Don't forget," Felix called after him, "the table is booked for seven-thirty, in case you were thinking of washing your hair."

"Nobody likes a smart arse!" came the disembodied, half-chortled reply. Once Philip was out of earshot, and Felix could hear him talking, he immediately reached for his own phone.

"Oh, sorry! I didn't mean to wake you. You got in last night? Yeah, that's for sure, none of us is getting younger. Okay, yes, that's right, that's the place. Seven-thirty. See you later."

He'd just put his phone back down when Philip came back in, swigging the dregs of a bottle. He belched and sat down heavily.

"Fancy another?"

"I haven't had the first one yet. I told you, I'm still working. What did he say? How are sales going?"

"Not there again. Just that annoying voicemail reply. Thank you for calling Thingummy Promotions, sorry we're busy, et cetera. Don't thank me, Leo, call me back!"

"Phil, he's a one-man band, just like Centrum Records. You do know that?"

"Well you do fine."

"Yes, but I have a lot of experience."

"Felix, he's young, he does things differently. The world

has moved on. He's keen, he's sharp."

"Meaning I'm not?"

"I didn't say that. Horses for courses. For making easy money from the past, you're the man. For the future, he is. That's all. Come on, relax and have a drink."

"Later, I promise. But this work must be done first. The easy money from the past doesn't actually take care of itself."

By the end of a lovely spring afternoon, Felix was regretting taking better care of the money than himself. He had insisted on walking to Muswell Hill, thinking of how his doctor would approve of that and despite Philip's protests.

"Look at us! We'll die!"

For once, he now thought that his friend might not have been exaggerating, as he came to another halt and leaned on a fence, breathing heavily.

"You didn't tell me it really was a hill."

"I told you that you were in no condition to walk there, not even the new health-conscious you. You're still a fat bastard, you know."

"I do know. Sorry. We should have got a taxi, you were right."

Felix looked utterly disheartened, hands on his knees and shaking his head. Philip clapped him on the shoulder.

"Come on, mate. I haven't walked up here in years, but I do remember there was a pub just at the top. We can recover in there. The restaurant's only a few minutes away."

But the pub, though still serving welcome pints to trilby-hatted old gentlemen in Philip's hazy memory, had gone. A billboard advertised the views to be had from the windows of apartments for professional people, although the two of them were standing in front of a building site.

"No," said Philip, "no. Nobody told me."

Felix returned the clap on the shoulder.

"Nobody ever does, my friend. *Tempus edax rerum.*"

"What?"

"Ovid. Time devours everything. Come on."

There were other bars on the Broadway, but none in which Philip would countenance spending money on "Mexican donkey piss", and so they went straight on to the restaurant. There were diners at several tables and two people at the bar, sitting at opposite ends. Felix breathed in deeply. As Philip was shaking hands and exchanging greetings with two of the waiters, the people at the bar half turned round on their stools. The young woman got up and came across.

"Lottie! Charlotte, I mean."

He pulled his daughter into a bear hug and punched Felix on the arm.

"You didn't tell me she was coming! I just didn't think you'd be interested."

While he was talking to them both simultaneously, he didn't notice the other person at the bar, who was now looking over at them. He was too absorbed in the pleasure of his daughter's unexpected presence and the absence of Tim.

"Oh, Dad. You are an idiot sometimes. I do go to restaurants, you know. I even like hanging out occasionally with boring old music guys who drone on. No offence, Felix."

"None taken," laughed Felix. So far, so good.

"Table for four was it, sir?" asked a waiter.

"That's right."

"But there's only three of us," interrupted Philip, "unless Tim's hiding in the toilets."

Felix gestured to the man at the bar, who slowly rose from his seat, picked up a silver-topped cane, and walked over to the group of people still clustered around the coat stand. Dressed in a purple three-piece suit, silk scarf and a beret, he limped heavily but carried himself with a certain bearing that reminded Philip of something, now that he had registered his presence. A long, white beard and wire-framed sunglasses added to a bohemian but daunting mien. The man nodded at Felix, who shook his head as if in reply to a tacit question.

"So," said the man, smiling at the other two.

"Hello, I'm Charlotte."

The man bent to kiss her extended hand.

"I am delighted to meet you, Charlotte. Felix has spoken of you most warmly."

There was a slight similarity to Felix's intonation, but Philip did not think that he was Dutch. There was something about him, something now rising to the surface of Philip's recollection.

"I knew your father, a long time ago," he continued.

"Jesus," said Philip, "it can't be."

"And yet it is, Philip, you know it is. Jesus to a Jew, but at least no Nazi regalia tonight."

"Bob Spendlove."

He took a step back and into the coat stand, which promptly toppled over against the door.

"Woah, Phil! Are you alright?" called the head waiter, rushing back over to assist.

"I think we'd better sit down, don't you?" said Bob, pointing his cane at a reserved table. He smiled at Philip.

"We don't want to cause any damage, after all, do we?"

It was the last day of March, and a fine evening in North London. Since Philip and Stephen had sat in the disappeared pub at the top of Muswell Hill all those years ago, most of the old neighbourhood shops on the Broadway at that time had also vanished. Through the window by which Philip was sitting, you could look up above the facades of the craft beer micro-breweries, the street food cafes, and the designer outlets, and still glimpse the traces of the genteel Edwardian suburb, but it was like seeing a ghost. That thought amazed Philip as he sat at the restaurant table, the thought that a part of his life could now be filed away as history. Some of those trilby-wearing old gents might have been at Dunkirk, or even in the trenches of Flanders. Now they, too, were all gone, devoured by time. Perhaps to the twenty-somethings of today, Philip's youth would be as distant as the world wars had been to him. The thought seeped into his growing apprehension about next day's show. Before it could take root there, he dismissed it, by slamming his empty glass onto the table.

"Philip! You are still with us. I realise this must be a shock, but we sat down ten minutes ago and you have said nothing other than my name. That's not the mouthy kid I remember."

"Lottie, this gentleman used to be our manager."

"Dad, he just told me that while you were zoning out."

"And did he tell you about when he stopped being our manager? He didn't hand in his notice, you know. And Felix. You planned this. You accepted my hospitality, you drank my beer, and all the time you were planning this. I don't know why, I don't know how you found him, but I do know that I told you all about what he did to us. So, Bobby boy, it's not me who needs to say something, it's you and this faithless friend."

"That's more like Monsieur de la Croix!" said Bob, as a plate of poppadums and dips arrived.

"Another pint, please, Viraj."

"Dad, calm down," murmured Lottie, "they both seem very nice."

Philip snorted.

"My dear girl, you're defaming me," said Bob, "and age has not affected my uncanny ability to hear everything said about me."

Dear God, now he's charming her.

"Phil, please, of course I owe you an explanation, Bob and I both do, but Lottie is right. Calm down. Stop shouting, just listen."

So Philip stopped shouting, and listened, and this is what Felix and Bob told him, as Lottie took it all in, enthralled. Old music guys weren't so boring, it turned out.

*

Bob had got himself in well over his head, he stressed this several times.

"I was a young man then, full of it, like you, Philip. I sailed close to the wind, I admit it, but I was never actually dishonest. I just had rough edges."

He had begun life as Jonathan Barnett, son of an estate agent. His parents were not ultra-Orthodox, but neither were they impressed by their only child's obsession with Bob

272

Dylan, or by his unwillingness to go into the family business. When he announced his intention to go to art college, he was told to expect no further financial support.

"So I got the hell out of Dodge, or Finchley anyway."

From that day, Jonathan Barnett was on his own. Within another month he had become Bob Spendlove and met Linda. They had married on his twentieth birthday.

"Spendlove's was an undertakers' near my parents' house. It seemed appropriate. I was very bitter then. Bob was of course Zimmerman, another Jewish rebel."

Bob and Linda, already in her first year at college when they met, worked on her parents' market stall to make ends meet, then took it over when her father decided it was time to retire to the Costa del Sol. Out went the sports jackets and cocktail dresses, replaced by velvet loons and tie-dyed shirts.

"Linda knew where to get the cheap stock and we dyed them in our bath. We couldn't believe it when all these trust fund hippies actually started buying the rubbish."

They had been able to afford better stock in a short time and began to specialise in vintage wear. Bob left art college when he realised that this was far more fun and made more money than painting ever would. He also decided to branch out into what had always been his real love, and began to import and sell blues, jazz and gospel records.

"Dylan? No, Felix, not Dylan. You could buy Dylan records anywhere. Anyway, he'd become so boring by then."

By then, Bob and Linda had met Martin, who had just arrived in London and had learned enough about silk-screen printing at the same college to persuade them to take some of his T-shirts.

"Oh my Lord, this scrawny boy with a thick Northern

accent. You couldn't help but love him, despite his unfortunate tastes."

They would run into Martin regularly, at various parties, gallery openings and 'happenings'.

"I still don't know what a happening was, my dear girl. I imagine you were about to ask."

By the time he and Emma told them about their new band one night, Martin was one of their closest friends. It was Bob's decision to branch out still further, into music management, that set him on course for some serious difficulties.

"I knew a few people in the business, in radio, I thought it would be a breeze, and I genuinely liked those early songs of Stephen's. My mistake was, how shall I put this, to over-extend my credit. Philip, I know you thought back then that Linda and I were making a fortune out of Generation 27 and robbing you blind. Maybe you still think that. I assure you, to this day I have not recovered a penny."

Philip stared into his beer. He had picked up on Bob's reference to the songs being Stephen's and wondered whether that was deliberate. Of course it was.

"Okay. So where did you go? Why didn't you tell us? Why are you back? And how come he's involved?"

"Amsterdam. I'm surprised you never guessed. We had to leave London overnight, more or less, believe me. Some of my creditors were not gentlemen. I say no more, in deference to the presence of the young lady. We therefore felt it unwise to tell anyone where we'd gone, for a few years anyway. Even Martin."

"That party, that Dutch girl who threw it. She was your cousin. I'd forgotten that."

"You had. Anika is in fact my second cousin, on my mother's side. I have numerous relatives there. We Jews are everywhere, Philip, after all, aren't we? It was the obvious place to go. As to Felix's involvement, I knew him before you did. He and Anika were engaged, you know."

Philip remembered the lovelorn young man on his sofa after the party.

"We came up to her flat, which was just around the corner from here, then left London the next day. Anika was sworn to secrecy, even from my mother. I've been there ever since. I now own a record store. A quieter but less stressful life."

"And Linda?"

"I have no idea. She returned to England after we broke up."

"So," said Philip, swirling the dregs around the bottom of his glass, "great story. You still haven't told me what you're doing here. You might be leading a quieter life, but you haven't turned into a bloke who does things just to be sociable."

Bob laughed out loud, something Philip could not recall him ever having done.

"Quite right, Philip. I have not turned into that sort of man."

Plates of curry, rice and naan bread had arrived.

"Let's eat," said Felix, "there is more to say but I'm hungry."

He and Bob asked Lottie about college. She plainly revelled in the attention of a louche-looking man with an exotic drawl, while Philip grappled with the realisation that her own father rarely showed such interest in her life. He is just as affected as he used to be, he told himself, and he's up

275

to something, and so is Felix.

"Phil, we are not up to anything."

He looked up from the food he had morosely been pushing around his plate, and for a moment wondered if he had spoken out loud.

"You know," Felix continued, "that is something about you I have always liked."

"You like something about me?"

"Yes, even when you're being sarcastic. I like that everything you're feeling is there on your face, you just can't hide it. It's a nice quality, but it's a good thing we don't all have it."

Lottie laughed at a story Bob was telling her.

"Phil, I didn't really know you back then. All I was told by Anika was that her cousin had moved to Amsterdam, and could I use my contacts at the radio station to help him find a job. I was desperate to stay in touch with her and so I was happy to help. By the time I got to know you, I had left the station, lost touch with Anika, and only ran into Bob once in a while. It just never occurred to me in the next few years to tell you about him, and anyway, I had promised to keep quiet about it."

"But he's here now, and you invited him."

"Philip, blame me by all means, but not Felix. He's just tried to be an honest broker."

"Honest! Ha!"

"That's not fair, Phil, there are things you don't know," began Felix, before Bob silently raised a hand, a gesture Philip remembered from the meetings in the Soho office, and not one that was going to silence him now.

"Don't raise your hand to me, mate. You're not my

276

manager, you gave that up, remember?"

"Fair point, Philip, and I will put my hand down, but it is now time for a reality check. Wouldn't you say so, Felix?"

Felix sighed, then nodded, and watched Philip carefully as Bob spoke.

"You're the only member of Generation 27 who remained a professional musician. Let's be honest, you were the only musician. But how did you make a living for all those years? Plenty of sessions work, yes, and you've produced records, but what else? Not your solo albums, that's for sure. Philip, I don't blame you for doing anything you could to get by. It's a tough business. Don't blame me for doing the same."

So Bob did know. Stephen had been, for a short time, a naturally gifted songwriter, but he had been ignorant and uncaring about maximising his talent for commercial gain, and he had never registered his songs with a performing rights agency. None of them even knew of such things then, but Philip eventually did, after Verity had started working for a music publisher. He had repeatedly justified the registration of the songs in his name, and the publishing deal he struck for them, by replaying in his mind's eye that summer day in 1980, when Stephen had told him that he wanted a break. Steve wasn't interested in that side of things, he would say to himself, and he'd want me to use the royalties to keep the spirit of the band alive. Philip had wanted to justify this to himself very badly indeed, and had eventually succeeded, even convincing himself that he had acted altruistically. But now Bob somehow knew that this was how he'd subsidised his income for so long.

"But look what you've done. Why am I not to blame you for that?"

"Oh, Philip. All these years in the game and you still don't know how it works. How do you think that Felix acquired the original Generation 27 recordings to re-release? And did you never wonder where the money from *So I'll Burn* went?"

Philip was by now uncomfortably aware that his daughter might be hearing things about him that he would struggle to explain to her, but she had apparently tired of the boring old music guys and was absorbed in texted declarations of devotion from Tim. He shrugged.

"I assume it all went to those creditors."

"Not so. Valediction Records never went bankrupt. I set up another company, bought all the assets, including the rights to the album, then wound up the label before anyone came calling."

"So you did rob us all."

"Philip, I repeat. I have never seen a penny. Listen. Sales of the album and the singles petered out after you went your separate ways. There is occasionally a minor resurgence of interest, but this has never amounted to serious income. Whatever money has come in has in any case gone to someone else, someone who was entitled to it and who needed it."

"Who is that?"

"Martin."

*

"What did I miss?" asked Lottie brightly, putting down her phone and taking in the silence of the three men.

"Boring business. Look, even your father has been subdued! How is your boyfriend? I am so sorry not to have

278

met him this evening."

Martin. The name hung there, while Bob slipped back easily into polite conversation.

Lottie made ready to leave.

"Dad, Tim says we should come along tomorrow to support you."

Philip grunted as she kissed him on the head.

"Have a nice evening, guys. See you tomorrow night."

"I look forward to it," replied Bob, raising his cane in salute.

"You're coming?", asked an incredulous Philip, as the door closed behind her.

"Of course. Why not?"

"Okay, Bob, gloves off. Lottie's gone. We can speak plainly. We've had your life story, but I don't believe you've flown in just to see my show, and you're now telling me that all the record sales since God knows when have gone to Martin."

"Philip, I have always spoken plainly with you, I think you will agree. My life story, as you put it, was by way of a background explanation, and now here we are. As a younger man, I operated on the margins, but I have never been without honour. You and Martin were also my creditors. Valediction Records was in debt to you, for the great music you made. Of course, you will never get back everything to which you were entitled, but the record sales, as I say, have been helping Martin, and I have given the original recordings to Felix, and therefore you too, and you will make something from your project with him. You also have Stephen's royalties – by the way, I only discovered this when Felix and I first discussed the project – and I do not judge you for that. He has been gone a long time; I didn't consider him when I talked to Felix."

Philip fell silent and withdrew into himself again, to further review all that had been said that evening. He was finding it almost impossible to marry the story of Bob Spendlove, as narrated by Philip de la Croix over the decades, with that of Jonathan Barnett, who had taken risks and made unwise decisions but, in the end, had tried to do the right thing by everyone. Not so different from Phil Cross, really. But he remained silent in the taxi home, even as Felix spoke.

"It was his idea, Phil. The reissue of the back catalogue. It was Bob's idea. He approached me, not the other way round. He really does see this as a way of making it up to you for past mistakes, although he would never say that to you."

"Hmm. You still haven't told me why he's here. He could have said all that over the phone."

"Like he said, Phil, he wants to come to your show tomorrow."

The taxi headed down the hill, passing the site of the old pub and disappearing into the darkness.

*

Oh my God, Stan was right. Self-important, narcissistic, that was this man in a nutshell. Surely not every one of them is this bad?

Theo had taken refuge in the union office at the top of the stairs from the performance space. It was a glorified cubbyhole, but he could hide here, calm down and collect his thoughts, which had been scattered widely since Phil de la Croix had arrived. At this moment, he was mostly vexed at

280

having to leave his credit card behind the bar, his original offer of food and drink having been dismissed as an insult to Phil's 'professionalism'.

"How do I entertain my daughter and my friends on that? You can put these names on the guest list, by the way."

And who's that fat old German guy he's brought along with him? His sound man. Sound man? There's only Phil and two guitars. You plug in and you sing. How is that so complicated? Why should I be paying for his dinner too?

He had bought himself a new pork pie hat that morning, which he thought made him look the part. He pulled the brim down over his eyes.

Thank God for small mercies, Phil hadn't asked him again about ticket sales. He'd have said, "Not bad!" if he had been asked. He was sure that plenty of people were just going to turn up on the night. Perhaps he could sit here quietly for another hour, then rush down to open the doors and sit there taking tickets and money. Except from the names Phil had given him, he supposed.

*

"I'm just saying that he's only a boy. He looked terrified when he left us. You were being a bit of a rock star, Phil. This is only a college show."

Having demolished double veggie burger and chips, Philip was sipping his third pint since Theo had left them to enjoy the hospitality that had been demanded. Felix was munching a bag of peanuts with his orange juice.

"A contract is a contract; the kid has to learn if he wants to get on in this game. Speaking of which, where's he disappeared to? We need to set up the stage and do a sound check."

"We don't need him for that, and it won't take long. Come on."

Felix was of course right, and they were back in the bar area after twenty minutes.

"Right, time for one more, then feet up in the dressing room before going on. You have got that new shirt I'm wearing?"

"Hanging up in the corner. How about leaving one more until after the show, Phil?"

Philip was already shouting.

"Leo? Leo!"

The barman pointed to a side door and called after Philip. "It's Theo!"

As he opened the door, Theo came through at speed and collided with him.

"Jesus, Leo! My beer's gone everywhere! You disappear for an hour, then you run back and spill my pint. Is the dressing room up there?"

"Oh, erm, yes. Yes, it is."

"Right, I'm going up there. You can bring me a replacement beer. Good man. Oh, and send my guests up there. Felix! Shirt!"

The door slammed behind him.

"Don't worry," said Felix to the boy, "I'll deal with the beer. There is no dressing room, is there? It's just an office, yes? I will deal with that too. You go do what you have to do."

Theo had earlier set up a table by the main doors to the performance area, which Philip had since covered with a few copies of *So I'll Burn* and many more of the solo records he'd made since then. He made a space for a cash tin, opened the doors, then sat down behind the table and waited.

Ransom Promotions' first show!

*

Felix surveyed the people crammed into the tiny room. He counted eight, including Philip and himself. He had managed to persuade Philip to not go back down to remonstrate with Theo about the lack of a proper dressing room, reminding him of his own stories of changing in public toilets. He was now regaling the room with a fund of similar stories. You had to hand it to the man, he could hold court. He could also drink a lot of beer and whisky without showing any apparent debility, but Felix glanced nervously at his watch as Philip poured another glass of scotch and accepted a joint from Nick, with whom he had once played in a band. At least he was now most definitely in a better mood, and so Felix decided not to tell him how many people were downstairs with just twenty minutes until show time.

Apart from Nick and Ray, another former bandmate, there was Jez, with whom Philip had apparently buried the hatchet, and of course Bob, with whom he was evidently trying to do the same, judging by the number of times he said, "Isn't that right, Bob?" after yet another story. Bob was smiling, but then he often was. In the corner were Lottie and Tim. Felix liked Lottie very much, and wondered how she could be Philip's daughter, but he didn't understand why she had brought Tim, who looked constantly uncomfortable.

Then Felix became aware of two new arrivals, standing in

the doorway. One of them was a man of about the same age as most of the other men there but dressed more conservatively and better maintained. His companion was a slender woman at least twenty years younger, wearing artfully ripped jeans.

"Red Mark!" yelled Philip, and the man made a theatrical bow.

"Everyone, I was at school with this scoundrel, he was my partner in crime, and now look. A rich lawyer!"

"A judge, actually," said Mark, shaking hands with everyone, "and this is Julia."

"Well don't you judge me," said a delighted Philip, clumsily embracing Mark.

"He does everyone else," said Julia, and everyone laughed.

"My God, it must be ten years and you look just the same. That portrait in your attic must be scary!"

"What can I say, my dear? Hard work, early nights, and the love of a good woman. You look pretty amazing yourself."

Spoken like a lawyer, thought Felix, eyeing the rear view of Julia as she leaned over to accept the joint from Jez.

"So glad you could fit this into your schedule, your honour. I wasn't sure you got the message. You got in okay? Leo should have had you plus one on the guest list. Nothing personal, Julia, but I could never keep up with this boy's love life!"

"Dad!" said Lottie in a warning tone, as Julia giggled.

"What, the kid sitting by the door? No, I gave him some money. I felt sorry for him. We squeezed through the crowd and here we are!"

Felix tensed himself. Oh dear. Here we go.

He looked over at Bob, who was looking back at him, one eyebrow slightly raised, and then he slipped out and went downstairs, trying not to be noticed. The walk back up the stairs just a minute later was slow, not just because he was overweight but because he did not want to go back into that room and tell Philip, in front of his friends, about the audience awaiting him. Surely Mark's sarcasm had been picked up? Clearly not, to hear the ongoing laughter just above him. He reached the top step to find Bob standing outside the door.

"How bad?"

"Even worse than I'd imagined. I'm going to need moral support."

"That's why I'm here."

Philip was mid-story, arm draped around Mark.

"So this man is beeping his horn, Steve's panicking about the police turning up, and I'm about to run out of paint!"

"Philip," said Bob, "a word."

Felix took a breath in the silence that followed.

"Phil, downstairs, it's not good."

*

The majority of the dressing room had decamped to Crouch End. Mark had wanted to join them, but Julia hadn't. The others had gradually drifted off and Lottie had disappeared to her room with an abashed-looking Tim in tow. Now only Philip, Felix and Bob sat around the kitchen table.

"I'm normally a fun drunk," said Philip, "but right now I'm not. April Fools' Day. Ha! That's me. The April Fool."

"You should call it a night, Phil. We can talk tomorrow."

"About what, Felix? You mean the post-mortem for my career? No, you've all been avoiding it since we got back. Why did the others leave so early? They were embarrassed, that's why. Embarrassed to be with me. Right, Bob?"

"Philip, we can talk about tonight right now, but only if you're going to be honest with yourself. There is no point otherwise. And I mean honest, not self-pitying."

Philip sighed heavily and his chin fell to his chest.

"I know, I know."

It seemed to Felix that at this moment his friend finally gave way under the weight of the events earlier that evening. When he had gone down to the performance area, prompted by Mark's throwaway remark, he had stood still for a minute, hoping that he might have missed something. You have to tell him, he had concluded, you have to tell him now, before he comes down those stairs in his new shirt. You have to tell him that the barman is watching football on his phone, that there's no background music coming through the PA, that Theo has gone, and that none of this matters because there are only two people here, drinking coffee at a table to the side. They have their coats on and probably wandered in by mistake. Everyone back upstairs had been mortified, except for Mark, who thought it funny, and of course Bob.

Unimaginably, the situation had further deteriorated when they had all trooped downstairs, with Philip anxious to find Theo and then leave immediately. It turned out that the coffee drinkers had intended to be there. They were a retired couple who had seen Generation 27 'a thousand years ago' and they were waiting for two friends, who arrived as Philip passed by, guitar cases in hand and violence on his mind.

"None of us drinks anymore," said one of the men, "but we still like to get out for live music when we can."

Philip had marched on and out through the doors.

"Oh, are we late? We wondered why no one was on the door."

Felix had said something off the top of his head about unforeseen circumstances and had left them asking the unconcerned barman about getting their money back. Philip had given up trying to find Theo after an aimless half-hour of wandering around the deserted campus, but only after Bob had convinced him that this was pointless. Now he spoke.

"Look at me, Philip. So, first things first. There is no point whatsoever in chasing that kid for your money, because he hasn't got it. What are you going to do? Beat him up? Take him to court for four hundred quid? You have to let it go."

Philip said, "Yes, but...", then paused, then waved his hand at Bob, who continued.

"Philip, this evening was not a harbinger for the end of your career. You are not star-crossed. You are not unlucky. You brought this fiasco upon yourself. When Felix told me about the show, and about your unwillingness to promote the Generation 27 reissue, I thought you'd lost your mind. That's why I agreed to come over, not to gloat, or say Felix told you so, but because you need your arse kicking, and Felix is too nice to do that. Now, give me an honest answer. Don't waste my time, or yours. Did you really expect an inexperienced student to bring in an audience of a couple of hundred other students to listen to someone they'd never heard of?"

"Jesus, you haven't grown more diplomatic with the years, have you?"

"Diplomacy is bullshit. Answer?"

"Well, when you put it like that, no, I suppose not."

"Indeed when I put it like that. As for the coffee drinkers…"

"They were wearing anoraks! Please!"

"They were your punters, the ones who'll come out to hear 'Trying To Explain'. You're lucky you got as many as four of them. What were you thinking of, vetoing all references to Generation 27 in the publicity?"

"I just don't want to be stuck in the past."

"But you are, you are absolutely stuck in the past. You are still a young, thin man with half a century ahead of him, except you're not. Philip, the country of the young is a cruel, unforgiving place, and we don't belong there anymore. Would you like some advice, just to sleep on?"

"Normally, I'd say no to that, but after this evening I'll give anything a shot, even advice from you. Go on."

"That's my boy. Okay, number one. Your golden age has gone, stop chasing another because you'll never have another. Number two. You can still bask in that golden age. Most people never have one, so be thankful. Number three. Never, ever do another show without publicising that golden age. Number four. Allow Felix and I to set up a lucrative tour of the clubs of north-west Europe. By all means, play a few of your newer songs, but give the coffee drinkers what they've come for. You will make a lot of money and have fun. Is that so bad, Philip de la Croix?"

Philip's eyelids were drooping.

"Tell him again tomorrow," said Felix.

*

Bob didn't need to repeat the advice the next day. Philip emerged that afternoon looking more rested than he'd been since Felix arrived in London.

"I'm starving. Fancy a bacon sandwich? Lottie's gone, so we're safe. You do the coffee. How soon can you set up those dates on the continent? Bob's still at his hotel, I suppose. Maybe we could meet him for a drink later? Give him a call. Hey, it'll be great to see Amsterdam again. What are you laughing at?"

"Nothing, Phil. Your moods are infectious, you know? In both directions. And what about tomorrow, may I ask?"

"What about tomorrow?"

"Monday, the third of April, Alexandra Palace. You have forgotten?"

"Does Bob know about it?"

"No, I told him nothing about that. He came to talk to you about our project, that's all."

"Hmm."

Felix would have left things like that. Bob had helped him to rescue the project, as he'd hoped, and he was appreciative (he had not told Philip that he had agreed a small percentage of record sales as a measure of that appreciation) but in truth he had always found Bob an unnerving presence, and wondered if he was planning to go home soon. Philip, on the other hand, now appeared to be warming to his erstwhile *bête noire*, which was typical of the man. So typical that, before he'd finished his first drink that evening, he had told Bob the whole story of the blood oath, the note and the plectrum.

When he had finished telling him, Bob took a sip of his whisky, put the glass down, and drummed his fingers on the table.

"Well. That is interesting."

"Bob, you don't sound surprised by what Phil has just told you."

"Very little surprises me anymore, Felix, but I am curious. I did know of your blood oath, Philip. Emma mentioned it when she was firing a broadside at me one night. My God, she ended up hating me more than you ever did. I remember her once insisting on me reading some sort of band manifesto she'd put together. Dear Emma. I never actually saw this oath, however, but clearly it wasn't just our sister who took it seriously."

The candle on the saucer between their glasses flickered briefly. Philip shivered, then blew his nose.

"The thing is, I think Martin might have sent the note and the plectrum, but I don't know that, and I don't know who'll be there waiting for me tomorrow. And I don't know why."

"Well, Philip, I can tell you with certainty that Martin did not send it."

"But he's still alive," said Felix, as if to remind Bob of something he'd forgotten, "isn't he? You have told us that he needed financial help and that you gave him the money from album sales."

"He is still alive, but he did not contact Philip. Of that you may be sure."

And Bob told them why he knew this. In the silence that followed, shock filled their eyes and Philip's voice.

"The poor old sod. But he can't be much more than seventy. Isn't that a bit young?"

"Apparently not, especially if you spent your earlier years up to your eyes in Afghanistan's finest produce."

"How often did we all just let that go? Maybe we could

290

have done more."

Bob shook his head.

"No, Philip, we couldn't. You must understand, Martin really liked doing it, he would never have stopped just because we shouted at him. He had a great time. He probably knew that he would pay for it eventually, but that was his choice. Anyway, how do you think Emma felt? I was there sometimes when she confronted him."

"So was I," said Philip, thinking back to one morning in an Edinburgh car park.

"Well then," replied Bob, "you know."

"So you stayed in touch with him all this time?" asked Felix.

"In irregular touch. He didn't know where I'd gone for a long time, any more than the others did. We heard about the end of the band, and I guessed he was in Manchester, with all that design work he'd been doing. I knew the guy he was working for so, once the dust had settled, I contacted him. He was my friend, you know, long before I knew you two."

Bob Spendlove was still Bob Spendlove, he betrayed nothing as he sat there recounting the terrible decline of Martin, but Philip was touched by his reminding them of how far he and Martin went back.

"I'm sorry, Bob, it must have been hard for you, seeing him fall apart."

"Not as hard as it was for Emma. After she'd gone, he ended up in prison. When he came out, I began to see him more regularly again. But yes, falling apart just about summarises that time."

Late into that night, Philip lay awake. He thought of Bob, whom he now believed he had misjudged for a long time, persuading Martin to go with him to a care home, setting up the direct debit for the fees from an account into which he paid the record sales proceeds, faithfully visiting once a month until the day he realised that Martin would never recognise him again. He imagined Bob helping Martin to gather his few possessions before leaving his bedsit.

"Just about two sets of clothes, no socks – I had to buy him some new, and a toothbrush and deodorant – and his briefcase, which he wouldn't let out of his sight, and Emma's guitar, just about the only thing of value he hadn't sold. Oh, and all his birdwatching stuff. He actually had a couple of pieces published in magazines, one when he was in prison, and he treasured them."

Poor Martin. He hadn't sent the note but neither had Steve. Philip remained certain of this without understanding why he did. It just wouldn't be Steve. But who? And then Philip thought about Emma. She had frightened him at times. He wondered if she would now. He would give anything to know, but he supposed that people who never compromise with life don't hang around for so long.

He couldn't remember how he'd he got Steve's phone number that day. Or was it his parents'? Yes, it must have been.

"Steve, it's Phil. Listen, sorry, I know this is out of the blue, but Martin just phoned me. There's some bad news."

And the child. Bob had said a girl, taken into care. Poor kid, poor Emma, poor Martin. Poor Bob. Poor Judith Friedman. Poor Uncle Pat. Send not to ask for whom the bell tolls, Philip Cross. He fell asleep, thinking of the people he'd lost from his life. They had just faded away, while he was off somewhere, chasing after something, something he'd never caught.

*

Monday, the third of April.

He woke suddenly, which was very unlike him, and he did not like the feeling. Why had he done that? The time.

He peered through the gloom at the clock on the dressing table. It was not yet seven, but he had just realised something. After days of reading the note over and over, it had only now come to him that today's date was not backed up by a time. Ah, he thought, so that's definite then, I am going.

"Actually, the thought occurred to me last night," said Felix, "but I assumed you knew, and I forgot to check."

He was also up early, drinking coffee and looking at his phone.

"Oh, and by the way, Bob left me a voicemail last night. It must have been after he got back to his hotel."

Bob was flying home this morning and had secured Philip's confirmation that he would honour a tour to promote the Generation 27 reissue, before making his farewells.

"Philip, I am glad we did this," he had said, opening the taxi door, "and I think you will be too. You know, we all fall off the *zeitgeist* in the end, but so what? The *zeitgeist* is overrated."

But he had forgotten to tell them something. Felix handed over the phone.

"My dear men, thank you for a convivial and most interesting evening. Regarding Martin, there was something else. He started writing a letter to Philip and Stephen, after he'd been diagnosed. A long letter, and I'm not even certain he ever finished it. He never let me see it. He was constantly agonising over whether to send it, and obviously he never did. He went into periods of denial about his condition, and forgot about writing it for a while, and then of course he forgot about it for ever. Anyway, just a thought. I hope that Philip finds his answers at Alexandra Palace, just like he used to. See you in Amsterdam."

"Mysterious as ever. He doesn't change."

"Indeed. So, what time do we go there?"

It was a bright, clear morning, the sort of which Robert Browning had thought when he wrote of his desire to be in England, according to Philip, and so they decided to go out for breakfast and then on to the meeting place. Whoever was going to be there would surely wait, as would they.

"And don't worry," said Felix, "no need for a pub to be open. Today we take a taxi."

*

The view from up here had changed. Philip could remember sitting in front of the landmark skyline, maybe on this very bench, looking out over the suburbs to the dome of Saint Paul's.

"Phil, I don't get this. How come the cathedral is over there? I'm lost."

He smiled as he thought of Stephen back then, how worried and perplexed he always was. He thought again of the last time he had spoken to him, of the silence that followed his telling him about Emma.

"Steve? Are you still there?"

A few minutes of uneasy conversation had stuttered along. That was it, Philip remembered now, he was back at his parents' home then, after a serious relationship had ended badly. What awful timing, he could recall thinking when Stephen had told him. He could hear his mother calling him in the background. Stephen! Stephen! Who's that?

"Thank you for telling me, Phil. Let's stay in touch."

And that was that. Thirty years had passed and here he was, wondering if a sixty-something Stephen was about to appear.

You had to look hard to pick out Saint Paul's now. He'd read somewhere that there were regulations protecting the best views of the cathedral from modern encroachment. If that were so, he wasn't sure that they were working very well. There was nothing blocking the view as such, but plenty on either side of it to distract. Towers, blocks, shards. Shards, for God's sake.

"When we build, let us think that we build for ever."

"What?"

He'd almost forgotten that Felix was sitting next to him, sharing the view and seemingly his musing upon it.

"John Ruskin. Whoever built those things, I don't think they had for ever in mind."

They sipped the coffees they'd bought from the café by the boating lake.

"How do you know so much?"

"I don't think I do."

"You know more than I do, about most things. You quote people I've never heard of. You speak better English than most Brits."

"You flatter me, Phil."

"And you're wise, Felix. You're a wise friend."

He patted Felix's knee heartily.

"Well, Phil, thank you for saying that, but you know, it's always easier to be wise about other people. Nobody is so rational about themselves."

He thought of the last time he'd spoken to Hannah, then he returned the pat.

"Phil, you should not worry. Stop beating yourself up about Saturday. It's gone. Listen, I don't know so much, believe me, but I do know the most amazing thing: there is nothing greater than being alive, being here right now. And look, you can still see Saint Paul's, and the sun is out!"

They sat there. Philip drained his cup.

"More coffee? We could be here all day. My turn to go, you wait here."

He disappeared around the corner. There were few people about on a Monday morning, and only an occasional car went past, but his attention was caught by a taxi pulling into the drop-off point where he and Philip had arrived an hour previously. He wiped his glasses on his handkerchief and peered down the road. The driver and a passenger were both now out of the vehicle and leaning back into the cab, slowly helping out another passenger. After the taxi pulled away, he could see quite clearly now that a woman, a young woman, and an older man were standing there, looking about them as if getting their bearings. The woman pointed up at the building above them. Then, as if decided where they were going, the two began to make their way up the road, arm in arm, watched by Felix.

He glanced back over his shoulder, but there was no sign of Philip. The couple were making slow progress but they were now definitely coming towards the bench where he sat alone, and he could make them out more clearly. A young woman and an elderly man with his arm through hers. For God's sake, Phil, hurry up. Whoever had sent the note and Valediction Records plectrum might be approaching.

"There you go, two sugars. Oh, I might have mixed them up. Have a slurp and tell me. Felix?"

He turned to face Philip, raised his eyebrows, and turned back to the couple, now less than a hundred metres away.

"Oh," said Philip, putting the coffees down on the bench, "do you think?"

"Oh yes, yes, I do. Recognise them?"

"I don't think so. Not the girl, I'd say she's only about Chloe's age. I can't really see the old guy, he keeps looking down, but he must be in his eighties. He can barely walk."

The young woman was constantly turning to her companion, as if cajoling him on, and then she pointed to where Philip and Felix were both now standing and looked directly at them. Philip took a step back.

"No. No, wait, that can't be. What the hell is this?"

"Hello," she called brightly, as they came nearer, "I think you might be expecting us? Is one of you Phil de la Croix? My name's Kelly. Wow! Is that Saint Paul's?"

*

"Kelly, I am delighted and relieved to meet you. We feared that we might be here all day. My name is Felix, and this is indeed Phil. We are old friends."

"Kelly," said Philip uncertainly.

"Actually, Eloise. No, sorry. I don't know why I said that."

I'm just a bit nervous. Kelly is fine."

"Ah," said Felix, "Phil?"

Philip was still looking doubtfully at the young woman, whom Felix thought strikingly fetching, and neither of them had given a second glance at the old man, who had been guided onto the bench and was now looking down at the park below.

"Phil looks like he's seen a ghost. I tell you what, Kelly, you must have this coffee, so long as you have a sweet tooth. The elderly gentleman can have the other. I will go and fetch two others, and you two can talk."

"Thank you, I could do with this."

Felix smiled and walked away.

"Kelly."

"Yes?"

"This is Martin, isn't it?"

"Yes. I thought that might shock you. Like your friend said, as if you've seen a ghost."

As if by consent, they sat down on either side of Martin.

"You've come from Manchester, I'm guessing."

"The posh bit, out in Cheshire really. We got a taxi to Crewe and then caught the Liverpool train. Terrible journey, the train kept stopping. Oh, you're crying. What is it?"

Philip sniffed and wiped his eyes.

"The thing is, I knew about Martin. A friend told us. So I knew he couldn't have sent me the plectrum, but I just knew it came from him, if you understand. As you were coming up the road, it suddenly became obvious. You sent the note, you brought him. Last night, when I was thinking about today, I had no doubt at all that he would be here, and I thought I'd steeled myself, but when I finally looked at him just then.

Well…"

More tears ran down his face, down where his beard had been.

"I'm so sorry. I've only really known him like this, it must be terrible for people who remember him as he was. But Phil, do talk to him, or even just touch his hand. He is still Martin. There's part of him still in there, I do believe that."

So Philip forced himself to look again at Martin. He would not have recognised him. They sat there together, high above London, as they had so often.

"So, who are you? And why? That oath, bloody stupid idea, we were just kids. Eh, Martin? Who are you, Kelly?"

By the time Felix reappeared, she had recounted the story, or a suitably edited version.

"Were you famous? I did a search but there wasn't much there."

"A bit. For a short time. You know what, Kelly? We burned, that's what we did. Didn't we, Martin?"

"You're still staring at me very intently, I might say."

"Well, I thought just for a moment back there that you were the ghost, that you were someone else, but of course you can't be. You're very forthright, though, aren't you?"

"And you'd say that to a man, I'm sure."

"Touché," chuckled Felix.

"Thank you, Felix. Kelly was telling me that she has brought me a letter, and that she thinks it's written by Martin to Steve and me, and that she found it in a bass guitar case. This here, if you hadn't guessed, is dear old Martin."

"Of course, yes, I thought it might be. So Bob was right about the letter. But Kelly, if you had Phil's address, why not just post it?"

"I couldn't be sure it was still his address. I thought this was safer. Anyway, they swore an oath. I wanted Martin to keep the oath. It's still important. Should one need the others. Well, he doesn't remember anymore, but he needed them, it seems, and here he is."

"Steve!"

"Where?"

"No, you silly old fart! But he knows. He knows about today. I passed the note on to him, and it got back to Kelly. So yes, where is he?"

Kelly and Martin disappeared in search of public toilets.

"He's still continent, but he needs a bit of encouragement."

They marvelled at her gentleness and her unflappability, and did not envy her the journey home. Philip was now turning over the thickly-padded envelope she had just handed to him.

"Aren't you going to open it?"

"That is Martin's writing. Only he would use copperplate for just that. G27. And no, not until Steve gets here."

"I understand. Phil, this young woman, she is quite remarkable, you do not think?"

"She is."

"But there is something else about her, is there not?"

"You noticed."

"I see it now, you saw it immediately, didn't you? But you knew Emma much better than I did."

"It's just a coincidence, Felix. She's a care worker who happens to care for Martin, that's all."

"I suppose you're right. Here they come."

Kelly opened the rucksack she'd been carrying.

"Anyone want a sandwich? I made far too many."

And the four of them sat on the bench, eating cheese and pickle sandwiches. Kelly wiped Martin's mouth and turned to face Philip.

"If you think this other man, Steve, is coming, we'll wait a while longer. But what about Emma? I wanted to meet you all, and for you all to read the letter. I wouldn't feel like I'd honoured the oath otherwise, honoured it on Martin's behalf. Is she no longer around? I know there was a line through her name. Was Martin in love with her?"

Philip couldn't look at her and kept his eye on Saint Paul's.

"Martin was probably in love with her once, but no, she's no longer around."

"He still remembers her. Well, he did. Anyway, I will need to get him back soon. I don't mind being sacked, I've had it with that place, but I don't want the police out after me for kidnapping a resident."

"I'll keep in touch, maybe come and visit him."

"No. You won't. And I'm not judging you for that. What would be the point? Don't worry, he'll be safe in the home, and I'll still visit him. He's like family to me."

While they were talking about him, and Kelly was holding his hand, Martin was looking fixedly into a clear sky, or to them he was. He had picked out the flight of a distant raptor, and was studying it, as if it were a fragment of memory taking form and coming closer.

Philip had taken his other hand and turned away, straining his eyes for a thin, dark boy, shyly waving as he walked towards them.

STEPHEN

"Stephen! Come on, Stephen!"

"Dad?"

"Try and sit up. Can you drink some of this water?"

Curious faces were peering around and over their seats at the man slumped in the corner, another man bent over him. The seething incredulity of travellers late for meetings gave way to a mix of interest and revulsion, as some noticed the trail of vomit down his shirt.

"You're still a bit warm, but clammy rather than a high temperature. How are you feeling now? Woah, steady, don't try and get up! That's how you ended up like this."

The man opposite. It was the man opposite, with whom he'd shared an exasperated look at the announcement of the delay. Back in focus, he looked a good deal younger than Stephen, with long hair, beard, and a friendly face. He remembered now. The train to London. But what had happened? And how did this man know his name?

"A bit shaky. Erm…"

"You fainted," he said as if in reply, "only for a minute or so. There you go, you dropped this."

He handed him the blue plectrum.

"You were looking a bit out of it, then you suddenly stood up. You were staring down the train. Then, down you went. You might want to wipe off the puke."

He handed Stephen a tissue, and sat back down in his own seat, facing Stephen.

"I called you Dad."

"Don't worry, I've been called worse."

The man was smiling, and Stephen felt the enormous relief of normality returning to his mind and body.

"God, I'm so sorry."

The excitement clearly having passed, the other passengers had returned to their phones.

"Really, not a problem. Actually, my job."

Confusion clouded Stephen's face.

"I'm a doctor. Gareth."

He extended his hand.

"Stephen. Oh, but you know that."

Gareth pointed to where Stephen had placed his booking receipt on top of his ticket, as he always did.

"It always helps to have a name."

Stephen felt foolish about an idiosyncrasy he couldn't explain, but it had been useful today and so the feeling passed.

"Do you mind me asking? As you're a doctor. Why do you think it might have happened?"

"I was just about to ask you that."

Gareth was direct but engaging, and Stephen found himself wishing that he had a GP like that, rather than old McFadden's son, who had taken over the practice but who was barely an upgrade on his father.

"Stick with the pills, Mister Elijah, there's a good chap."

The pills. I wonder, thought Stephen.

"Well…"

He would wonder later how he had come to tell a stranger not only that he had suddenly withdrawn from antidepressants, but that he didn't want to take them anymore.

Gareth watched him gravely, occasionally holding up an index finger to either ask a question or offer an opinion. He's listening to me, thought Stephen, he's actually listening to me, as he tried to explain why he'd spent so much of his life taking various prescribed drugs, and why he didn't want to do that anymore. He finished by telling him that, just before he'd fainted, he thought that he'd seen Emma.

Then the train jerked forward and began to roll along, picking up speed. After a mock round of applause, the passengers returned to fussing over their laptops, bags and coats. Stephen dared not move. It was at least another fifteen minutes to Euston, and he was anxious not to miss a word of what Gareth might have to say.

Gareth leaned back, folded his arms, looked above him, then leaned forward on the table between them and looked steadily at Stephen, who fiddled with a jacket button and wished he'd wiped his shirt more thoroughly. Did it smell?

"Stephen, I'm not a psychiatrist."

"Oh. Yes. Of course."

"But I can tell you a couple of things with near enough certainty. You've been on antidepressants for a long time and you've suddenly come off them. Without telling your GP, I'm guessing?"

"Erm. Yes."

"Sudden withdrawal can have some pretty unpleasant side effects. First, that would explain the disturbed sleep patterns and the weird dreams, even your imagining that you saw someone you used to know. Second, it would account for the dizziness and the throwing up. I get what you said, that you hate feeling constantly drugged and dependent, but come off them gradually. Talk to your doctor, maybe think of counselling. See your doctor anyway, just to rule out more sinister things."

"I will."

"Good. Now the cod psychiatry."

To Stephen, it did not sound like any sort of psychiatry. It sounded like the self-evident being pointed out to him. Gareth told him nothing that he didn't know already, but it felt like an epiphany. It was okay to prefer poetry and folk music to electric guitars these days – "So you're a Renaissance man, Steve, you're a grown-up!" – and it was definitely okay to be embarrassed by his mother and resentful of his dead father, but it was also time to let go of all that wasted energy.

"Throw it away, Steve. Upbringing, ancestry, inheritance. It's weighing you down, all that baggage, so dump it. Your psychiatrist was right, you can't keep everyone happy, but you're still stuck on that roundabout. You have been for a long time, haven't you?"

And it was time to let go of Emma.

"I wrote a song about her, a long time ago. I never played it to anyone."

"Play it for the others, they should hear it. You all miss her. But Steve, things can go wrong, and you're not always to blame. It's not your responsibility to make everything alright. You couldn't have saved your band; you couldn't have saved Emma. There is some darkness in life, and it overwhelms some people, and it's sad, but you just have to accept that sometimes it's no one's fault."

The music began to fade. She lifted her head from his shoulder and gently pulled free of his arms, kissed him on the cheek and walked away, turning back one last time to smile at him, before disappearing.

"I'm sorry, I just…"

"It's fine, don't be embarrassed. Have another tissue. Missing someone is normal. Carrying the weight for everyone isn't. Look, we're approaching Euston. Are you alright? Where are you going now?"

"Well," replied Stephen, rubbing his eyes, "I wasn't sure but now I am. I have a meeting to get to."

They shook hands on the platform.

"Steve, it's been a pleasure. I hope I was able to help. Look after yourself, you hear?"

"You helped me more than you know. Thank you."

Gareth shouldered his bag.

"Steve," he called back, "the past is gone. Live now. Live well."

With that he joined the bustle away from the train, leaving Stephen to wipe his shirt again and gather his bearings.

"I will," he said, and then he stepped forward, along the length of the platform and up to the concourse, filled with April sunlight. He paused again briefly and smiled.

"Hello. I'm back."

Then he moved on, his stride lengthening with each step.

*

Godspeed, Stephen Elijah.

The train was gone, and the fields returned to their abiding silence, broken only by the plangent cry of a kite.

Weeeoo wee-oo wee-oo wee-oo.

Borne on long, narrow wings, cleaving the bright air,

306

forked tail twisting it through the heavens, it circled higher and higher, rising above the age-old land, until it disappeared into the rising sun.

G27

Little brothers,

I bet you never thought you'd hear from me again. That is, if you do hear from me. I keep tearing this up, then rewriting it, and I'm still not sure I'll ever send it, or even where I'll send it. Ha! This old-time script might look impressive, but it doesn't mean I know what to say. I'm beginning to appreciate what Steve went through when he used to write those songs.

If you do ever read this, one thing I do know is that a long time will have passed since we were all together, so I should start by telling you the story of my post-Generation 27 life. It's not a story in which I look good, and I don't suppose that will surprise you.

To begin at the beginning. You'll remember that Emma and I moved to Manchester for the job I landed. Of course you do. You must have been so mad at me then, and I don't blame you. But to start with, everything went better than expected. The record company really took off. Big name signings, hit singles. Right place at the right time. The money being made then was unbelievable, and some of it came to me. I even had my sleeve designs in an exhibition. One of my old art teachers came to see it! Emma got an admin job with the company, and all was good in Martin's world. But it was not. For a junkie, it was precisely the wrong place at the wrong time. Emma tried to tell me, and sometimes I listened – I even started on a recovery programme once – but mostly

I didn't listen, or I couldn't. I was up to my eyes in debt by the time the label went to the wall. I even sold some of her jewellery behind her back.

There's always a big pause here. Maybe I'll get past it this time. Right, so this bit's hard.

I know she could be unpredictable, even scary at times, but the truth is that Emma was a lost girl, a lost soul. She had her own demons, and I was never what she needed. I knew inside how unhappy she'd become but I wouldn't face it, and when we had the baby, I thought that would make everything right again. Imagine that, me, a father! I even went straight for a few months after Eloise was born, but it didn't last. One day, Emma left the baby with a friend and drove away. God knows where I was. The car was found abandoned in a place called Withernsea, on the east coast. They recovered her body a few days later, washed up somewhere. Apparently, she had filled her coat pockets with stones, then just walked in. She left no note, but I didn't need one. I'm sorry to give you the details like this, my boys, but I couldn't tell you at the time. It wasn't a cool, rock n roll, Virginia Woolf death. It was cold and dark and lonely. I went there a long time afterwards. The sea and sky go on for ever, it was like looking at eternity.

I'm also sorry about the funeral, but I didn't want anyone there. Just two weeks after that, I was picked up for dealing and duly became a guest of Her Majesty. My folks were both gone by then, Emma's dad the same, and her mother had disappeared with a new man, so the baby was taken into care.

They say prison's the worst place for a junkie to go, but I actually got help inside and I got clean. When I came out, some decent people were there for me. I got a job as caretaker at my Dad's old church, and a place to live. And here's a surprise for you: Bob Spendlove started visiting! He had written to me in prison, and now he sort of keeps an eye on me, like a friend does. I know you had issues with Bob, so did I, but you know what, he has a good heart. He offered to help me trace my daughter, but I thought best not. She'll be better off where she is.

That brings me to the reason why I'm writing to you both after however many years. This is also difficult to write down, to see it there on the page before me. I have Alzheimer's.

At first I just thought that years of abuse were catching up with me when I forgot where I was going, or couldn't remember someone's name, but Bob suspected that it might be worse than that, and he was right.

I got the diagnosis eighteen months ago. Sometimes I wish I hadn't agreed to go to the doctor, but I suppose I needed to know what I was up against.

I'm only in my sixties. Only! But I'm told that my 'lifestyle' could be a 'contributory factor', so yes, the years have indeed caught up with me, as they do with all of us in the end. Me just a bit sooner than I'd have liked. But no complaints.

So, brothers, things are only going in one direction now, and speeding up. Bob – brutal as ever, bless him – tells me that I must start considering a suitable place to move to. He can't be here all the time, neither can the people from the church or anyone I still know around here, and I know the day is coming when I won't even be safe here in the flat. I have read a lot of terrifying leaflets!

If I am to finish this letter, then, it has to be now. Words are disappearing as the days go by, another reason it's taken

310

me so long. Thank God for Roget's Thesaurus*! Bob got me a copy.*

So what do I want to say to you? These will be last words, after all.

Okay. Phil. I have followed you from afar. Those solo records you made, those new artistic directions (did you really say that in an interview??), the shows when you wouldn't play the old songs. But Phil, didn't we have a great time? I remember you telling me once how desperate you were to get away from your childhood on that estate, how you needed to find your own place in the world. You found it, Phil. It seems to me that you've spent all the time since then on a search for that place, when you were there all along. It's not a place you're missing, my dearest man, it's a time, and that time has gone. Remember it with pride, don't disown it.

Steve, my genius boy. Still and always. That's why we loved you so much. Did you ever understand that? Probably not. I know nothing of your life since Generation 27, although Emma once told me you'd won a poetry prize – that didn't surprise me, you wrote songs like a poet – so I am talking to the Stephen Elijah of long ago. Still the boy who carried the weight of the world on those narrow shoulders, I am sure. Bob is fond of telling me that I was a 'drug-addled zealot' back then, which is fair, but I saw more than you thought. Deep into those dark eyes, I saw how everything mattered so much. The band, the ideals, Emma. I think she was a little in love with you, too, because you were the only one who saw beyond her anger. I wish I'd been able to do that, Steve. I remember you in those final days before it all ended. You were full of pain, the sort of pain that never leaves poets. But Steve, don't ever feel guilty. I fucked up, not you. You have a righteous heart, and you are cherished.

My boys, I have a favour to ask before I sign off. You don't hang around for very long with this thing. When I'm gone – I'm sure Bob will let you know (I'd love to hear how he phrases the announcement!) – I'd like you to help him find my daughter. I'll be safe from all her questions by then! There won't be much of an estate to pass on – Bob's helping me out as it is – but I'd want her mother's old guitar to go to her, and there's an old photo frame of my Dad's I've become attached to. She might want that. I wouldn't begin to know how to find her, but I'm sure you'll do your best. If you do find her, tell her all about our adventure. In an unvarnished but glorious light. Now there's an epitaph! Tell her we burned, just like her mother said.

A last thought. Have you ever seen The Resurrection, Cookham, *the painting by Stanley Spencer? I used to disappear off to whichever gallery it's in (sorry) all the time, just to look at it. It's all about how the wondrous can be found everywhere. How the divine is within us all. Brothers, that's about all I've learned in my decades in this world. I don't believe there's a state of constant happiness. No one gets to live like that, on some sort of permanent high (and I should know), but you can feel a deep satisfaction that you're living your life fully. A quiet and gentle contentment. That's the ticket.*

In the likelihood that we shall not meet again, I'm signing off with love, for two of the dearest friends a man could wish for. I have been most fortunate.

Your brother always,
Martin Rogers

ACKNOWLEDGEMENTS

I was inspired to write this book by a conversation among a group of twenty-somethings I overheard on a train. It set me to thinking about youth and age, and how, as Marlowe wrote, we have neither, but 'as it were, an after-dinner sleep, dreaming of both'. I can't think of a better description of the passing of time, but I have also tried to write about it here.

The story of the band *Generation 27* is set in late seventies London, a time and place forever etched in my heart. By good fortune, I was there when punk and new wave exploded. It was the most exciting thing that had ever happened to a rock-and-roll-obsessed kid, and it opened up a world of possibilities. I salute the visionary musicians and artists who lit up my young life then, not least Joe Strummer, Mick Jones, Paul Simonon and Topper Headon of *The Clash*: their spirit runs through the fictional history of *G27*.

The issues of dementia and mental health are woven into *Valediction Records*. These are subjects that most of us recoil from discussing but, as our own lives pass, we almost inevitably run into one or the other. We need to be braver about this, and I acknowledge the work of the incredible doctors, nurses and carers who combat these crippling illnesses. Some of them helped me, others have helped people I knew, and I thank them.

Thanks to my publishers, Cranthorpe Millner, for their belief in me and for giving an unknown a shot, and many thanks also to John Hollingsworth, for his stunning plectrum photograph, used on the cover.

Finally, I am indebted to the readers of my early manuscript. Their feedback and encouragement helped to convince me that it was worth staying at my desk and finishing the thing I'd started. David Parry, Liz Reynolds, Claire Lewis, Zoe Lewis, Jo Apted: thank you.

Last, but very far from least, I can never repay Gabrielle Monk for the support and love she has given me, and for the dark moods she has tolerated. But I will try.